Coming in here had been a bad idea. He needed to leave. Now.

He turned toward the door.

"Mac?"

He stopped and squeezed his eyes closed. Kate.

"Hey." Her palm touched his back.

Slowly, he opened his eyes and turned. "Hey."

Her smile was warm as she looked deep into his eyes, assessing him. "Are you okay?"

"I'm fine." He tried to drag out something casual. Or any words would be welcome. His brain had frozen at the sexy, happy sight of her. Her chocolate-colored eyes gleamed under the overhead lights, her cheeks flushed and her body damn near perfect in an open-necked shirt and tight black jeans.

She frowned. "Well, as much as I'm getting used to your permanent scowl, you don't look fine. What are you doing here?"

He stupidly dropped his gaze to her mouth and memories of how she tasted flooded him. He snapped his gaze past her shoulder and shrugged. "I came looking for you."

Dear Reader,

Welcome back to Templeton Cove. I'm sad to say this will be our very last visit to my favorite English seaside town.

This final installment revolves around a very special lady: Marian Cohen, the beloved, feisty, amazing matriarch of the town who stole my heart (and the miniseries!) from the very first book.

A Stranger in the Cove introduces Mac Orman, who has come to town searching for Marian, his biological grandmother. Unfortunately, one of the first people Mac meets is no-nonsense, protective, loving Kate Harrington. As a charity worker, Kate has seen her fair share of cases where people are hurting and angry. It isn't long before she makes up her mind that Mac is in town to cause trouble for her close friend Marian.

This book encapsulates the joy I've had writing Marian's escapades throughout the miniseries. She means the world to me! Throughout Kate and Mac's journey, I was reduced to tears of happiness and sorrow as I finally revealed Marian's past.

I hope you enjoy this book, and if you're visiting Templeton Cove for the first time, I urge you to read the rest of the series.

It's a sad goodbye from me to a town I love with all my heart.

Rachel

Twitter: @rachelbrimble
Facebook: Rachel Brimble

RACHEL BRIMBLE

A Stranger in the Cove

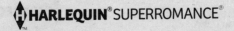

Recycling programs
for this product may
not exist in your area.

ISBN-13: 978-1-335-44908-5

A Stranger in the Cove

Printed in U.S.A.

Rachel Brimble lives with her husband and two teenage daughters in a small town near Bath in the UK. After having several novels published by small US presses, she secured agent representation in 2011. Since 2013, she has had eight books contracted with Harlequin Superromance (Templeton Cove Stories). She also has four Victorian romances with eKensington/Lyrical Press.

She likes nothing more than connecting and chatting with her readers and fellow romance writers. Rachel would love to hear from you!

Books by Rachel Brimble

HARLEQUIN SUPERROMANCE

Templeton Cove Stories

Visit the Author Profile page at Harlequin.com.

This book is dedicated first and foremost to Susan, Clare, Debbie and Karen Brooks, my husband's birth mother and sisters with whom he was reunited almost three years ago. I love you so much, ladies, and we feel so blessed to have you, your partners and our new, precious nieces and nephews in our lives.

I'd also like to dedicate this book to my fabulous editor, Piya Campana—there aren't words to express how much your expertise, knowledge and support over the five years of our working together means to me. I wish you all the luck in the world as our careers take a new path. Let's make sure we keep in touch!

CHAPTER ONE

KATE HARRINGTON'S ENTIRE body trembled with annoyance when the not-so-honorable Mayor Binchy abruptly ended their phone call. She slammed the phone receiver back into its cradle.

The nerve of the man!

She glared around Templeton Cove's Teenage Support office. It buzzed with activity, her colleagues busy talking on phones or scribbling notes, heedless that dusk fell beyond the plate glass window.

Frustration boiled dangerously inside her. She and the rest of the staff had dedicated every hour possible into making the upcoming fund-raiser a success. Tickets had been selling well for months, and the team was on track for an impressive donation to the local hospital's new young mother and baby unit.

But how was she meant to impress the three or four major donors to the event in three days' time if the mayor had deemed the entire day and night a "non-priority"?

Young, unmarried mothers who'd been kicked out of their homes or had found themselves all alone with a baby to care for were a *non-priority*? Kate ground her teeth. She'd like to make a priority of ramming a red-hot poker up Mayor Binchy's ass.

"Whoa…" Her colleague Nancy Marshall approached, pushing her glasses up her nose. "What, or who, has put that look on your face?"

Kate scowled. "The look that says I might just wring someone's neck?"

Nancy nodded. "Uh-huh, exactly."

Kate tipped her head back and groaned. "This fund-raiser means so much to all of us and I really wanted the mayor to show his support on Saturday." She dropped her chin and glared. "Is that too much to ask of the man who supposedly champions the town and supports the community? Mayor Binchy is a waste of space if he deems lone mothers a non-priority."

Nancy's smile vanished, and she flicked her long black hair over her shoulder. "He said that?" Her eyes widened. "To *you*?"

"Yep."

"The man must have a death wish."

"Agreed."

"And what did you say *after* he said that?"

"He cut me off somewhere around, 'shall I bring a few of these mothers to your place so you can explain where you stand?'" Kate blew out a breath and sat behind her desk. "Forget him. We don't need some stuck-up know-it-all to front this fund-raiser. All we need is plenty of press interest, and that's pretty much a done deal. We've got music, food, marquees galore…not to mention the Moon Shadows." Kate felt marginally appeased that one of the UK's up-and-coming country rock bands backed their campaign. "So, did you want my help with something?"

"If that's okay…" Nancy grimaced. "Although now is probably not the best time to let you know about another no-show for Saturday."

"What?" Kate's optimism wavered once more. "Who?"

"The lead guitarist from the Moon Shadows is sick. The bassist has promised he'll find a replacement. I'm just worried how the crowd will react to not having Jason Stewart there. He's the main man, after all."

"Since when has a guitarist been the main man? What's wrong with the lead singer?"

"Nothing. It's just Jason is…" Nancy's dark eyes glistened with mischief. "Well, Jason."

"Hmm." Kate picked up a pen and tapped it on her desk. "As long as they find a replacement and the show can go on, it will be fine. I'd like to think people in the Cove will be there for the cause…even if the mayor isn't."

"True." Nancy pressed her ever-present clipboard to her chest. "Is there anything else I can take off your plate? You look so stressed."

"I'm fine. Really." Kate pushed the curls from her brow and forced a smile. "See? All good."

Her colleague raised her eyebrows, her gaze disbelieving. "If you say so. I'll see you in the morning then, okay?"

"Sure. Have a nice night."

Kate dragged some papers from the overflowing tray on her desk and resigned herself to another late night. Her eyes itched with tiredness, and her body ached from the hours she'd put in over the last month trying to pull together what she hoped would be a fundraiser to beat all fund-raisers.

She put the final touches on the last press

release before the event and emailed it to the *Cove Chronicle*'s editor. With any luck, Claire Neale would run a story about the event on page two, even if she wouldn't promise Kate the front page. The local radio station had been great, and Kate's entire team had worked social media to the breaking point, but still, any last-minute ticket purchases would be welcome.

She picked up the phone and dialed the *Chronicle*'s number. Considering the last press release she'd sent had gone astray, Kate needed to be sure this one was safely received.

"The *Cove Chronicle*, Claire Neale speaking."

"Claire, it's Kate."

"Hi. What can I do for you?"

"I just sent you the press release for Saturday's fund-raiser. I'd really appreciate you running it tomorrow, if possible."

"Can't do tomorrow, Kate. You should've had this with me days ago if you wanted it in tomorrow. I'll tell you what, as you've got the Moon Shadows coming, I'll put it on page two on Friday. Okay?"

Should she tell Claire about the lead guitarist? No. What good would that do for the cause? "Great. Okay. That's good. Thanks."

"You're welcome. Now, get off this phone. Some of us want to get home before nine, if we can."

"Sure. Have a good one."

Kate hung up and leaned back. She stared out the window toward the purple-gray clouds beyond. Only a few skeleton staff remained in the office, none of whom she really knew past work. She took a long breath. She was in need of some company. Some fun company. It niggled that she'd not managed to secure the mayor's attendance and that the main draw of the Moon Shadows would be a no-show. What else could go wrong?

She needed to get out of here and lighten her mood.

Shutting down her computer, Kate grabbed her purse and headed out the door.

A couple of drinks and some friendly company at the Coast and she'd be feeling more positive, ready to fight for some more backing tomorrow. Her charity work mattered— to her, and to the teenagers she tried to help. She would not be beaten down from working for mothers who'd had the courage to go through their pregnancies and the birth of a new baby alone.

She pressed her hand to her stomach. She would've found that courage if the baby she'd once carried had made it…if she'd managed to keep her child safely cocooned in her womb.

Kate's heart grew heavy as fresh doubt and a sense of ineptitude pressed down on her. She quickly buttoned her coat against the February chill and shook off memories that would only serve to upset her. Lately, it felt as though she was losing her fire, failing herself and others. She could not give up her work or her determination to succeed. If she did, she'd have nothing left but the haunting memories of the baby she'd lost and how that had brought her to work at the center in the first place.

That, and Marian's support, of course.

Kate smiled as she thought of the town's matriarch and baker, Marian Cohen. A wonderful woman who had also been a surrogate mother to Kate through one of the worst times of her life. She'd never take Marian's continuing love and comfort for granted. Not ever.

With that thought, Kate's steps lightened, and a slow smile appeared as she strode toward the Coast.

MAC ORMAN WALKED to the window of his room above the Coast. Light snow swirled around the parking lot, and the old-fashioned streetlamps shuddered in the gathering wind. Maybe the idea of starting his search for Marian Ball, or Marian Cohen as she was known these days, could wait until morning.

He walked to the small desk in the corner of the room. Papers were strewn across the top, along with his father's notebook. The chaos reflected Mac's frame of mind. Despite knowing before he came here two days ago that Templeton was a small town, the lack of activity—and the increased chance of being noticed as a stranger—was worrying. For a fleeting moment, he'd wondered if he had made a bad decision coming to this seemingly sleepy town where a newcomer would undoubtedly be scrutinized like a rare museum piece.

The last thing he wanted was a bunch of nosy people wanting to know him and his agenda.

He'd been exposed to the same suspicion

repeatedly as he'd walked along the high street until he'd found the Coast. Why his pretty average appearance could evoke such blatant evaluation was beyond him. Not that it mattered. Self-righteous and judgmental people he could deal with. It was comfort and sympathy from others that irked him.

Mac walked back to his bed and flopped backward against the pillows, picking up one of the letters the adoption agency sent to his father. Whatever happened next, he was here now, and he wouldn't leave until he'd achieved his goal. Closed community or not.

There would be no going back once he started making enquiries, and many people in this small seaside town might be affected by his actions. He dropped his gaze to the correspondence, feeling guilty.

Marian Ball, married name Cohen— Now resident in Templeton Cove. Approx. 65 years old. No other children.

He folded the letter and exhaled.

God only knew how things would go. Judging by the stony welcome, there would be plenty of people wanting to know who he was and what he was up to. Mac smiled wryly.

Well, all they'd know was he had a job to do. A job he was keeping from his family, one with the potential to turn his world—and theirs—upside down.

Templeton Cove, with its rows of seafront shops, B and Bs with vacancy signs hanging from fancy posts, tempting restaurants and bustling offices, was where he would find his biological grandmother. Marian Cohen had given Mac's father up for adoption, and, according to his father's research, she now lived in the Cove. She'd been married for eight or nine years but hadn't had any more children.

Mac clenched his jaw as further resentment whispered through him.

No other children.

Reading between the lines of his father's sometimes indecipherable notes, the circumstances surrounding his father's conception had not been ideal. The implication of possible abuse, neglect or abandonment had been alluded to, which was why his mother had asked him to let the search for Marian Cohen go. To leave the past in the past now that his father had passed.

The strain of keeping this trip a secret from his mother and older sister had bothered him for weeks, but now he was here, there would be no going back. He closed his eyes.

His family didn't feel the same drive to find Marian as he did. Why would they? It was Mac who'd lost his girlfriend and their unborn child, and the future happiness that had been torn from him by a drunk driver.

Anger burned in his chest, and Mac snapped open his stinging eyes to glare at the ceiling. Life was too damn short to ignore a person because you might not like what they had to say, where they'd been or what they'd done.

Rightly or wrongly, Marian Cohen deserved to know what kind of man her son—his father—had been. She deserved to know Dan Orman had cared for his family, worked hard and tried to be everything a good husband and dad should be, but time and again he'd failed.

Insecurity and self-doubt had incessantly plagued Dan's personal life, no matter how successful his business. Over time, he had pushed away his wife, barely managing to keep the love of his children. Abandonment and unworthiness had pulsed in his blood.

Mac knew all too well the legacy his father's biological mother had left him with—

and Marian Cohen was to blame for her son's every failing.

Guilt didn't belong in Mac's mission, only determination…and resolution.

Neither did the cowardice of a phone call. Marian Cohen would look her grandson in the face.

Pushing up from the bed, he walked into the bathroom. A quick shower and change and then he'd head downstairs for a beer or two. The Coast, with its polished ship's wheel hanging in pride of place on the wall, ropes looped across the ceiling and the whole interior decorated to resemble a galleon from years gone by, was as corny as any little seaside bar could be.

Yet when he'd arrived, the place had been packed, a three-piece band playing on a raised platform and the small dance floor in front of them decently full for a Wednesday night. From what he'd gathered from the people who frequented the place, the Coast was quite probably the most popular bar in town.

Mac undressed and stepped into the shower. He'd be lying if he said the Coast's inexplicable familiarity hadn't influenced his decision to stay here. He'd immediately relaxed a little and allowed the informality to seep inside him and bolster his reasons for being here.

In bars, no one cared who or what he was. When he played and sang, all they cared about was that his music relieved them of their worries.

The sense of loss that squeezed his chest confirmed how improbable it was he'd ever share real love with anyone again. Jilly had been gone three years, and although Mac dated, was open to what might be with someone else, no woman had come close to rekindling his belief in true, lifelong love.

If everything he'd once dreamed of—marriage, kids, a home—wasn't to be, he could accept that. But what he wouldn't accept is Marian Cohen not knowing what being given up for adoption had done to his father's confidence.

Mac was here now and God damn it, he would come face-to-face with Marian Cohen no matter what.

CHAPTER TWO

Kate took a sip of her rum and Coke and laughed. "Vanessa, you can't be serious. Since when have you tossed anyone out of the bar without good reason? Just tell me what she did."

The Coast's landlady glanced at her husband, who stood at the other end of the bar chatting with a couple of guys. "Dave will have something to say about me gossiping, but…" She wiggled her eyebrows. "Let's just say the girl was in here looking for trouble. Whether that trouble landed her in bed with one of the locals or not."

Kate shook her head and smiled. "That isn't even a story. After all that build-up, I thought…" She looked at the guy who moved in beside her. *Good Lord, of all things male and glorious.* She cleared her throat and dragged her gaze back to Vanessa. "Anyway—"

"Well, hello there." Vanessa deftly side-stepped and stood in front of the burning hunk of love who had just approached the bar. "How was your day? Is there anything you need?"

Kate feigned intense interest in the mirror behind the bar, surreptitiously checking the stranger out. His gaze briefly met hers in the reflection, and she quickly turned toward the pool table, smiling into her glass.

The man's eyes were bright blue against his tanned skin. His hair was longer than she normally liked on a guy, but he wore it well. His shoulders were broad and sheathed in a worn, leather jacket, with only a rectangle of white T-shirt temptingly visible beneath.

"Spent most of it in my room, if I'm honest." His voice was deep and just the right side of husky. "Everything's good, though."

"Glad to hear it." Vanessa smiled. "What can I get you?"

"I'll have a beer. Thanks. Oh, and some dry roasted nuts, if you have any."

"Nuts?" Vanessa voice faltered. "Oh, *nuts*… of course. Coming right up."

Fighting the urge to laugh, Kate faced the bar again and risked another glance at him. He'd leaned his back against the bar, his eyes narrowed as he stared toward the band playing onstage.

Nice, strong jaw. Wide shoulders. Dark lashes surrounding his phenomenal eyes. She lowered her study to his hand resting on the bar. Men's hands had always been her thing.

Her mouth dried. Big and strong-looking, his nails nicely trimmed and veins popping in just the right way. The man's hand bolted him at ninety miles an hour from the starting line to the winner's podium in her book.

"One beer." Vanessa placed the glass, none too gently, on the bar and smiled at Kate before turning to Mr. Bad Boy. "And one bag of nuts."

"Thanks." He lifted the beer and drank.

Kate stared at his throat as he swallowed, aware Vanessa was staring, too. He lowered the glass, and Kate snapped her study to the mirror.

He swiped his hand over his mouth. "Do you have any other bands lined up for the week?"

Vanessa exhaled. "Not this week, as we're hosting a big fund-raiser on Saturday. It's going to be a lot of fun. You should be there." She glanced at Kate. "Shouldn't he?"

Kate took a deep breath and forced her gaze to his. "Sure." She held out her hand.

"Kate Harrington. I'm in charge of the fund-raiser. Nice to meet you."

Ignoring her hand, he nodded, his gaze intent on Kate's as Vanessa moved away to serve another customer.

Kate stared back. His refusal to shake her hand made her attraction wane. "I manage the Cove's Teenage Support charity. You might have passed by the office. We're just off the main promenade."

"Can't say I have."

She narrowed her eyes as he turned back to the band. What was this guy's problem? She wasn't sure if it was her, Vanessa or the entire town that made him behave like a jerk, but she as sure as hell wasn't going to let him ignore her. Sometimes manners had to be taught. "So, you're visiting? Anyone I might know?"

"I doubt it."

Tension radiated from him as he took another slug of beer. Not to be put off, Kate picked up her drink. "Saturday's fund-raiser is for a new mother and baby unit that opened at the hospital a few months ago." She waited for him to look at her.

"Mothers and babies?" His bright blue eyes burned into hers. "Great cause."

Surprise mixed with pleasure and, at least

momentarily, quashed her reservations about him. She smiled. "Glad you think so. So how long are you staying in Templeton?"

He sipped his drink, his gaze moving back to the band. "I don't know yet. At least a week."

He faced her and lifted an eyebrow. "Is that a problem?"

Her cheeks warmed, clearly her annoyance with him showed in her voice. "No. Not at all."

He slowly ran his gaze over her face, lower to her neck, lingering on her chest for just a second longer than necessary, before he focused on the stage again.

She lifted her glass to her lips. Every inch of her body was intensely aware of him, and she didn't like it. Not one tiny bit.

The guy was aloof, standoffish…maybe even downright rude.

Good looks and even better bodies were not to be trusted. This guy could be just as much of a cheater as her ex. Even more so, if his terse manner was anything to go by. So why did she want to keep looking at him?

He leaned his elbow on the bar and faced her. "So…" He took a sip of his drink. "Do you live around here?"

Feigning nonchalance, she sat straighter

on her stool and put forth as much of a welcoming attitude as she could. It wasn't this stranger's fault he'd briefly—very briefly—attracted and intrigued her in one very dangerous blow. "Yes."

He lifted his eyebrows. "That's all I get?"

"That's all you get." She held his unwavering gaze. His voice was rich and deep and had the same warming effect on her as a shot of whiskey on a cold night. "That is, until I know a little more about you. Your name would be a good start."

He drank. "Mac. Orman."

"Pleased to meet you."

He studied her for a moment before he took a drink. "So, what else do you want to know?"

Her gaze dropped involuntarily to his mouth, most likely betraying her nonchalance. She shifted on her seat and lifted her eyes to his. "Why don't we start with what brought you to the Cove?"

The seconds ticked by, his blue eyes darkening.

Kate's nerves whispered with tension. "Was that not a good question to start with?"

He flitted his focus to the band once more. "I'm here on business."

She frowned. "In Templeton?"

"It's as good a place as any, isn't it?"

She hazarded a guess that his cold tone was meant to make her believe it was no big deal why he was in Templeton. Little did Mr. Bad Boy know, she was blessed—or sometimes cursed—with the ability to read between the lines and notice when something wasn't quite right with a situation. Her senses pinged to high alert with this guy, at the stiffness in his body, his clenched jaw and, quite frankly, his whole defensive demeanor.

She eyed him over the rim of her glass. "You don't strike me as the type to have work in a small town. You have city nightlife, city women and city trouble written all over you."

He faced her. "Why trouble? Because of the way I'm dressed? The fact I'm in a bar on my own?" He shook his head. "Give a guy a break, won't you?"

She fought to keep her cool and shrugged. "You seem, I don't know, a little guarded, that's all."

"Is that right?" Another sip of his drink. "Then why don't we talk about you?"

She frowned. "What about me?"

"Well, I know your name's Kate. I know you work at a charity. Why?"

"Why what?"

"Why a charity? Why *that* charity?"

"Does it matter?"

"No, but I wanted to see how open you are to sharing with strangers, seeing as you're expecting so much from me." He lifted his beer and looked around the bar. "As I thought. None of my business. Like why I'm in town is none of yours."

She narrowed her eyes as she glared at his profile. "Fine."

Vanessa reappeared and slapped a ledger on the bar. "Wow, we are fully booked for Saturday, Kate. It's going to be a good one, judging by the people traveling in from out of town." She glanced at Mac and frowned. "I know I promised you a double room if one became free, but are you okay with a single until after the weekend?"

He shrugged. "Sure. Can't see any reason I'll need a double." He glanced at Kate, and the first semblance of a smile lifted his lips. "At least not for the first week."

Her mouth dropped open, but nothing quick or smart emerged.

He faced Vanessa. "Where do you recommend I go for breakfast tomorrow?"

Concern flitted into her gaze. "You haven't enjoyed the breakfast here?"

"It was fine, but I want to venture out. Discover a bit more about this little town."

Little town? Kate shifted. The derogatory way he referred to the Cove niggled.

"Well, there are some good cafes on the seafront, a bakery if you want some ridiculously delicious pastries and superb coffee. Other than that, the Christie offers full English, but they're kind of pricey."

He sipped his beer. "Great. Thanks."

Kate drained her drink. Suspicion whirled inside her about this man and his motives for being here. Mac Orman brimmed with confidence. His whole character screamed that he knew where he was going and what he was doing.

Yet, something about his cold gaze told her he wasn't quite as self-confident as he made out. If his interest in the fund-raiser was anything to go by, he *could* be the caring type.

He nodded toward his empty glass. "Could I get another one of those?"

Vanessa picked it up. "Sure."

"And one for the lady."

Kate flinched. "Me?"

He nodded, his gaze steady on hers.

Damned if the man thought he could faze her. She lifted her chin. "A rum and Coke would be great. Thanks."

Vanessa grinned. "You're so funny, Kate. As transparent as a sheet of glass." She shook her head. "I'll go grab those drinks."

Kate shot a glare at Vanessa's turned back before taking a deep breath and facing Mac. She forced her mind to the matter at hand rather than wondering if he was ever going to take off his leather jacket so she could see what was underneath. "What sort of work are you in?"

"Work?"

"You said you were here on business."

"Business, yes. Work, no."

Kate frowned. "What does that mean?"

"It means I have business with someone."

The band finished, and he clapped, his gaze shrewd as he stared at the trio. "Are they local?"

Perplexed and more than a little frustrated by his change of subject, Kate glanced toward the band. "No, but they play here every other month, or thereabouts." She studied his profile, her unease intensifying. "So, this someone is who brought you here…to this *little town*?"

Vanessa slid their drinks on to the bar. "Right. I'll leave you two alone. I need to get some work done before that husband of mine bursts a blood vessel." She leaned closer to Mac and lowered her voice. "He's always a little overly suspicious of the good-looking guys who come in here. He's got a bark like a Doberman, but he's as soft as a teddy bear. Just don't tell him I told you that."

Vanessa walked away, and Kate studied Mac's turned cheek.

"To answer your question…" He picked up his drink. "I'm looking for someone."

Inexplicable protectiveness wound through her for the people in the Cove. "Who?"

"That's not really something you need to know."

Her senses screamed with warning as he faced the band once more, his jaw tight as he watched them pack up their gear.

"It's personal."

His clipped, no-nonsense tone stopped further words from spilling from her too often unstoppable lips. She snapped her mouth closed.

The atmosphere was strained between them, and her mind raced as she ran her study over his neck and shoulders. Would he bring trouble to town? Looking to wreak some kind of vengeance? To right a wrong? He certainly bore the expression and stance of someone incredibly pissed about something.

Her best friend, Izzy, often accused Kate of running full-throttle and letting her overactive imagination leave her sanity behind. Yet, she couldn't ignore the foreboding running through her. Her past made her suspicious. She didn't like people making judgments. Assuming things when they had no idea. But she was doing exactly that with Mac. He wasn't to blame for her ex. For her mother. For her sister.

She drained her drink, wincing as she swallowed. She needed to get out of here before Mac said anything else. She needed to leave the guy the hell alone. "Okay, well, it was nice to meet you. I'd better get home. I have a full day tomorrow."

"Sure." He kept his gaze averted and took another drink. "Maybe I'll see you around."

"Maybe you will."

With all the poise she could muster, Kate slipped from her stool and brushed past him, deftly weaving through the thinning crowd and out the door.

She was known throughout the Cove for her

lightning wit and her savvy comebacks, not to mention her no-holds-barred fund-raising strategies. Yet tonight, this stranger had reduced her to a suspicious crime-busting detective at best…or a dumbass, suspicion-fueled idiot, at worst.

She pulled her phone from her purse and texted Izzy.

Just met a man who could be here to cause one hell of a stir for someone in the Cove. I'll pop by the gallery tomorrow morning xx

MAC RETURNED TO his room, but once inside, he found everything annoying, even the window's sea view. He tipped his head from side to side. The tension in his neck and shoulder muscles indicated sleep would be a long time coming.

The feisty woman, with her dark brown eyes and thick, curly brown hair, had been a welcome diversion, but now she'd gone, guilt had returned for the reason he was here and the task he had ahead of him. Kate Harrington's questioning had only increased his determination to confront Marian. The doubts he was doing the right thing by telling her about the man her son had been, would not make Mac hesitate any longer.

He strolled to the window and opened it, breathing in the cold night air. Restless, Mac stared at the remaining three or four cars visible in the lamplight as the bar emptied for the night. His conscience pulled at him to call his mother. It wasn't unusual for days to pass without him calling her, weeks, if he was on the road with some band or other. But if he called her now, her instincts would tell her something was up.

The last thing he wanted was to rouse his mother's suspicions.

He closed the window and walked to the desk. He retrieved one of the envelopes and shook its contents on to the bed.

A photograph of his father landed face up and Mac picked it up. His dad smiled at the camera, one arm slung comfortably around Mac's mum's shoulders and his other hand resting lightly on Mac's older sister's waist. His fourteen-year-old self stood tall beside her, his chest puffed out and his first guitar proudly held in front of him.

Happy times. Good times.

His smile faltered as loss snagged his chest. Times that would never be repeated now his father was dead. The futile hope his mother and father might one day reunite crushed. According to the dates in his father's notes, he hadn't yet started his search for his birth mother when this picture was taken. And it had taken many years after before he'd finally found her.

Exhaling, Mac dropped the letter, damning the cardiac arrest that had taken his father just three months before. Walking back to the desk, he picked up a red, hard-backed notebook and opened it. He scanned his father's notes. Through these writings, Mac had realized how his father's search for his biological mother had consumed him. His notes were intense and methodical…pretty much like the man himself.

Yet, his father had chosen to keep his findings a secret and had never contacted the woman who had given him up.

Mac swiped his hand over his face. A sure sign of his father's habitual insecurity. Yet another example of how Marian's abandonment must have impacted her son's life—unbeknownst to her, of course.

But now Mac was here in Templeton, and he would find Marian Ball. Find her and make sure she learned what kind of a man her son had been.

He could start his pursuit of the old lady tonight. The last two days he'd either been holed up in his room trying to pin down a strategy or he'd wandered aimlessly around town looking at the various townhouses, wondering if Marian lived behind one of their doors, his indecision about speaking with her hounding him. But now, as frustration and impatience overtook him, his hesitation vanished. Mac gathered up the papers and stuffed them in the desk drawer along with his father's notebook.

Snatching up the keys he'd been given upon arrival, Mac left the room, and headed downstairs Once he'd locked the back door behind him, he glanced at the upstairs windows. No doubt his departure at this time of night would cause talk. No curtains twitched and no shadows were cast behind glass.

Satisfied he hadn't been seen, Mac walked through the garden to a small gate that took him on to a back street. He breathed deep. The cold night air was invigorating and washed away the uncertainty of whether being in the Cove was a betrayal to his father. His mother had confessed to him after the funeral that she'd dissuaded his father from looking for Marian years before, fearing what a second rejection could do to her then husband.

That reason had been weak, almost cowardly, in Mac's opinion. Even if the circumstances that led to his father's adoption turned out to be upsetting, his father should've had the guts to hear them.

As well as the notebook, his father had left behind a diary in which he had recorded his feelings and thoughts throughout his investigations. Mac's mother's pleas had not fallen on deaf ears. Not only had his father heard them, his inner demons had echoed them.

Mac scowled.

Well, his father's heart had decided to call it a day…suddenly and brutally, leaving his family flailing. Since the death of his girlfriend and their baby, Mac had had trouble dealing with grief. So he'd done the only thing he could.

He gotten busy finishing what his father started.

Mac stalked through the side street until he emerged onto the main thoroughfare, which ran alongside the beach. Crossing the road, he walked across the wooden-planked promenade and gripped the railing. The guilt for abandoning his family in their hour of need pressed down on him, and he battled the sting in his eyes as he looked toward the blackness of the ocean, its waves crashing.

Conflicting determination and doubt warred inside him, and Mac turned his back to the beach to stare across the street. He hadn't walked this far along the seafront since he arrived.

He stilled, every hair on his body rising.

Marian's Bonniest Bakery.

The bakery's awning was pulled back, and its latticed, cottage-styled windows were unfettered by curtains or blinds. It looked homey, inviting…motherly.

He narrowed his eyes as adrenaline caused his heart rate to speed up.

He slowly straightened from the railing and walked forward as though pulled by an invisible rope. He barely glanced in either direction as he crossed the street.

Once he reached the other side, he flitted his study from the bakery's name to its window. Over and over, he repeated the sequence, his mind scrambling. What were the chances his father's birth mother owned this place?

He stepped closer to the window and curved his hands around his eyes as he tried to see inside. In the shadowed darkness, he saw pine tables and chairs, a few booths along the window and a counter in back. The place was a decent size, and a profound sense of welcome permeated its light-colored walls dotted with sketches of cupcakes and loaves of bread.

Jolting away, Mac turned and marched along the pavement, his fists clenched as trepidation unfurled inside him. In his mind, he'd purposely decided Marian Ball was someone who put herself first. A woman who had left her baby behind to seek an untethered life without husband or child to hamper her. That had been the easier scenario to carry until he learned the truth.

Templeton Cove might be small, but certain sections were high-end and expensive. So he'd envisioned her living out a wealthy retirement by the sea, heedless of her long-abandoned child trying to track her down.

As unfair as that might be, considering a woman's limited choices almost fifty years ago, it helped Mac to bury his anger. He wanted to find Marian Ball and lay his father to rest. He hadn't come here to find a grandmother he might like.

The bakery didn't fit with any of his imaginings, and that scared him.

What if she was welcoming and warm? What if she'd had other kids and his father was mistaken?

He gritted his teeth, focusing on the pain of all he'd lost. The woman needed to know how her decisions had affected her son and, in turn, his children.

Yet, the enormity of what might happen next continued to badger him. He needed to think some more. Tomorrow he would come back here, order some breakfast, check out the locals and, of course, check out Marian and her bonniest bakery.

CHAPTER THREE

KATE PUSHED OPEN the door of the View and entered the chic art gallery.

Across the room, Izzy, her best friend and the gallery's manager, stood in front of a painted landscape, her arms crossed and her head tilted in contemplation.

"Iz?"

"Mmm?"

Kate prodded her friend's arm. "Hey."

Izzy turned, her eyes glazed in obvious thought. "What do you think of this piece? I'm trying to decide if I like it or not." She turned back to the painting. "Jay acquired it on one of his business trips. He loves it, but I'm not sure."

Kate glanced at the painting and shrugged. "Sea, sand, sky. What's not to like? Now..." She gripped Izzy's arm and pulled her to one of the cushioned seats in the center of the gallery's open floor plan. "We, me and you, have to figure out what we're going to do about Mac Orman."

Izzy frowned. "Who?"

"Mac. The guy I texted you about last night."

Izzy raised her eyebrows as they sat. "What *we're* going to do? You have noticed I'm working at the gallery full-time now, as well as trying to organize my wedding. Do you really think I have time to worry whether or not a mysterious stranger who just arrived in town is going to end up sleeping with my too highly strung, too much in need of sex, best friend?" Izzy sighed. "Sorry, my life's far too busy right now."

Kate feigned a glare and playfully swatted Izzy's shoulder. "Are you actually trying not to laugh?"

"Of course not."

Kate narrowed her eyes and nudged Izzy again. "Nothing about this guy, nothing about my text to you last night is funny. Absolutely nothing."

Izzy's blue eyes glinted with undisguised glee. "This is priceless."

"What is?"

"You."

Kate's cheeks warmed with indignation. "Some friend you are."

Izzy frowned, and when she spoke, her tone was less amused. "You need to calm down." She searched Kate's eyes. "My God, this guy has really gotten to you, hasn't he? Just how good-looking is he?"

"He's…he's… Oh, damn it." Kate slumped. "He's hot. Really, really hot, but that doesn't mean he's trustworthy. He's up to something. Something that can only mean bad news."

"Just because some guy strolls into town and puts your knickers in a twist doesn't mean he's up to anything. Maybe you don't trust him because he's made you think about sex for the first time in far too many months."

Kate huffed a laugh. "Ah, see? That's where you're wrong. I think about sex *a lot*. It's the doing I haven't done for months. That's by the by. The point is, Mac admitted he's in town looking for someone."

"And?"

"And the look on his face, all chiseled jaw and flashing blue eyes, when he said it, told me that when he finds this unfortunate person, he isn't going to give them a hug. No, siree. The man looked more likely to bite their head off and feed it to the seagulls." Kate shook her head and pushed the curls from her cheeks. "I don't like it. Not one bit."

"But you like him."

Did she? Even after a night of almost zero sleep and hours of thinking about Mac, she still wasn't sure what to make of him. "Yes. No. I don't know." She stood and walked around the seat before facing Izzy once more. "I have no choice but to find out what he's up to. What if my instinct's right and someone we know is going to be upset by Mac's arrival, or whatever it is he plans to do or say to this person? Won't I be in some way culpable?"

"How?"

"Because I could've forewarned them. Maybe helped to smooth a few of Mac's clearly ruffled feathers. You didn't see his face. He's up to something, and it doesn't bode well."

"But he'll only see you as nosing into his business."

"I'm not nosing, I'm concerned. For him and whoever he's here to see." She planted her hands on her hips. "Anyway, I'm trained for this sort of thing."

"What sort of thing? Prying?"

Kate glared. "Caring. I'm a charity worker. I care about people. It's what I do."

Izzy stood. "Look, if this guy is looking for someone, there's not a lot you can do about it. Leave him be. If, on the other hand, you like him, why don't you drop by the Coast tonight and talk to him? Maybe he'll tell you more about the reason he's here. But if this is another one of your lost soul missions, Kate, you need to steer clear. I get the impression he spooked you. Maybe it's better you leave him alone."

"Spooked me?" Kate laughed, ignoring the pang of truth she felt at Izzy's words. "Since when has anyone spooked me? Let alone a long-haired, teeth-flashing, blue-eyed, incredibly tall...man."

Izzy raised her eyebrows. "Are you forgetting who you're talking to? What about Dean?"

"What about him?"

"He hurt you. Badly. Maybe this Mac guy spooked you because he reminds you of Dean."

"He's nothing like Dean."

"Are you sure about that?"

Kate opened her mouth, but no words came out. Instead, a hundred comparisons between

Mac and her ex flickered through her mind. She swallowed. "Okay, fine. You've nothing to worry about because Mac doesn't seem at all interested in hooking up with a woman. He practically sneered at everything I had to say, and he was by no means impressed with Vanessa's teasing."

"Then the man must be an ass. Which is exactly what I thought about Dean when I first met him."

"That's not fair." Kate whirled away and strode toward the painting Izzy had been staring at when Kate came into the studio. Her friend had hit on the nerve that had been the cause of the most fitful night Kate had suffered in months. Mac did have the same dark hair and broodiness about him as her filthy, cheating ex. Yet, there was something different about Mac. Something she wanted to explore.

Needing to change the subject and simultaneously lash out, she chose a new target. "Jay Garrett has really bad taste."

"You think?"

"Well, not in gallery managers, obviously." She flashed Izzy a smile over her shoulder. "But in paintings, yes."

Izzy came to stand beside her and draped

her arm around Kate's shoulders. "Why don't we talk about my wedding instead? Maybe that will take your mind off Mac Orman."

"How are the plans going? Is there anything you want my help with?"

"Not right now, but you could come over later and help me drink a fine bottle of Chablis."

Kate grinned. "Absolutely. Look, I'd better go, but I'll come by your place around seven."

"Perfect." Izzy walked Kate to the front door. "So, what are you going to do about Mac?"

"I don't know. Yet. But you're right. I can't afford to get mixed up with a bad boy again."

"Dean was a long time ago. You can't let one bad relationship put you off the type of guys you're attracted to forever."

"I'm not attracted…it's just that for a fleeting moment he seemed genuinely respectful of what I do for work. I liked that. My gut is telling me somewhere behind that angry exterior is a decent bloke." She crossed her arms. "Maybe I could help him."

"Kate…"

"What? All I'm saying is, if I can stop him going in all guns blazing, I will. I know what it feels like to be backed into a corner. Mac seemed ultra-tense. Like he's got no real idea how to speak with this person when he finds them. It was…weird."

"Weird? Or just something you couldn't immediately solve?"

Kate sighed. "Both. I'd better go."

"Okay. See you later."

Kate left the gallery and made her way along the high street toward the Teenage Support office, buttoning her coat against the late winter chill. Her head bent low, she wondered when it would ever feel like summer again in Templeton.

What she needed was a hot cappuccino and one of Marian's breakfast rolls. A guaranteed diversion from Mac. She pushed him to the back of her mind and forced her focus on the day ahead.

Deserving and desperate kids and their families needed her full concentration and dedication. Maybe Izzy was right and Kate should butt out of Mac's life. What drove her to reach out to people was her work with those who had been bullied—and experiences she had with her mother. Mac was a big boy who most likely knew exactly what he was doing.

Feeling more positive, Kate pushed open

the door of the bakery and shook out her curls, already turning to frizz, thanks to the cold sea air. When she looked up, her eyes were drawn toward one of the booths. Mac Orman sat with some papers in front of him as he stared toward the counter, his eyes narrowed.

What looked to be a half-eaten breakfast had been pushed to the side. He turned his focus to the open notebook in front of him and scribbled something on the page, his expression grim with stony concentration.

Kate's suspicions rocketed. Was whoever he was looking for in the bakery right now? Was he writing down their actions or day-to-day business for some reason? Was he stalking someone? She looked around. Nobody seemed to be taking any notice of Mac and his notebook. She took her time hanging her jacket on the old-fashioned coat stand as she furtively watched him.

There it was again. He looked at Ella behind the counter and made a note. Then he looked at an older woman Kate didn't recognize. Made another note. What was he up to?

Mac glanced toward her and flinched. Aha! She lifted her chin. Caught red-handed. Whatever he was writing certainly wasn't innocent. She straightened her spine and walked toward him as he quickly shut his notebook and slipped it on to the seat beside him.

MAC FORCED A slow smile and tried his best not to be distracted by the sexy, disheveled sight of Kate Harrington. Her deep, dark eyes were almost hypnotic, but he'd have to be half-blind not to notice the concern in her gaze when she'd questioned him last night. She seemed nice, sweet…and all sorts of sexy mixed in. Another time, another place, he might have been interested.

But not here. Not now.

He needed Kate to keep her nose out of his business. To let his cold façade slip would risk his pursuit of the elusive Marian Ball.

Judging by the suspicion in Kate's gaze as she marched toward him, she'd seen him checking out the locals. She glanced toward the counter and back again, annoyance etched on her pretty face. Her shoulders lifted as though she were bracing herself before she dropped them and stood right beside him.

Here goes…

He stood in the hope she wouldn't sit. "Morning."

She stared. Her eyes assessing, judging.

He raised his eyebrows. "Getting breakfast?"

"And coffee. Lots and lots of coffee." She eyed him carefully. "You?"

He tilted his head toward his table. "Breakfast done and pretty nice it was, too. This Marian, whoever she is, must be one hell of a cook."

"She is, but Marian's out of town. It would've been Ella or one of the other girls who fixed your breakfast."

He stilled and tried not to inhale as her words knocked the wind out of him. How could he not have considered Marian Ball might be out of town? He forced his expression into cool nonchalance, but from the way Kate's gaze bored into his, alight with interest, he knew he'd already been analyzed, and a calculation had been made.

He slid back into the booth. "How well do you know Marian?"

"Why?"

"Why?"

"Yes. It's a simple enough question."

Annoyed, Mac said, "I'm trying to be friendly here. Make a little conversation. If you don't want that…" He tilted his head toward the counter. "Don't let me keep you."

"Fine. I know Marian really well." Uninvited, she slid into the booth opposite him. "As do most people in town."

Mac studied her. How much could he say, or ask, about Marian Ball without arousing Kate's obvious distrust. "Is that so?"

"Uh-huh." She held his stare, her eyes giving away nothing.

He blew out a breath. "So, this place is hers?"

"I'm pretty sure she owns it now, but it was Jay's, and his father's before him."

Mac frowned and glanced toward the counter. "Jay?"

"Our resident millionaire. He's as cute as hell and richer than Rockefeller, but the guy only has eyes for two women in town."

"Two women?" Mac smiled. "You don't strike me as the kind to talk so fondly about a guy dating two different women. You got a thing for him?"

"No, but Jay's a great guy. He's kind and generous, my friend's fabulous boss, a loving husband, and a great father to his little girl, Sarah."

"Ah, his wife and kid. I get it."

"Do you?"

He frowned as wariness clouded her gaze.

"He's married, he's a daddy. That's the two women in his life."

She leaned her forearms on the table, her brown eyes dark with warning. "You need to understand something about the people in this town, Mac. For the most part, we're good and caring. We look out for one another. Certain people have done amazing things for me and they've asked for nothing in return. That makes me protect them and do all I can to ensure their happiness. So, if you're here looking for somebody, I hope you're not intending to upset or hurt them in any way."

He clenched his jaw. "I'm here to resolve some unfinished business, remember?"

"Yes, I do. Personal business. Which, judging by the way you're looking at me, might irritate the hell out of me."

She slid her gaze to the side of his seat. "So, why the notebook?"

He glared. Who did she think she was? "Are you kidding me?"

"Far from it."

"You think I'm going to sit here and let you question me again? For the love of God, I only met you last night." He leaned forward, matching her posture. "You need to forget you met me. Forget why I'm here. I'm in the Cove for good reason—a reason that has nothing to do with you."

Her cheeks flushed, but her eyes only hardened further. "Be that as it may, you've got me concerned."

He sat back and crossed his arms. "Why? What business is it of yours who comes into the Cove? Regardless of their purpose."

She stared at him before looking around the bakery. "I…" She met his gaze and slumped. "Fine. You seem on edge. If I can help—"

"You can't."

"Is it Marian? Is that who you're looking for? Because if it is, you need to know she's the boss around here."

God, the woman was canny. He'd give her that much. He sighed, no more able to stay angry with a pretty woman than he could with his mother. "I kind of figured that."

"Not the bakery. The town. Marian is the boss of Templeton."

He searched her expression for the flashes of teasing and laughter he'd seen in her eyes at the Coast. She stared back at him, her gaze solemn.

"So, she's a dragon? Is that what you're trying to tell me?"

"A dragon? Marian?" She huffed a laugh.

"Marian is the furthest thing from a dragon you're going to meet. Of course, on occasion, she can be way too bossy, but her heart's in the right place. She's kind, caring, and supportive to everyone. Sure, she might breathe fire now and then if someone upsets one of her brood, but she's got the people who deserve her love at heart. Which means, Mr. Orman, if you upset one of us and are still here when she and George return from vacation, your ass is going to be pinned to the wall before you have any chance to flash that sexy smile of yours."

Marian flew from his brain, and he smiled. "Sexy?"

"I'm serious."

"Well, thanks. I'll take the compliment gladly."

She looked away with a scowl. Mac studied her profile. He couldn't decide if he was more attracted to her when she flirted or when she was angry. Either way, he wouldn't be acting on it. Not in a town where the woman who could be his father's birth mother lorded it over the residents as though she were some kind of guardian angel.

If Marian the baker was his biological grandmother, she was the woman who'd given her child up for adoption. He needed to know why and how that happened. The woman Kate described didn't sound like she could be the Marian he was looking for. Would someone maternal, caring and protective really be okay knowing she had a child out there somewhere?

Kate slid from the booth. "I have to go." She stared at him. "Just take my advice and don't go upsetting anyone in town. Whatever your issue is, think it through carefully. I've known far too many people who have come close to destroying themselves by holding on to anger, planning revenge, or forever regretting something they can't change. None of those things solve anything. Believe me."

The sudden sadness in her eyes made his chest ache, and he touched her hand before he could consider the crack such physical contact would create in his veneer. "Hey, you okay?"

She glanced toward the door. "I'm fine."

"Has someone hurt you?"

"Of course not." She hitched her purse higher on to her shoulder. "Just be careful. That's all I'm asking."

She hesitated, her focus falling to his mouth before she nodded and headed for the exit, breakfast clearly forgotten.

Mac watched her rush along the street until she was out of sight. Whatever had caused her unchecked sadness, Kate Harrington was strong, feisty and full of determination. God only knew how the unfortunate guy who ended up falling in love with her would get through their years together with his balls intact.

Picking up his notebook, Mac slowly rose before walking to the counter. He smiled at the young girl serving. "Can I settle the bill, please?"

"Sure." She rang up his purchases. "That's seven twenty, please."

He handed her a ten-pound note. "So, when does Marian get back from holiday?"

"Next week. She's going to be full of stories. I can't wait."

"Stories?"

"Oh, yeah. Her and George, that's her husband, are a blast. So funny…" Her eyes twinkled with laughter. "So naughty, if the truth be told. Here, that's two eighty change."

"Thanks." He dropped the coins into a pot on the counter and glanced at the leaflet taped to its side. *Proceeds for the fund-raiser at the Coast. Contact Kate Harrington for details.*

He looked up and met the girl's gaze. She

tilted her head toward the pot. "You should come along. It'll be a fun night."

"Oh, I will." He smiled. "Most definitely."

CHAPTER FOUR

KATE EMBRACED THE adrenaline flowing through her as she ducked into the marquee that had been erected at the back of the Coast. Although a little harassed, she thrived on the pressure of creating successful events. Despite the light snowfall, the lit space was warm and inviting. People had been wandering in for the last hour. As the time for the Moon Shadows to play neared, that trickle became a steady stream.

Couples and families milled around, some grouped by the heaters, laughing and enjoying their drinks amid the growing anticipation of the fun ahead. As the colored fairy lights along the top line of the marquee danced across the faces of the revelers, Kate scanned the room.

The fund-raiser needed to go off without a hitch. The money already collected was fantastic, and two of the four major donors who'd arrived looked to be enjoying themselves, seemingly impressed with the decorated marquee, stalls and family games scattered around. She glanced toward the makeshift stage at the far end of the marquee.

Now all she had to worry about was the Moon Shadows delivering three no-holds-barred, hour-long sets to take the crowd into the evening. Then Nick Carson would take over as the DJ for the late-night dance party.

Kate narrowed her eyes. As far as she could see, only four members of the band had arrived. Where was the replacement?

"Kate?"

She turned at the light touch to her shoulder. "Hi, Vanessa. Everything okay?"

"Sure." Vanessa adjusted her hold on the crate of glasses she carried. "I'm just going to deliver these to the drinks table. Hopefully, with an extra bar set up, we can easily cater to the number of people we're expecting."

"I hope so." Kate glanced around. "There are far too many young mums in the Cove. It's imperative we do all we can to help them."

Vanessa's gaze softened. "Hey, you do all you can to help everyone. Don't be so hard on yourself. Everything's going to be great."

"Hmm, I hope so." Kate cleared her throat. "So, have you seen anything of Mac today?"

Vanessa's smile faltered before she lowered the crate to the floor. "No, have you?"

Concerned by the sudden unease in Vanessa's eyes, Kate frowned. "He hasn't done something to upset you, has he?"

"Not as such. No. I'm sure it's nothing."

Kate touched her friend's arm. "Hey, what's going on?"

Vanessa sighed. "His attitude worries me, that's all. Dave and I have done all we can to make Mac welcome, but he doesn't seem to want what we have to offer." She grimaced. "Maybe I'm too used to people enjoying themselves when they're here."

"He hasn't been asking you personal questions, has he?"

"No. Why?"

Hating that Mac Orman held a secret that was pretty much guaranteed to affect someone she knew, Kate crossed her arms. "I'm just concerned he might be in the Cove for all the wrong reasons."

"Such as?"

"I don't know."

"Well, I for one, trust your judgment. If you think I need to give Mac some space—"

"I didn't say that. In fact, I think we need to do all we can to keep him close."

Vanessa smiled and wiggled her eyebrows. "There wouldn't be an ulterior motive in there somewhere, would there?"

"No." Kate feigned a glare. "So, you can stop looking at me like that. Considering I caught him in the bakery the other day looking as though he was taking notes on some of the people in there, you can say I entirely distrust the man."

"Taking notes? What do you mean?"

"He had this book and he was scribbling in it as he studied people. The minute he spotted me, he snapped it shut clearly not wanting me to read anything."

"Isn't that understandable? The guy's entitled to his privacy, right?"

"Hmm."

Unease whispered through Kate as it had time and again since she'd left Mac at the bakery. Right along with memories of the way he'd spotted her vulnerability at the end of their conversation. "Something's definitely up with him."

"And you're going to find out what."

Kate nodded as determination rose inside her once more. "Yes, I am."

"Good. I'll see if I can find out anything, too. But in the meantime, let's be nice to him.

I'm sure he'll turn out to be an okay guy, and this notebook is nothing to worry about. He's probably plotting a book or something."

"A book?" Kate huffed. "Plotting, period, more like it."

Vanessa picked up the crate and shook her head. "I'll see you later."

As her friend walked away, Kate exhaled a shaky breath and headed toward the band as they warmed up their instruments and checked leads and microphones. She really needed to focus and forget Mac Orman. For now, at least. "Hey, guys."

She recognized the lead singer from the band's poster as he came toward her, his smile warm and his hand outstretched. "Kate Harrington, right? Joe Masters. It's good to finally meet you in person."

Kate shook his hand. "Same to you." She looked over the stage. "It seems as though you have everything under control. Will you be ready to kick things off in fifteen minutes or so?"

"Absolutely."

"Only, I was a little worried the replacement guitarist isn't here."

"He's not."

Her heart picked up speed. "And that doesn't bother you?"

"He'll be here any second, I'm sure."

"You're sure? But you're due on in minutes."

Joe winked. "Relax. Everything will be fine."

She opened her mouth to protest, but he jumped onto the stage and proceeded to talk with the drummer. Kate took a deep breath. She had people to greet, donations to lock in the safe as well as a hundred and one other things to check on. If Joe Masters said his band would be ready, she'd have to trust him. But if a new musician didn't show up in the next ten minutes, she'd be on the phone to every local band she could think of to ask if their guitarist would spare a night to play with an up-and-coming band for charity.

Stopping to chat and greet people as she went, Kate made slow progress toward the food stand. where Dave, the Coast's landlord, was, happily cooking burgers in a closed, mobile oven.

Kate leaned on the counter beside him. "It's going well, isn't it?"

"Never had a doubt." Dave pointed his tongs toward the main bar inside. "There's plenty of people in there who will make their way out here once the Shadows start." He frowned as his attention landed on something over Kate's shoulder. "He's a strange one, that Mac Orman. Not sure what to make of him, even though Vanessa, God love her, tries to convince me he's all right."

Kate turned and her heart kicked. Dressed in blue jeans and a black shirt beneath his ever-present leather jacket, Mac looked just as ridiculously hot as he had when she'd seen him in the bakery a couple of days before. She thought over Vanessa's observations, interested to hear Dave's take. "What do you mean by strange?"

"Well, the guy clearly isn't lacking in the looks department, if the way Vanessa was watching him earlier is anything to go by. He seems pretty sure of himself, but..."

She faced Dave, pleased she wasn't the only one impervious to Mac's charms. "What?"

He turned back to the oven. "Something tells me that guy is here with an agenda. I don't like strangers with agendas."

Kate looked at Mac again. He stood near the band, wearing a stony expression and holding a bottle of beer. "No, me neither.

Maybe I should try to uncover that agenda. What do you think?"

"By all means, if you think you can. Just do me a favor?"

"What?"

"If anyone asks, this little bit of digging was all your idea, not mine. Okay?"

Kate smiled. "You're not actually scared of Vanessa, are you?"

"'Course not, but if she thinks I'm causing trouble, I'll be sleeping on the couch. At my age that doesn't do my back any good, if you understand what I'm saying."

"Understood. I'll keep my investigating to myself."

He nodded and Kate took a deep breath before she headed toward Mac. He turned as she neared, almost as though he sensed her approach. He clearly struggled to change his expression into something less hostile as his slow study drifted over her body, seeming to assess every part of her.

Kate's stomach knotted with attraction. But there was no way of knowing who Mac was, or what he was capable of. Her guard needed to be in place at all times.

She forced a smile as she stood in front of him. "Mac, nice to see you again."

His gaze lingered on her mouth before he met her eyes. "I'm surprised to hear you say that, but thanks."

Deciding she would make a better detective if she smoothed the tension between them, she laughed. "Just because I'm concerned why you're here doesn't mean I don't like you. You seem pleasant enough. So, did you come in for a look around? Or do you plan on staying awhile?"

"I thought I'd check out the band. The Moon Shadows are pretty good."

She glanced at the band, more than a little concerned that the guitarist hadn't shown up. "I'm not much for country rock, but from what I've heard, they aren't half bad."

"What sort of music do you like?"

She shrugged. "Acoustic, Ed Sheeran, that sort of stuff." She faced him. "And I'm partial to some ballads and smooth jazz on occasion."

He nodded, his gaze intense on hers. "Good choices."

Their eyes locked, and the noise around them faded. Kate struggled to look away, struggled to speak. "Any more luck finding the person you're looking for?"

"Not yet, but it's early days."

"Early days?" She faced him. "You plan on staying longer than a week?"

He took another gulp of his beer. "If I have to."

"But you can't."

His blue eyes brightened with amusement. "Why not? I thought it was Marian who was the boss around here. So far, no one named Marian has tried to push me out of town like you are."

"I'm not trying to push…" She glared. "Stop doing that."

"Doing what?"

"Tormenting me."

He raised his eyebrows. "I torment you?"

"No." Her cheeks burned. "You infuriate me."

"Then my aim has been met."

She opened her mouth to respond when the leader singer from the band joined them. "Kate? Could I have a word?"

Grateful for the interruption, she faced the singer. "Sure. What can I do for you?"

He grimaced. "Bad news. I just called the replacement guitarist. He can't make it."

Her stomach dropped. "And he's only told you now? Can you get by without him?"

"No can do, I'm afraid. Can't play our songs without a lead guitarist."

"Then what am I supposed to—"

"I'll help you out." Mac stepped forward and extended his hand to the lead singer. "Mac Orman. Guitarist."

Joe shook Mac's hand. "Joe Masters."

Kate stared wide-eyed at Mac, her heart beating fast. "You? You'll step in?"

He flashed her a smile. "Anything to help out a lady." He turned to the singer. "I'll just run upstairs and get my guitar."

Joe frowned. "How well do you know our music?"

Mac nodded. "Really well. Big fan, in fact. Well, except for the times I'm looking for some ballads or smooth jazz."

Kate's mouth dropped open, but words failed her as Mac headed inside the bar. She stared at the empty doorway and snapped her mouth closed.

Joe patted her on the shoulder. "There you go. Panic over. Told you I had everything under control."

He strolled away, leaving Kate standing alone and flailing in a sea of attraction, grateful to a man she really didn't want to lean on. But apparently with Mac, she didn't have a lot of choice.

MAC HUMMED A Moon Shadows tune as he let himself into his room, reliving the look of shock, then relief on Kate Harrington's face. That had been worth a million pounds. It had been a long time since he'd wanted to be the one to ease a woman's stress and worry. He wanted to do both for Kate, even if his reasons weren't entirely honorable. He needed a way to lessen the woman's distrust of him so he could get on with his mission.

The question was, why had she made his business *her* business?

He grabbed his guitar from where it lay on a chair and took his phone from his pocket to silence it. His mind wandered to Kate once more. She looked fantastic in a pair of tight blue jeans, black boots and a peach knit top. Decent, yet almost indecent. Just the right side of sexy.

He dropped his gaze to his phone, and his smile promptly disappeared.

The display showed three missed calls from his older sister. Immediate guilt warred with his need to keep what he was doing in Templeton to himself a while longer.

But if he avoided her, Dana would only keep calling. His sister was never one to be impeded by anyone, especially her younger brother. He pressed the button to return her call.

She answered on the second ring. "At last! I've been trying to reach you all day."

Mac shouldered the phone and grabbed a pick out of his guitar case. "What's up?"

"What's up? Where are you? I can't believe you'd take off like this. Not when we need you here."

Culpability pressed down on him. "Why do you need me there? I know Mum's upset about dad, divorced or not, but it's you and her grandchildren she needs around her, not me. What can I do to ease her grief? You know what I'm like with that kind of thing."

"You mean sympathetic? Empathetic? Caring? Don't talk rubbish, Mac. You're amazing with Mum, with me, with all of us. Your disappearing makes no sense."

He squeezed his eyes shut. "I had a commitment for a gig. I couldn't get out of it." He left the room, closing the door behind him. "There's nothing I can do but to see it through and then I'll be back. Okay?"

"No. Not okay. We need you here. I can't be

with Mum 24/7 when I've got two kids and a husband away working. Please, will you just come home?"

"I can't. Not yet." He hurried down the stairs and through the bar, steadfastly ignoring the curious stares directed toward him and his guitar. "Dana, look, I've got to go. I'll call you later, okay?"

"Where are you? It sounds kind of noisy."

"That's because there's a crowd of people here waiting for me to get on stage. We'll talk later. 'Bye."

He ended the call, doing all he could to banish his sister's words. Right now, he needed to concentrate on erasing the suspicion from Kate Harrington's beautiful eyes and have her look at him with respect, maybe even a little wonder if he played well enough. His new, slightly worrying, reasons for wanting to do so were as dangerous as they were stupid, considering he'd recently acquired the troublesome desire to know if her lips were as hot as the rest of her.

He liked her spirit and the way she didn't let anyone—including him—push her away or around. He had a feeling she'd make a much better friend than enemy. If his playing could allay her misconceptions about him, all the better.

She stood talking with an older couple, and as he walked by her, she turned and touched his arm. "Mac, just a second." She smiled apologetically at the couple. "Will you excuse me?"

"Of course." The man nodded. "Good luck with everything. You do the town proud."

"Thank you. Enjoy yourselves." She faced Mac, her brow furrowed. "Are you sure about this? I'm just about to introduce the band, and I don't want you to think I've put you under unwanted obligation."

He stared into her worried eyes, and an entirely unanticipated concern for her swept through his chest. Why did it suddenly feel preferable to have her angry at him, rather than looking so anxious? "I'm doing this because I want to help you out. Nothing more, nothing less. It looks amazing in here, and if people are having a good time, they'll stay longer and spend more money. We both know the Moon Shadows are a big part of today's attraction. Let me do something toward making today a success. Okay?"

Her cheeks flushed and her shoulders relaxed. "Thank you."

"Anytime."

He walked up the three steps to the stage.

Joe Masters came forward and slapped his hand to Mac's shoulder. "You're a lifesaver, man. Let me introduce you to the band." He pointed as he spoke. "Over there, we have Josh on drums, Will on bass and Lola, who will be singing backup vocals."

Mac raised his hand, acknowledging the band's curious but welcoming study. "Mac Orman. Pleased to meet you all."

The next few minutes passed quickly as Joe talked Mac through the proposed set. Once Mac had convinced the lead singer he knew each of the original and cover songs well enough to keep up, Joe left the stage in search of Kate.

Mac took up his position and released a slow breath as he looked out at the audience. Women smiled at him, while guys focused on his guitar or the rest of the band. Every face looked happy, comfortable. Potentially, a really good crowd. The familiar buzz pooled in his stomach as it did every time he played. His gaze fixed on Kate as she emerged through the throng and climbed the steps onto the stage.

She didn't so much as glance in his direction as she walked to the microphone. "Good afternoon, ladies and gentlemen. I'm thrilled to see so many of you here already. There are burgers and hot dogs near the rear of the tent, as well as drinks available at the temporary bar or inside. As you know, today is all about raising money for the hospital's new mother and baby unit. Please, give what you can for this worthy cause.

"Okay, that's enough from me. I'm thrilled to leave you in the capable hands of the Moon Shadows and special guest guitarist, Mac Orman."

Mac stared at the back of her head as a jolt of unease pierced through him. Why hadn't he considered that she might offer his name to the whole damn town? So much for melting into the background.

She clapped along with the rest of the audience as she made her way down the steps in her sexy, high-heeled boots. He struck up the first note, watching her progress through the tent. It wasn't until she tossed a triumphant smile over her shoulder at him that Mac realized the public announcement of his name had been intentional.

Clearly not content with her own careful

watch on him, she wanted the whole town on high alert.

Kate Harrington didn't trust him, didn't like him and wasn't going to be happy until he left town for good. That much was obvious. He glared at her as she started chatting with a group of women in their twenties who enveloped her affectionately. Mac turned to the audience, purposefully catching the eye of another twentysomething female.

He tipped her a wink, and she returned the compliment with a bright smile and glittering eyes. But it didn't calm his frustration that, no matter what he did or said, nothing seemed to lessen Kate's curiosity about him.

Well, one way or another—he strummed the opening bars of the first song—he'd see through what he came to the Cove to do. Whether she watched him like a bloody hawk or not.

CHAPTER FIVE

KATE STOOD AT the temporary bar and rejoiced in her ingenuity. Mac thought he was so cool, so full of bravado and smugness as he continued to keep his mission secret from her. Well, he might have the new knack of freezing her tongue while simultaneously inflaming her body, but flooring her by stepping onstage to save her from certain disaster had backfired on him big-time.

Now she'd publicly introduced him. The well-known busybodies in the Cove would be all over him.

Her triumph faltered. So, why didn't that sentiment feel as good as it should?

She swallowed. Could it be because he hadn't given her enough reason to be outed that way? He might enjoy tormenting her, but he'd not actually done anything to anyone— yet. What he had done was help her out of what could have been carnage, considering the number of Moon Shadows fans present.

Shame warmed her cheeks as she watched him onstage. His skillful playing easily held rhythm with the rest of the band, his furrowed brow and concentrated gaze reflecting his determination to do a good job.

What was wrong with her? Why did she keep hounding him, just because he seemed determined to keep her, Vanessa, and everyone else, at arm's length? All she had to justify her suspicions was his refusal to share with her. She might be able to talk with teenagers who came into the center, but that didn't make her someone people were willing to divulge their intimate and personal stories to.

She had no idea what Mac was dealing with by coming here. No idea of what it meant for him to find this person. Yet, something about him gave her reason enough to *want* to know. Her sense of foreboding had not abated since the night she'd met him. That had to mean something, surely?

Her mind drifted back to his questions about Marian, and Kate's apprehension escalated. What if it was Marian he was searching for? What if he was after the woman she owed so much to…possibly her life?

Kate's eyes burned as images of the night she'd miscarried her baby in Marian's home reared up. Poor George, Marian's devoted husband, had rushed to call the ambulance while Marian rocked Kate in her arms on their bathroom floor. Her hidden pregnancy had been revealed to at least two people in the most horrendous way.

Yet Marian hadn't only respected Kate's wishes for silence about the baby, she'd stayed by Kate's side for two nights in the hospital and then offered her a bed in her own home until Kate felt strong enough to walk about town as though nothing had happened…her heart silently breaking.

She pulled back her shoulders and glanced in Mac's direction.

One way or another, she'd get him to admit Marian *wasn't* who he was looking for. The anger, resentment or whatever it was that made the man so damn hostile would not be directed on her beloved friend.

Turning away, she lifted her hand to Vanessa. "Can I get a glass of white wine?"

"Sure." Vanessa frowned as she reached for a wine bottle in an ice bucket. "How you doing?"

"Good."

Vanessa glanced toward the stage. "Are you sure about that? I know I said I'll see what I can find out about Mac, but maybe both of us are plain out of order."

Kate took her glass of wine. "I've just been thinking the same thing, but I don't trust him. I'm overprotective of certain people, and I don't like the idea of someone coming into town and causing them grief."

"But is he, though?"

She put down her glass and lifted her hand, counting off her fingers. "He's snarky. Rude. Arrogant. And, as you've said, practically unapproachable."

Vanessa nodded toward the stage. "I wouldn't exactly call him unapproachable. Would you?"

She walked away to serve some people at the bar, and Kate looked at the crowd around the stage. People were clapping, smiling and cheering as Mac played a solo bridge. She narrowed her eyes. So, people liked his music. Big deal. It was still his fault that her deepest, darkest secret had reared its ugly head now that she thought Marian was the one in Mac's firing line.

Kate had hidden her pregnancy and miscarriage from everyone, including her family. And she'd failed to keep her baby safe. So she punished herself by staying single and keeping her tragedy to herself. If she ever became intimate enough with someone that she trusted him, she'd undoubtedly want to share her burden.

But for now, she didn't want anyone, apart from Marian and George, knowing what happened that day.

She'd already lost friends with her snappishness and bouts of withdrawing. She didn't want to lose anyone else. Kate blinked against the burning in her eyes…she'd desperately wanted to keep her baby.

Vanessa sidled up to the bar, her gaze shrewd. "I know what's going on with you. I've figured it out."

Kate's stomach somersaulted, her heart thumping. "What?"

"Maybe you have a *thing* for him."

Releasing her held breath, Kate laughed. "I do not."

"No? Then I'd say he might have a thing for you."

"Don't even go there." Did he? She sipped her wine as pleasure twisted inside her. "Why would you say that?"

Vanessa smiled. "Because I noticed the atmosphere between the pair of you the moment you met. Electric."

Kate huffed a laugh, heat warming her cheeks. "We couldn't be more different. He's as secretive as they come…which is incredibly infuriating. Plus, I get the impression he's used to living out of a suitcase, whereas I love having the Cove to call home."

"So?"

"So, Mac Orman and I couldn't be less suited."

"So?"

Kate glared. "Will you please think of something else to say?"

"If he doesn't want to share his business, maybe that's his prerogative. Maybe it would be better for him *and* us if you find a way to get along with him while he's here." Vanessa turned to another customer who had come up to the bar. "What can I get you?"

Rolling her eyes, Kate turned toward the stage. What did Vanessa know? So something about Mac had gotten under her skin. The intensity in his eyes, the coldness of his attitude was exasperating, yet he'd stepped up to help her and was even smiling at the audience. A little. The guy was a contradiction, and it bugged the hell out of her; she wasn't ready to trust him.

She'd let her guard down with Dean and

look how that had ended up. She hadn't spoken to her sister in two years. And she missed Ali so much more than she ever missed her ex.

Mac left his spot farther back on the platform and strolled up to the microphone. Kate's melancholy about her sister vanished as her heart stumbled. Mac's stride was confident as that soft smile played at his lips. What was he doing?

He nodded his thanks to Joe Masters and gripped the microphone with one hand, casually pushing his too-mussed, too-sexy hair from his forehead with the other. He flashed a smile. "Afternoon, ladies and gents. Joe asked if I wanted to do an acoustic version of one of my own songs as a way of introducing myself and my music. Would anyone mind?"

Kate's heart beat a little faster. Had Joe actually offered Mac this solo time or had he asked Joe if he could sing in order to torment her again? A part of her longed to hear him sing…longed to know how bad he might be, despite today being about people getting their money's worth. The thing was, some incompetence on his part might at least go some way to crushing her emerging attraction to the man.

The crowd whooped and clapped their approval as Kate took a generous mouthful of wine, her gaze on Mac.

As soon as he struck up the first note, Kate's stomach knotted with a horrible, traitorous thrill.

Then he sang.

Every hair on her body rose.

She closed her eyes and let the music…let Mac…wash through her senses. She couldn't stop her smile, and she couldn't halt the tingling infusing her skin. Slowly, she opened her eyes.

He looked straight at her, and, even from a distance, she could see the no doubt intentional temptation in his gaze. She should've walked away. Instead, her feet remained rooted to the floor, her eyes on his.

The realization of just how much trouble she could find herself in mixed with the physical effects of his rich, melodic, utterly beautiful voice. How was she supposed to stop herself from acting on the sudden desire pulsing through her? It had been months since she'd even looked at a man, let alone felt this incredible pull toward one.

She wasn't naïve. She knew this was pure lust that hung between her and Mac. Old-fashioned, come-to-mama attraction crackling across the space that separated them.

Kate quickly turned away and picked up her glass of wine, steadfastly ignoring the way it trembled as she drank.

"Hmm." Vanessa leaned her forearms on the bar and whispered in Kate's ear. "Like I said, electric."

Accepting defeat, she put down her glass and covered her face with her hands. "Why now? Why when I'm so far away from trusting a man again does one have to turn up who looks like that?"

Vanessa straightened. "We don't get to choose the timing of these things. Surely you, of all people, know that after all the heartbreak you've seen in your work."

She walked away, leaving Kate feeling both afraid and shamefully enthralled. Turning toward the stage again, she studied Mac; thankfully, he was concentrating on his guitar strings. Maybe she needed to act cool about his being in the Cove and looking for someone. Act as though it was no big deal.

A bit less animosity, might help them both. If she adopted a no-nonsense business approach to him, surely that would douse the fire and fuse the electric. One thing was for certain—now that Mac had stepped in to help her fund-raiser, she had to speak to him, had to show her gratitude. Avoiding him was out of the question.

MAC BOWED TO the rapturous applause that reverberated throughout the space and tried his hardest not to search the crowd for Kate. The occasional sadness he saw in her eyes was slowly increasing the burden of his subterfuge, making him want to get to know her better…to prove to her he was a good guy. Mostly.

Straightening, he raised his hand in thanks and slipped his guitar strap over his head as he exited the stage. Accepting the back claps and nods from the people he passed, Mac headed to the bar. A cold bottle of beer would quell the strange blend of euphoria and self-doubt rippling through him.

There was no denying the warmth that emanated from the people around him, no denying his relief at their congratulations and easy acceptance of him considering the less than favorable welcome he'd received from certain individuals. He didn't like small towns. Never had, never would. He lifted his finger to Vanessa at the far end of the bar. Why he didn't like them escaped him, though. Was the dislike his own or something he'd been taught by his family? As far as he knew, they'd never even lived in a town the size of Templeton.

His father had known for a while Marian Ball lived here. Had he inferred something to Mac in the past that made his son overly cautious about communities he knew nothing about? Most likely. Kate was problem enough, but he had to keep everyone else at an enforced distance, too, or risk divulging something about why he was in town. He had to ensure Marian was the first to know, nobody else. He might want closure to his father's search, but Mac also wanted the woman to hear what he knew from him and only him.

"Hey, Mac." Vanessa opened the fridge behind her and pulled out a bottle of his preferred beer. "You did good out there." She flipped off the top and slid it across the temporary bar. "That one's on the house."

"Thanks, but as the proceeds are going to charity…" He tossed a few coins into the bucket on the bar and took a lengthy slug. "All in the name of helping out those less fortunate, and all that."

"Hmm, not sure Kate sees your helping out that way."

His defenses immediately slammed up. "Why? What's she been saying?"

"Whoa." Vanessa raised her hands, her brow creased and her gaze irritated.

Mac briefly closed his eyes. "Sorry."

"So you should be. I'm just the messenger, after all."

"The messenger?" Mac stilled. "Of what?"

Vanessa shrugged. "I just think the pair of you could get along quite nicely if you gave each other a chance."

Matchmaking. Another reason he didn't like small towns. He sipped his beer. "You're way off the mark there. Kate and I are..." He scowled. "Working each other out."

"Oh, that's what you're doing, is it?"

Vanessa's eyes turned infinitely softer as he hovered his beer at his mouth.

She glanced over his shoulder and grinned. "Hi, Kate. I'll leave you to it. I've got some thirsty customers who need serving."

Slowly, Mac turned. Kate held her chin high, her chocolate-brown eyes burning with annoyance, her cheeks flushed and her hands firmly perched on her slender hips. "I came over here to thank you for playing, only I

didn't expect you to be chatting so offhand-
edly about me to Vanessa. Do you know she's
one of the worst gossips in town?"

Despite, or maybe because of, her clear
irritation, amusement rolled through him.
"Then it's just as well I didn't give her anything to gossip about."

She rolled her eyes and, slid up to the bar
beside him. "If you're not careful, you'll con-
stantly be walking into a whole lot of trouble."

"Is that so?"

"Yes, that's so." A sly smile curved her lips.
"Which leads me to the conclusion it might
be to your benefit to enlist some local help."

"Help? With what?" Then realization
dawned and he laughed. "No thanks. I've
got it covered."

Her smile vanished and her cheeks reddened. "Why are you so stubborn?"

"Why are you so nosy?"

Her mouth dropped open. "I'm not nosy,
I'm concerned. You'll be chewed up and spat
out if you go nonchalantly poking around in
people's lives. You've told me you're looking for someone but won't tell me who or
why. Why don't you let me in a little? I know
Templeton and its people well. I'm betting I

can help you find who you're looking for in a matter of hours."

"Hours?"

"Fine. Days."

He raised his eyebrows, unable to resist provoking her temper. "Because if you can find them quicker than I can, I'll be out of your hair all the sooner, right?"

"Right."

"Is there an unwritten rule somewhere that a person can only stay in the Cove so long before they're ejected by the locals? Why I'm here is my business, Kate. It's got nothing to do with you."

She held his stare as indecision flitted through her eyes. The noise around them faded as his heart beat a little too fast, indicating just how much he liked her. He shouldn't like her. Her argumentative nature, her stubbornness and self-assumed right to get up in his business seriously irked him. Still, it was hard to ignore her thick, dark, curly hair that tumbled past her shoulders, leaving him itching to know if it was as soft as it looked. It was even harder not to want to fall headlong into her deep, dark eyes.

Blinking, he turned to the stage. "I don't

need your concern, okay? I'm a big boy. I can handle myself."

"Who said my concern was about you?"

He shook his head, took another sip of his beer. "Touché."

"Here's the thing. I'm concerned for who you're looking for."

"You've made that pretty clear."

"So convince me I've nothing to worry about."

"You haven't."

"Not good enough."

Frustration pulsed through him as his defenses against her weakened once more. That damn worry glinted in her eyes again. He blew out a breath. "I just want to speak to this person. Get some things laid to rest. There won't be any bloodshed if that's what's worrying you."

Her eyes widened. "I wasn't worried about that until now."

He shook his head. "Look, this person is connected to my family. Okay? I just want to talk to her."

Triumph flashed in her eyes. "Aha. A her." Then, like a switch had been flicked, the triumph dissolved into apprehension once more. "Let me help you. I work with families all the time. I could at least act as a mediator or something."

"No."

"But—"

"I won't need a damn mediator, Kate." He clenched his jaw. "Just leave things alone."

"No."

He swiped his slightly trembling hand over his face. "Why does my being here bother you so much? Are you sure your nervousness is about someone else? Or more about you?"

She swallowed. "Someone else."

Care for this woman and the inexplicable way she'd reacted to his presence since meeting him wound through him. There was something disconcerting in her eyes…the odd flicker of deep sadness, or shame, that made him want to hold her. Tell her everything would be okay.

"Hey." He gently placed his hand on her arm. "I can tell something's happened to you. What, I don't know. But believe me when I say I'm not here to cause you more pain. Everything will work out as it's supposed to. End of story."

She snorted and turned, tears glinting in her eyes. "Nothing ever works out how it's supposed to, and why should I trust that you don't mean to hurt this woman? People hurt each other all the time." She eased her arm from under his hand. "More often than not, the things people want, the things they hope for, never happen. If you don't know that, you must have lived a more privileged life than most."

The tear that rolled over her cheek made him catch his breath, and he battled against his weakening defenses. God, if only she knew how acutely he'd experienced the brutal destruction of hopes and dreams. Of heartbreak so bad, he'd never be the same again.

He leaned against the bar, felt the warmth of her arm alongside his. "My life has been far from privileged, believe me."

She stepped in front of him, her dark gaze burning with frustration. "Fine. But by going up on that stage, you saved me from having a lot of disappointed people demanding God knows what from the center. I'm in no doubt that because of you, the fund-raiser will be the success my team and I hoped it would be. I owe you. Let me help you, Mac. Please."

"I don't need your damn help." Yet inexplicable want edged far too close to his heart. He didn't want her help, he wanted her in his bed; wanted her to look at him with lust, not pity. He tightened his jaw. "If that changes, you'll be the first to know. So, please, just leave it be."

"Mac—"

"Enough." He slammed his bottle on the bar and tried to brush past her.

She gripped his arm, her eyes dark with determination. "So I've been hurt. You're right. But I can see that whatever has brought you to Templeton is hurting you, too. Am I right?"

Shame that he could be so transparent to anyone tore through him. He'd felt isolated since he'd lost Jilly and the baby. Here, in Templeton, where no one knew him, he could be who he was before. He had the opportunity to laugh. At home, laughter felt inappropriate. At home, he was the man to feel sorry for; the man who'd lost his pregnant girlfriend in a car accident.

Why else did he sign up for as many gigs as he could? Stay away for months at a time.

On the road, he was anonymous. He could be who he wanted to be without judgment or guilt.

Or so he thought.

What the hell did Kate want from him? He'd been bloody horrible to her. The tattoos on his chest and arms relayed in perfect patterned honesty how he felt about life. Rejection, loss and disappointment were what life had to offer…they were all *he* had to offer.

"Mac? Are you listening to me?"

He glared. "Stop talking."

"What?"

"I said stop talking." Tears burned behind his eyes. "Right now."

Her brow furrowed as she intensely studied him. "My God, you really are hurting, aren't you?"

He had to stop her talking, had to stop her seeing any more of him. Without thinking, he reached out and pulled her close. Her gasp whispered into his mouth as he covered her lips with his and kissed her hard, sharing every ounce of his hurt, anger and passion. She tensed in his arms, her body rigid…and then she softened.

Her lips pressed against his, and she tangled her fingers in the hair at the nape of his neck. Jesus… He gripped her tighter, kissed her deeper, and she returned his demand with her own. His heart pounded as the sweet taste of her lips and musky scent of her perfume infused his senses, sending his desire deep into his groin.

The fire. The need. It was too much.

He eased back and stared into her wide, beautiful eyes. Her breasts rose and fell with each harried breath, her mouth swollen and her body tense.

Mac squeezed his eyes shut before snapping them open. "I've got to go."

He stormed past her and into the crowds, through the bar and out into the parking lot. He bent double and breathed in the cold night air as though dying from lack of oxygen. Feeling calmer, he straightened and stalked between the parked cars toward the exit.

What the hell had he done?

CHAPTER SIX

KATE CARRIED A steaming cup of coffee into her living room, and curled up under a blanket on the settee, exhausted after the previous night.

She turned on the TV, and canned laughter flooded her apartment. Not that she had any interest in watching anything right now. It was the noise she needed.

Dropping her head back, she picked up her coffee and took a sip, her thoughts filling with Mac. She'd finally crawled into bed at nearly two in the morning, the fund-raiser having gone better than she could've hoped. An early estimate indicated they had surpassed the intended monetary target. From the moment Mac had left the bar, Kate had done everything expected of her. She'd mingled, she'd laughed, she'd taken the microphone and thanked donors, the public, the band and Dave and Vanessa. Yet her focus had wandered to the doors as futile hope lingered that Mac would return.

He hadn't.

But he had kissed her. No, devoured her. The few stolen seconds in his arms had engulfed her with a yearning she'd purposefully buried for good reason. Kate closed her eyes. Why had she let him kiss her? Why hadn't she stepped *way* back and told him off? Instead, she'd pulled him closer and deepened their kiss until all she wanted to do was drag him upstairs to his room.

The man was dangerous…and not only because he was here to cause trouble. In her job, Kate had witnessed people inflicting harm, upset, even occasional abuse on each other. But she'd sensed a gentle kindness buried beneath Mac's exterior.

Somehow, he'd perceived the pain from her miscarriage. The pain she tried so hard to hide—from her miscarriage and then, more recently, a tentative leap into romance with a man who had blindsided her. A man who tore two previously close siblings apart, and taken off, never to be seen by Kate or Ali ever again.

Kate opened her eyes and sipped her coffee, glancing toward her phone. Nothing stopped her from calling Ali, but in the two years since Dean's departure, her sister had moved on while Kate lingered in no-man's land. What could she say to Ali after all this time?

How the two of them would ever get past what happened, Kate didn't know, but her mother had told her Ali now had a new man and a super-expensive engagement ring flashing on her finger. The hurt of Dean's betrayal had most definitely burned deeper in Kate than her sister.

Hating her resentment, Kate put her coffee on the table and walked across the living room, the throw wrapped around her and dragging along the floor. Unlocking her patio doors, she stepped onto the balcony, the frigid morning air making her shiver. Her slow exhale sent forth a stream of white vapor.

She looked left toward the town's fairground and then right along the promenade where the Coast was situated a few streets away.

Mac.

He was a mystery, but she'd be a liar if she didn't admit that was part of his appeal. Who was he? Who was the woman he looked for and how long did he plan to stay in the Cove?

These questions coiled inside her like contracted springs.

As for her? Well, apparently, she was an open book. A woman who held no mystery whatsoever.

It was terrifying to think her pain showed so clearly in her eyes. Yet hadn't she recognized the pain in Mac's, too? He was the first person in months who'd acknowledged her unhappiness. No one else, apart from Izzy and Marian, knew how much Kate still hurt; how much she refused to trust again.

She tentatively touched her lips, and her heart swelled traitorously. How could she deny how good it felt to have a strong, capable man like Mac take control? Even for such a short moment, it had felt wonderful to lean into him.

The ringing of her apartment doorbell ripped through her melancholy, and Kate flinched. She looked to the door and then her watch. It was barely eight thirty. Who would be calling on her at this time in the morning?

She walked inside and pressed the buzzer at her door. "Hello?"

"Darling? It's Mum."

"Mum?" Kate frowned and mentally flicked

through her calendar. Nothing. "Did we have something in the diary?"

Her mother laughed. "No, but can't I pop by for a visit when I have the chance? Can I come up?"

"Of course. Sorry."

Kate pressed the entry button, pulled open the front door and quickly began tidying her apartment, shoving magazines under cushions and slamming glasses and plates into the dishwasher. Hurrying into her bedroom, she whipped the duvet into place and snatched pillows off the floor, plumping them and arranging them in a tragic display of domestic ineptitude.

She hurried back into the living room just as her mother's footsteps sounded at the door. Tightening her sleep-mussed ponytail, Kate swiped her fingers under her eyes, pulled back her shoulders and slapped on a smile. She took a deep breath and faced the doorway. "Mum! It's great to see you."

"Oh, and you, darling." Her mother pulled Kate into a hug and stood back, her canny gaze appraising Kate from head to toe. "You look…tired."

"I was at a fund-raiser until the early hours. Coffee?"

"Lovely."

"Great. Take a seat." Kate walked into the kitchen, separated from the living area by a long granite-topped counter. "So, what are you doing in Templeton?"

"Having finally put to bed a deal I've been working on for three months, I spent last night in a hotel in the city. We've secured a huge two-year contract. I thought as I'm due a couple of days off, I'd pop by and see my baby."

A couple of days? Kate's smile strained as she stirred her mother's coffee. "You know I have to work, right? I can't take time off right now. After last night, I need to—"

"Oh, darling, you're so sweet." Her mother took the cup of offered coffee from Kate's hand. "When I said a couple of days, I have no intention of spending them in Templeton. God forbid. I thought I'd stop by for a quick chat before I head home for a fabulous spa break with the girls."

Relief lowered Kate's shoulders. "Oh. Well, that's great."

"But…" Her mother sipped from her cup and raised her eyebrows. "Wow, this coffee is surprisingly good, darling. Anyway, I came to invite you home for a few days next month. As you know, Alison is engaged and they've set the wedding date for June. Just four months away. I think the pair of you need to bury the hatchet before it becomes a problem for her big day. Your father and I refuse to have her wedding spoiled by something that happened two years ago."

Kate lowered into an armchair beside her mother, a horribly familiar inferiority coming over her. As much as Linda Harrington loved her daughter, she also managed to make Kate feel like a vagrant in the face of her perfect makeup and haute-couture clothes.

Not to mentioned how lowly she considered Kate's chosen vocation, when compared to her own and Alison's. Was it any wonder Kate had never breathed a word about her miscarriage to her mother?

Sadness swept through her, and Kate buried her thoughts back into the deep recesses of her heart. "Why would you even think I'd intentionally spoil Ali's wedding day? Have you even asked if she wants me there?"

"There's no need."

Kate widened her eyes, disbelief of her mother's presumption riling her, as it always did. "Of course there's a need. The last thing a bride needs on her wedding day is unwanted guests."

"Don't be so ridiculous, Katherine. You're her sister. Her only sibling. Not only will she want you there, I should think she'll have an intimate role in place for you, too."

Doubt mixed with an inkling of hope as Kate sipped her coffee. "I'll believe that when I hear it from Ali."

Her mother sighed. "I wish you'd talk to one another. Ali needs you there. Just call her. I'm sure you'll both come around. I'm not bullying you, Katherine. I'm going to descend on Alison, too. Enough is enough."

Deciding compliance was the only way to provoke her mother's departure, Kate raised her hand in defeat. "Fine. I'll call her."

"No."

"No?"

"No. I want you to go and see her. It will be best for you to talk face-to-face."

"Mum—"

"Katherine, Ali is a successful business-woman who runs a hairdressing salon that's growing bigger every day. You can't expect her to drop everything the same way you can."

"I see." Kate's hackles rose, and her cheeks

grew warm. "I just play around with teenagers in dire situations, do I? Situations that neither you, nor Ali, can even come close to understanding in your rich, successful existence. Obviously, there's no reason I can't just shut the office and come home for an unscheduled holiday. Is that it?"

Her mother glared. "What you do for work isn't the same as what Ali and I do, darling. You know that. You're running yourself into the ground worrying about other people… strangers. Look at you. You're exhausted. Your hair…" Her mother shook her head. "Maybe you should come with me to the spa?"

"No, thank you." Frustration burned hot in Kate's chest. "I love what I do, Mum. I work hard and make a difference. Why can't you be proud of me? Why can't you see what I do is worthwhile? That my work makes me happy?"

"Does it?"

The skepticism and concern in her mother's gaze slashed at Kate's conviction. She lifted her chin. "Yes."

"Then why haven't you smiled since the unfortunate incident with Dean? You spend less and less time with your family, choosing to spend every waking moment in this tiny town."

"Because the Cove is my home now, Mum. Templeton is where my friends are and where I'm the happiest. I'm sorry if that's hurtful, but it's the truth. You know I come home to visit Nana as much as possible. I can't commit to any more than that."

Pain flashed in her mother's eyes, and feeling responsible for putting it there, Kate touched her arm and softened her voice. "Mum—"

Her mother shook her head. "Don't you think there's a possibility you use your work to immerse yourself in other people's problems rather than face your own?"

"Of course not." But Kate's throat dried and her hands trembled. She stood and walked to the patio doors. "If you've only come here to put me down, I'd rather you left."

"I'm worried about you, darling."

"Really?" Kate spun around, embracing her anger and humiliation. "Well, there's no need. I'm fine."

"You need a break. Why don't you let your father and I pay for a holiday for you? Why don't you take a risk and go on a date or two?"

Mac flashed unbidden into her mind, and

Kate pulled back her shoulders. "How do you know I'm not seeing someone? I don't have to tell you everything, you know."

"Are you?"

"No, but—"

"Darling, please. Just consider what I'm asking." Her mother stood, her purse under her arm. "Call Alison and arrange a time to get together. If nothing else, you'll enjoy discussing the wedding. You need more in your life than surrounding yourself with the misery you're so adamant you enjoy. You need to have some fun, some laughter—" her mother wiggled her eyebrows "—some sex."

"God, really, Mum?"

Her mother laughed. "You're passionate, opinionated and strong, Kate. Some men absolutely love that. The trouble is, you're not going to find a man strong enough to complement you in Templeton. Mark my words. You need somebody who doesn't know how you fall for every sob story going rather than deal with your own mistakes." Her mother held out her arms. "Come here."

Reluctantly, Kate moved forward. The sooner she hugged her mother, the sooner she'd leave under a cloud of Chanel No. 5.

"I love you." Her mother hugged her. "I'm

only doing what I think is for the best, and telling you some hard truths is definitely what's best right now." She pulled back and held Kate at arm's length. "Call Alison."

Kate nodded, feeling ever so slightly nauseous when she considered speaking to her sister. Two years was a long time before calling her out of the blue. "I'll think about it."

"Good."

Kate stood stock still as her mother swept toward the door and wiggled her fingers in semblance of a wave. The minute the door closed behind her, Kate collapsed onto the settee.

She stared blindly ahead as tears trickled from her eyes. Was her life really as sad as her mother believed? Or was it time to prove her wrong? Wasn't it time for her and Ali to have a conversation about what happened with Dean? Wasn't it time her sister explained her actions? And most importantly, wasn't it time for Kate to start living again?

Swiping at her tears, Kate got up and strode into the kitchen. She grabbed her phone and scrolled through her contacts. When she found Ali, she hovered her finger over the call button before releasing her held breath and slowly placing her phone back on to the counter.

Maybe she'd call her tomorrow.

MAC STOOD FROM the small desk in his room above the Coast and ran his hands through his hair. He stared at his father's papers and notebook as his mind raced with indecision. Factors, such as Marian Ball's hometown, her age and the number of years she'd been married, all confirmed that Marian of the Cove's Bonniest Bakery was his paternal grandmother.

He was becoming strangely used to this small town. Something about Templeton pulled at him; something that made him falter from his original plan. Now his strategy was beginning to feel wrong. Should he still find Marian and tell her who he was? That the son she'd never known was dead…after spending a life so fearful of abandonment that he'd pushed everyone away?

The longer Mac stayed, the less his scheme sat comfortably on his shoulders. That, and of course, Kate's suspicion he intended doing wrong. Which he did…or had planned to.

He blew out a breath. His intentions felt steeped in arrogance.

Things were no longer simple.

His determination to channel some of his pain on to someone else had begun to cool the longer he spent here…the longer he spent with a certain brown-haired, brown-eyed woman. A woman he'd kissed and couldn't stop thinking about kissing again.

Things were never meant to get this complicated.

Before he'd come to Templeton, the fire in his gut had burned too hot to consider anyone's feelings outside of his own.

Who was to say if Marian reacted badly, others in the town might not turn against him, too? Did he really want to leave the people in Templeton, who had treated him so kindly, with a bad taste in their mouth? That thought wouldn't sit well.

Every time he saw the genuine concern in Kate's eyes, his eagerness to carry through with his original plan waned. She cared about these people. Even after only a few days, Mac had begun to understand why.

He tossed the papers on to the desk and strode to the window. Gripping the frame, he stared toward the promenade. What had he really wanted to achieve by coming here? What did he want to happen next? Did he really believe that by hurting Marian Ball, his pain would heal and he'd move on?

Tears burned.

He'd lost a happiness he'd never thought possible when Jilly and their unborn baby had been killed. Was that really the fault of some woman who was merely related to his family by blood?

"Christ, you're a mess, Orman."

He pushed away from the window and snatched his leather jacket from the back of the desk chair. He shrugged it on before picking up his wallet, phone and keys and leaving the room and hurrying outside. The last thing he wanted to do was to bump into Dave or Vanessa.

The day was dry, sunny and cold. An almost perfect winter's day, if it wasn't for the storm of mixed emotions inside him. There was nothing for it. He needed some sensible, unbiased advice. He needed to open up to someone about why he was here. He just prayed his selfish motivation behind those two things wasn't treated with the derision he suspected they deserved.

Stuffing his hands into his pockets, he watched people weave past him on the busy beachfront. Even in February, Templeton was a hive of activity. What must it be like in the height of summer? Mac steadfastly ignored an unexpected need to see it for himself. It was whimsy. Nothing more, nothing less. He needed to resist the infuriating way this place had begun to grow on him in such a short time.

Desperately looking for something—anything—to tell him the best way forward, Mac turned down a side street. He passed a few small boutiques, interspersed with old townhouses, and came across an office with a wide plate glass window.

Templeton Cove's Teenage Support Center.

His stomach flipped. The center where Kate worked. Could she be the one to help him? He'd wager, as she dealt with teenagers, she had experience with unwanted pregnancies, maybe fostering and adoption, too. He stepped out of view and leaned against the wall of the house beside him, his mind spinning.

She'd asked to help him and he'd rejected her.

And then he'd kissed her…and enjoyed it far too much. Her waist had fit in his hands perfectly, her fingers on his neck a new and welcome wonder he wanted to experience again.

Could he really share everything with her about his father and what it meant to Mac to find his biological grandmother and tell her how her choices had affected her son? That he hoped by doing that his anger and grief would be sated? Surely, if Kate responded with empathy, it would only increase his attraction toward her.

He straightened and glanced at the center's window again. Or maybe once she knew his situation, she would tell him to get the hell away from her, leave town and never come back. At least that way, any attraction would be snuffed out.

So why did he dread seeing hatred in her eyes?

Tough. He'd brought that risk on himself.

Striding forward, he pushed open the door and walked inside.

The busy beachfront was a graveyard compared to the office. People milled about, phones rang, voices shouted from one end of the open-plan space to the other, and bursts of laughter pierced the air as a popular radio DJ advertised the latest fifty-grand competition.

This was meant to be a sanctuary for desperate and anguished teenagers, for crying out loud. Yet, the staff didn't seem to be taking anything seriously, let alone the kids they claimed to help. Coming in here had been a bad idea. He needed to leave. Now.

He turned toward the door.

"Mac?"

He froze. Kate.

"Hey." Her palm touched his back and heat rose.

Slowly, he turned. "Hey."

Her smile was warm as she looked deep into his eyes, her gaze assessing. "Are you okay?"

"I'm fine." He tried to drag forward some casual words. Or any words would be welcome. His brain had stopped at the sexy, happy sight of her. Her chocolate-colored eyes gleamed under the overhead lights. Her cheeks were flushed, and her body was damn near perfect in an open-necked shirt and tight black jeans.

She frowned. "Well, as much as I'm getting used to your permanent scowl, you don't look fine. What are you doing here?"

He stupidly dropped his focus to her mouth, and memories of how she tasted engulfed him. He quickly looked past her shoulder and shrugged. "I came looking for you, but judging by the mania in here, you're busy. I'll go."

She gripped his forearm. "Hey, it's always like this in here."

"Really? And how do the kids who come in here looking for help react? I can't imagine it evokes a lot of belief in your abilities."

She released his arm and crossed hers. "Is that so? And you deal with teenagers a lot, do you?"

"A few. I play music, remember?"

"Right. And, of course, the kids that come to see you play are alone, afraid, without parents or family, right? They don't know where their next bit of cash is coming from? Or know for sure where they're going to sleep when they leave the cozy bar you're playing at? Does that about sum up your fan base?"

The longer he looked into her eyes, the brighter his stupid, misplaced self-righteousness shone. He blew out a slow breath. "Sorry."

She glared. "For?"

"Being an ass."

"Right. Good." She dropped her arms and gripped his elbow, steering him toward a quieter spot to the side. "The kids like the noise. They like the crowds of people in here. It gives them a sense of anonymity, like no one is watching them. It gives them a safe place to talk without risk of being overheard. Do you understand?"

"Yes." He looked past her. A few teenagers were sitting at different desks, some sullen, some tentatively smiling at the adult speaking with them. "I understand."

"Good. Now, why don't you tell me why you came looking for me? Is something wrong?"

Forcing his gaze to hers, Mac tried to concentrate on his situation rather than how this woman made him realize pretty damn quickly that his words and actions sometimes made him a complete jerk. "I was hoping, although I've probably messed up my chance, that you might still be willing to help me."

She smiled, the concern in her eyes melting into relief. "Well, that's excellent news." She released his arm and raised her forefinger. "Wait here just one minute. I'll be straight back."

Before he could think what he was doing, he grabbed her hand. "Where are you going? Can't we talk here?"

She raised her eyebrows and slowly drew her fingers from his grip. "No. You're not a kid in trouble, Mac. You're an adult. I don't need any staff speculating why you're here. Trust me, it will be for the best if we go somewhere more private."

Somewhere private. Like her bedroom? *Yeah, sure, that's just what she'll be thinking right now.* "Got it."

"Two seconds, okay?"

He nodded and she walked away. Stuffing his hands into his pockets, Mac met the curious glances coming from every direction. He tipped a smile at them, suspecting that if any of these people thought him the least bit untrustworthy, they would try to protect Kate. A confrontation was the last thing he needed.

Not that stepping in for the absent Moon Shadows' guitarist had been the best move as far as remaining inconspicuous was concerned.

Kate had warned him that in this town, people looked out for one another.

She hurried toward him. He ushered her toward the door, somehow not able to resist laying his hand on the small of her back as they left her office and walked onto the street.

CHAPTER SEVEN

TRYING TO IGNORE the heat that radiated from Mac's palm on her back, Kate plastered on a smile. Keeping upbeat was the only chance she had of making his scowl disappear. The man was tense. Very tense.

"So…" She looked at him as he walked beside her. "Do you want to grab some lunch?"

"Sure."

"The Seascape?"

"Let me guess. A fish restaurant?"

"I knew as soon as I saw you that you were one of those guys who lets nothing get past him. A regular Sherlock."

A smile played on his mouth. "Funny."

"So, yes or no?"

"Yes. Sounds good."

Kate drew in a breath and stepped up the pace. A semblance of a smile from Mac was enough for now. If she was honest, a semblance was far easier to deal with than his very occasional full-on smiles. Those were knee-buckling. She suspected that whatever he had to tell her would merit her undivided attention, rather than her continuous yearning for him to kiss her again.

That particular desire needed to be pushed back.

"Here we are." She led him along the short pathway to the Seascape's closed double doors. "This place is famous for its seafood. Hope you're hungry."

She pushed open the door, relieved the restaurant was relatively quiet. The bright blue-and-white décor was accentuated with splashes of orange by way of the ceramic crabs, lobsters and buckets on shelving or hanging on the walls. A mix of cloth-covered tables, some long and some intimate, meant the restaurant welcomed couples and families alike. It was usually a place Kate came for informal get-togethers. Yet now, with Mac so tense beside her, nothing felt informal. Judging by his somber expression when she spotted him coming through her office door, whatever had led to him wanting to talk to her meant something was bothering him.

Caroline Hedley came toward them, two menus pressed to her chest. "Kate, good to see you. It's been—" Caroline grinned "—at least five days."

Kate laughed. "What can I say? I love your food." She turned to Mac, whose solemn gaze roamed the restaurant. Kate cleared her throat. "This is Mac Orman. He's in town for a while. Mac, this is Caroline Hedley. She owns the restaurant with her husband, Lee."

Caroline held out her hand. "Nice to meet you."

Mac slid his stony gaze to Caroline. "Pleased to meet you, too."

"Well…" Caroline blew out a breath. "Let's get you a table, shall we?"

Kate struggled to suppress her temper as they followed Caroline to a table for two in one of the restaurant's many alcoves. Mac could at least *try* to be friendly. The ability was there, after all. She'd *briefly* experienced flashes of it herself. She glanced at him. Maybe his distance was related to the Cove as a whole rather than just the woman he sought.

Caroline's voice broke through Kate's reverie.

"Here you go." Caroline offered Kate and Mac menus. "Can I get you something to drink?"

Kate smiled. "A Diet Coke would be great."

Caroline nodded. "Mac?"

"I'll have the same. Thanks."

"Great. I'll be right back with your drinks."

Kate leaned her elbows on the table. Mac met her stare, his expression unreadable. The more she got to know him, the more her wariness with Mac grew into exasperation. She'd shared a kiss with this man, he'd had his hands on her body. Surely, he realized she had the right to know more about why he was here.

She folded her hands on top of the table. "Talk to me. I'm listening."

He held her gaze a moment longer before opening his menu. "Let's order first, okay?"

Uneasy, Kate stared at his bowed head. "Sure."

Caroline came back with their drinks and took their orders. The second she moved away, Kate raised her eyebrows at Mac, impatient for him to speak.

He pushed the hair back from his forehead before slipping his hands on to the table. "The woman I'm looking for…"

"Yes?"

"She could be related to me."

Surprised, Kate leaned forward. "Okay."

"She could be my biological grandmother."

"Could be?"

"My father was adopted. Given up at birth." His jaw tightened and his blue eyes darkened. "I'm not certain of the circumstances surrounding her decision to do that, but I'm here to find her. To tell her about my dad and his family."

"I see." Kate stared. Adoption. A baby. What would it take for a mother to give up her child? She'd worked with many teenagers desperate to see their babies adopted by good families. For a way to know their baby would be loved and cared for. Had Mac's grandmother been a pregnant teen? "So, you're, what, twenty-four? Twenty-five?"

"Twenty-five."

"And your dad had you at what age?"

"Twenty-three."

"Right." Kate narrowed her eyes as she calculated, and her stomach knotted. "So, if your grandmother gave birth when she was a teenager she could be in her early to mid-sixties now. Right?"

"She's sixty-five."

Kate stilled. Marian was around that age. Sure, there were other older ladies around town, but this information landed far too close to her friend. She took a sip of her drink to ease the dryness in her throat. "You sound angry that she gave up your father for adoption."

"Maybe I am."

Kate frowned. She often dealt with misplaced anger in her work…and time and again, she witnessed how destructive it could be. "You shouldn't be."

"Wouldn't you be mad if it was your father?"

"No."

"No?"

"Not unless the circumstances dictated neglect or cruelty. So far, all I know is a woman gave birth and gave up the child. Was it at the hospital?"

"Yes, why?"

"That means she did it in a safe place where the staff would know how to start the adoption process. That shouldn't make you angry, and I want to be sure we're on the same page. Especially if I know this person."

"What does that mean?"

Kate leaned back and crossed her arms, the simmering fury in his gaze igniting her own. "It means I don't like to think I'm having lunch with a man capable of haranguing or frightening a woman old enough to be a grandmother. Let alone a woman who *could* be his own grandmother."

He glared. "Wow, you really think that little of me, huh?"

"What I think of you is neither here nor there. What matters is, do I walk out of this restaurant right now? Or do you promise me you're going to try to calm yourself *way* down should you find this woman?"

He held her gaze, his cheeks flushed and his lips tight.

"Fine." She uncrossed her arms and leaned forward. "There are certain people, certain women, of that age in Templeton who have done a lot for me. When I say a lot, I mean they could've saved my life or, at the very least, my sanity. So, if you think I'll stand by and let you—"

"I'll show some tact, okay?"

"I'll need more than that."

He shook his head. "Jesus, woman."

Kate raised her eyebrows.

He glared. "I'll be calm, okay?"

"Promise?"

A muscle in his jaw twitched before the anger in eyes softened. A little. "Promise."

"Good." Kate exhaled. "So, does your dad know you're in Templeton?"

He looked across the restaurant. "He's dead."

Understanding and sympathy rolled through her. "He was looking for her? Before he died?"

"He'd already found her."

"Mac?" She touched his hand where it lay on the table. "Look at me."

Slowly, he turned his head, his focus dropping to their hands. Kate swallowed, her heart aching for the first flash of sadness she'd seen in his eyes since they met. He needed comfort. The man was hurting, but from what she knew so far, his pain wasn't his grandmother's fault. No matter how difficult it might have been for him to discover his father was adopted, his grandmother had acted in the most caring way possible.

Kate tightened her fingers around his. "Do you know this woman's name?"

His gaze bored into hers, and as the seconds passed, her unease grew. The way he looked at her was unnerving. As though he was about to say something he knew she wouldn't want to hear. Unwelcome possibility tensed her shoulders as she considered the disconnection between the members in her own family. Surely, a long-lost member of Mac's family couldn't be linked in some way to her. Was that why he suddenly looked so apprehensive?

She slowly eased her hand from his. "What is it? Does this woman have something to do with me?"

"I came to you because I'm pretty sure you deal with uncertainty and getting the answers to questions a lot more often than I do. I know you're suspicious of me, Kate. From the moment we met you had me marked as someone to watch."

Heat warmed her cheeks. "And I was wrong to do that. You're okay." She smiled. "As men go."

A glimmer of a smile lifted his lips. "Gee, thanks."

She smiled. "What's her name?"

"Her name's Marian. Marian Ball."

Relief lowered her shoulders. "Well, the only Marian I know in the Cove is Marian Cohen. Bakery Marian. She can't possibly be your grandmother."

He sat forward, his gaze intense on hers. "Why not?"

"Well, for a start, she's never had any children."

"As far as you know."

She stared. He was right. How could she possibly know if Marian had given birth to a child she gave up for adoption? It was hardly the type of thing to drop into casual conversation. But surely Marian would've said something about a son when she'd been with Kate at the hospital? Or even during the many times Kate had cried on her shoulder since? After all, that was the Marian she knew and loved.

Mac sat back. "It's just a feeling, but I think Marian Cohen was once Marian Ball and my father's mother. If you only know of one Marian, why couldn't it be her?"

"Well, it could be, but—"

"Rest assured, if it is her, my intention of telling her who I am has gotten a whole lot less appealing."

"Because?"

"Seems to me she's well-liked and respected by everyone. I was hoping to say what I need to say to her and leave, but it appears everyone is concerned with everyone's business in Templeton. If I approach her, it's unlikely to be a quiet 'hello, my name's Mac and I'm your grandson.' It's likely the whole town will know about our connection within minutes."

Kate frowned. "Marian likes to talk, but

I can't see her telling anyone and everyone about something as personal as a child she gave up for adoption. You know, there's worse women you could have as a potential grandmother. Marian's practically a Disney version of a good nana."

He shook his head and took a sip of his drink. "You don't understand what I'm saying."

It wasn't aggression on Mac's face but frustration. Her initial shock melted into sympathy. "Look, I can't possibly know how you're feeling." She leaned her forearms on the table, resisting the urge to touch him again. "But Marian is a very special lady, Mac. I can't stand by and let you turn her world upside down. I won't."

Annoyance flashed across his gaze. "Fine. Then will you at least help me approach her? You know her. You'll be able to judge a lot better how I say what I need to say."

"And what is it you want to say, exactly?"

He stared at her before his gaze darkened and he looked away. "I'm not sure yet."

The shutters had been erected once more and Kate's wariness of Mac and his intentions returned. She couldn't give into his request for help. Not yet. Marian deserved Kate's loyalty and protection. Mac was a stranger. An angry stranger. If Marian had kept an adoption secret, Kate would do all she could to honor that secret.

Mac's wooden gaze and stiff body language entirely convinced her he was deeply and emotionally invested in his search. Which meant the result could be incredibly distressing for him *and* Marian.

Forcing herself to think logically rather than act on emotion, as her too-soft heart often led her to do, Kate said, "Marian's been in the Cove about nine or ten years and not once has she, or anyone else, mentioned she's a mother. Regardless of whether she might have given her child up for adoption. Marian's pretty open with everyone, as we are with her. How else would she get us to tell her the things we do? If she'd given up a baby, I'm sure I would've heard about it one way or another."

He faced her, suspicion darkening his gaze. "She's never had any family visit?"

Kate scrambled through her memories. "Not that I can think of."

"Friends?"

Confused, Kate picked up her drink. "Come

to think of it, I've never seen Marian with anyone who doesn't live in the Cove."

"Don't you think that's kind of strange, considering how liked she is?"

It *was* strange. Why hadn't she questioned that before? Everyone had past friends, didn't they? "Maybe."

"Then we have to consider the possibility that Marian Cohen, *if* she's Marian Ball, had a whole other life before she came to the Cove. One that no one knows about or has taken the time to question."

Uneasy, and Kate opened her mouth to protest, to underline Marian's good character, but Caroline came to the table. Kate forced a tight-lipped smile as Caroline put down their plates.

"Anything else I can get you?" She glanced between them.

Kate shook her head, her gaze on Mac's.

He shook his head. "We're good. Thanks."

"Great. Enjoy your meals and shout if you need anything else."

Caroline walked away, and Kate stared at Mac as apprehension sped her heart. If his suspicions about Marian were true and she turned out to be someone different than the person the Templeton residents had known all these years, it would shake the town to its core.

MAC ATE A piece of sea bass. Damn, the fish practically melted on his tongue. He met Kate's gaze, and she smiled as she picked up her knife and fork. "Good, huh?"

"Phenomenal."

"In my opinion, there's no better fish restaurant in the county."

He focused on his food. Their interrupted conversation about Marian hung in the air, weighing the atmosphere down with tension. Kate's confirmation about Marian's lack of visitors opened a whole new avenue of possibility. Clearly the people who thought they knew Marian didn't really know her at all. That made the prospect of telling her what her decisions had made his father become, all the more tempting.

He'd had love, anticipated the birth of his and Jilly's first baby together.

Had Marian not felt the same excitement? Turned her back on her baby? Or was she forced to give him up? He had to have answers. Losing his baby had broken his heart. Broken his belief in happy ever after.

Could a woman, a mother, ever just walk away? He couldn't believe Marian could.

He had to speak to her. Had to know the truth of what happened all those years ago.

Maybe she'd been free to choose, but she wasn't free to ignore the consequences.

He looked up to find Kate watching him. "What?"

"There must be more to you wanting to find Marian."

"Why?"

"Because to me, Marian did the best she could in what I suspect were frightening circumstances. How can you not see that? There must be more to this than you're telling me, judging by your hostility."

Mac clenched his jaw. "There isn't."

"No? Then prove it. You look so angry again. I won't let you near her until you've got a grip on your emotions. Marian's a good person, and I hate the thought that your arrival might upset her. Announcing you're her grandson when she didn't know you existed will be one hell of a shock. If you want my help, rather than have me standing in your way, you have to promise me we'll tread carefully."

He picked up his drink, studying her over

the rim as defensiveness simmered deep inside. "How and when I speak to her is my decision."

She held his gaze. "Which terrifies me."

He closed his eyes at the thought she might ever have reason to be afraid of him. "I'm not a barbarian."

Their gazes locked.

He wanted her help, wanted her to like and trust him, but there was little chance of that happening until she understood him. But the thought of telling her about Jilly and the baby...that wasn't happening.

He softened his tone. "Look, I get what you're saying, but when I discovered my dad had searched for his birth mother, I felt betrayed. It was as though he had this whole other life going on that my sister and I had no idea about and that hurt. Whether I had any right to feel that way is up for judgment."

"Did your mum know?"

"Yes, and she was as concerned as you are about the implications should he find Marian. It's possible the circumstances around his birth were not ideal. Mum was worried how that would affect Dad."

"And what were the circumstances?"

"I don't know, but unmarried mothers were

thought of in a very different way than they are today. It could be that my grandmother was alone. Maybe the father and her family abandoned her." He looked deep into her eyes, hating that he could explain things so easily to her when, inside, the adoption evoked such ugly emotions in him.

She sighed. "I've seen that scenario far more times than I'd like."

"Exactly, and even though I don't want to be the one to shock an older lady, I need some answers and I need to tell her the sort of man my dad was."

She nodded, disquiet once more darkening her gaze. "These situations often have huge ripple effects, Mac. What if Marian's your grandmother and wants nothing to do with you or your family? What then?"

Mac put down his fork and stared across the restaurant, uncertainty burning inside him once more. Loss, abandonment—were these things a goddamned Orman family trait? "Then I'll know more than when I arrived."

"Is that enough? You could just go back to your life as though her rejection hasn't affected you?"

He looked at her, and she shook her head,

sending her soft, shiny curls swinging. "I don't believe that. Not for you."

He frowned. "Not for me?"

She lowered her gaze. "You seem too sensitive to just walk away."

Mac huffed a laugh. "Well, that's a first. Nobody's called me sensitive before. Insensitive, on the other hand..."

She smiled, and his whole reason for being in Templeton seemed to lose some importance. Even if only temporarily. Mac fell into her dark brown eyes, his body yearning to be close to her like they'd been at the Coast. If he kissed her again, held her, he wasn't so sure he'd leave Templeton with the speed he'd been planning. She wasn't only beautiful, she was smart, savvy and kind, attributes that appealed to every part of him.

She picked up a chip. "No one can sing and play guitar like you and not be sensitive. Your music is beautiful."

"Thanks." Pride swelled inside him, and he turned back to his plate, trying to find the right words to explain how he felt. "If Marian's my grandmother and you think there's a chance she'll send me away, why do you consider her such a good person? From what you've said about her caring for people, she sounds pretty maternal to me."

"She is. That's why I know she would only have given up a child if she had no other choice. She has every right to keep silent about the adoption, but I can't believe that's something Marian would've found easy to do, considering her friendships in town. Which means she has a really good reason for not wanting anyone to know. Maybe she still feels guilty or bitterly regrets the decision." She paused, her eyes shadowing and her cheeks flushing. "Or maybe something happened back then that she never wants to speak of again." She stared into his eyes, and he could've sworn she was holding back tears. "What if having you turn up unannounced rips open old wounds? We have no idea what was going on for her then. What if you evoke memories she doesn't want to be reminded of?"

Culpability weighed heavy on Mac's conscience as he fought to maintain eye contact with her.

She sighed. "What if this ends up hurting more people than Marian? Would you seriously be okay with that?"

"I just need to meet her, Kate."

She stared at him, her gaze considering. "Are you sure that's all?"

"Yes. Well, and to find some answers, too. Dad should've gone through with his search. An explanation might have been all he needed to gain the sense of self he never seemed to find."

"And what about you?"

"What about me?"

"Don't you want to know if Marian is your family for you, too? You mentioned a sister. Do you have other siblings? How do they feel about what you're doing?"

He picked up his drink. "One sister. Older. And she doesn't know I'm here."

"Why aren't you including her in this?"

He sighed. "There's no point in telling Dana what I'm doing. She'll only freak out. She thinks Mum is all we should be concentrating on right now. Dad only died a few months ago and she's grieving despite being divorced from him for a couple of years. But I can't do anything to help her through that. Anyone who loses someone too soon and too suddenly has to find a way to get through it themselves. She has Dana. She doesn't need me, too. At least, not every minute. In time, Dana will see that."

She frowned. "You sound frustrated again."

"I am." He pushed his half-eaten meal away as his appetite disappeared. "I'm close to my family. If this goes wrong and I bring more pain to their door, I'll never forgive myself."

She covered his hand where it lay on the table. "Look, why don't you come by my apartment later and we'll talk more. I have to get back to the office, but I'll try to help you. Okay?"

Relief washed through him, along with a hefty amount of self-doubt. Was he doing the right thing by pursuing Marian Ball? Or was he hell-bent on a path that could be destructive to both Marian *and* his family? Something he hadn't considered before now.

He nodded. "Okay, later."

She smiled and released his hand. "Later."

CHAPTER EIGHT

A COUPLE OF HOURS LATER, Mac contemplated the activity surrounding him in Marian's bakery as he nursed his second cup of coffee. Why was he sitting here? After his conversation with Kate, his instincts were screaming at him to get the hell of out Templeton. The more time he spent in the bakery, the more he learned about the woman who could be his grandmother. He'd loitered over two cups of coffee and listened to the conversation around him whenever Marian was mentioned.

The woman's generosity and popularity made him waver between feeling nauseous to unexpectedly and uselessly proud.

He'd heard stories of her packaging leftovers for the homeless and giving extra bread rolls, pastries or bottled drinks to those who struggled financially or were having a rough time. He'd heard how she gave her time and ear to folks who needed it, how she'd even opened her home to people whose needs merited it.

Each new piece of information only served to make him question his motives. What if she turned a spotlight on his selfish reasons for pursuing her? What if—he swallowed—he succeeded in turning Kate's slowly emerging fondness for him to disgust?

He looked through the window toward the promenade. She had been right to question what he'd do should Marian reject him.

Yet, Kate and this small town somehow seemed to be seeping into his body and totally messing with his mind. She'd challenged his resentment of Marian, which had diminished his hostility a little. Now he was unsure what he should be feeling about Marian, his life…absolutely everything.

And that uncertainty was due to Kate and what her wisdom and kindness had unraveled inside him. She was making him feel again, thawing the ice around his heart.

He stared at the people strolling along the boardwalk or sitting at tables outside a couple of restaurants. Templeton was a friendly place. An interesting place. He turned and studied the customers chatting with the young women behind the counter. The relaxed atmosphere had caught him off guard once again, and he smiled along with the people around him as they shared a joke or gently ribbed one another about their clothes, jobs, girlfriends or boyfriends.

The small-town camaraderie should have been suffocating. Instead, he wondered what it would feel like to be a part of it. To walk into a place where everyone knew your name, wanted to help with your problems or congratulated you on a recent accomplishment.

It appeared people in Templeton were kind and attentive to everyone, regardless of whether they were family. He scowled, his usual pessimism whenever he thought of long-lasting relationships reemerging.

His phone vibrated on the tabletop and he glanced at the display.

Exhaling, he pressed the button to accept the call. "Dana, hi. What's up?"

"What's up is Mum asked me the weirdest thing at lunch today. She asked if I thought there was a chance you could be in Templeton Cove. Now, why would she think you would be in a tiny town miles from home when you're needed here?"

Mac winced. "I've got no idea."

"No? Well, Mum did. She seems to think

you might be looking for Dad's mum. Our grandmother. Please tell me she's wrong, and, of course, you wouldn't act on something that she specifically asked us to leave alone."

Mac thought of excuses and lies, but what good would it do to delay the truth? Sooner or later he'd come clean to his mum and sister. It was impossible to keep anything from them.

He took a deep breath. "Fine. She's right. I'm in Templeton."

"What?"

"I said—"

"You're in Templeton? What are you thinking? Have you found her? Have you spoken to her? My God, Mac, Mum will go ballistic. You going off on some genealogy mission is the last thing she needs."

He lowered his voice to keep others from hearing this conversation. "Will you calm down?"

"You had no right to do this. No right at all."

"Look." Mac swiped his hand over his face. Whether his mum or Dana approved, knowing his grandmother and her knowing him mattered. Maybe his desire to punish her had diminished, but nothing had changed in his determination to come face-to-face with Marian Ball. "The only woman I've found who has any possibility of being our biological grandmother isn't even here. She's on vacation. I haven't said or done anything yet, so you can stop panicking."

"Good." Dana huffed down the phone. "So now you can get yourself back here and put Mum's mind to rest. She told us she didn't want Dad looking for that woman, let alone us doing so. What on earth possessed you to go against her wishes? This isn't like you, Mac. You usually care so much how Mum, me and the kids are feeling."

As disloyalty swept through him, Mac dropped his hand to the table and lowered his voice still further. "This woman is part of our family." He swallowed as the force of his love for his family rose. "Who knows why she gave Dad up? Maybe he was adopted against her wishes. Maybe she was forced. I can't leave this alone until I know the truth."

"And what if the truth causes you more pain? Losing Jilly almost destroyed you. I can't believe you're willing to open yourself up to—"

"That's my choice, isn't it?" Pain pierced his heart. "Not yours."

"You lost your new family, something I

can barely imagine. But finding this Marian woman isn't going to bring Jilly and the baby back, no matter how much I wish it would for you."

"You think I don't know that?" Did he? Wasn't that what his coming here had been all about? That he could pass his pain and hurt to a stranger who meant nothing to him? So, how was it that he was starting to take Marian Ball's feelings into consideration?

Dana sighed. "Look, I'm worried about you, okay? You said you were playing a gig. I didn't think you lied, least of all to me."

"It was hardly a lie…more of a half-truth."

"Meaning?"

"It means I've played while I've been here. They were a good crowd. A great crowd, in fact."

"Crowd? I was under the impression Templeton is tiny."

"It is. That doesn't mean they don't enjoy music. Kate was heading up a charity gig and the Moon Shadows' guitarist—"

"Who's Kate?"

Damn it. He grimaced. "What?"

"You said Kate. Who is she?"

"A woman."

"For the love of God, do I need to come

down there? Not only are you looking for a woman Mum specifically asked us not to find, but you're sleeping with some random woman?"

"I haven't slept with her, and Kate is not some random woman." Mac squeezed his eyes shut. "What I mean is, she's nice. Kind. So whatever you're thinking, you've got it all wrong."

"Nice? Kind? I haven't heard you use those words about anyone in years."

"So?"

"So, what's going on?"

"Nothing."

"Mac, listen to me. You can't go through with looking for Dad's mum, okay? It will only upset Mum and—"

"I'm doing this *for* Dad."

"You're doing this for *you*. Dad's dead, remember?"

Mac gripped his coffee cup. Sometimes his sister drove him near insanity with her insensitivity. Maybe that was why Kate had called him sensitive. He'd had to overcompensate a million and one times to make up for his sister's tactlessness. He leaned back, his attention drawn to the girl behind the counter, who held a phone to her ear and excitedly gestured to her colleague. The few people lining the counter stepped closer to listen.

With his gaze locked on the girl, he spoke into the phone. "I've got to go, Dana. I'll call you if and when I find anything about Marian Ball. Okay?"

"No, not okay."

"Just give me a couple of days. If I don't find anything, I'll come home."

"Two days?"

"Two days."

"And what am I supposed to tell Mum?"

"Nothing, because there's nothing to tell. I'll call you."

He hung up on her protests and turned his phone to silent, watching the commotion at the counter. Bursts of laughter came from the small gathering, their smiles wide, some even wiping away tears. Mac stood and edged closer.

"You did what?" The young girl behind the counter widened her eyes and pressed her hand to her stomach. "You took George's swimming shorts? In front of everyone around the pool? Marian! Why didn't he have them on in the first place?" She laughed. "You convinced him to take them off? In a public pool? Eww."

The crowd erupted with laughter, one guy holding on to the counter as though he might crumple to the floor. Mac smiled. Whether or not Marian was his grandmother, it seemed she was more than game for a laugh.

And wasn't laughter what his family could use right now?

He turned and headed for the door before he acted on the sudden need to know what else his potential and, currently elusive, grandmother could be up to.

KATE WORKED ON her laptop, aware Mac would be arriving any minute now. She needed a little more time to finish her initial research into Marian Cohen, once Marian Ball.

Though it had been easy enough to find Marian online, it soon became clear Kate knew little to nothing about Marian before she came to Templeton...and wasn't likely to uncover anything unless she dug deep. Really deep.

The search engine provided plenty of information about the bakery and Marian's charitable work. Even a few pictures of her wedding to George on Cowden beach. Next, Kate needed to find out if it was possible to see a copy of her birth certificate, maybe check a census or two from way back.

Kate inhaled a shaky breath.

It felt so wrong to probe into Marian's past. The older woman had gone above and beyond for Kate during and after her miscarriage, and now Kate was repaying that kindness by digging around where she didn't belong. But where Mac might.

When his anger had turned to quiet need, it had driven Kate to want to help him any way she could.

A genuine yearning had rung in Mac's voice. As though meeting Marian might hold something profound for him. Still, if she sensed any maliciousness on Mac's part, she would do everything she could to shut him down and to escort him out of town, far away from Marian.

She closed down her laptop, putting it to the side of her on the couch. Her suspicion arose from the way she'd recognized his sadness. Mac had lost something in his life. Something big…just as she had.

Dropping her head back, Kate pressed her hand to her stomach. Pain and wanting slithered into her heart, biting and pinching. Why had she thought everything would eventually return to normal? That she could forge a career and not imagine the face of her child over and over?

Marian hadn't lost her baby. She'd carried him, nurtured him in her womb and then given him to a family who could love him. Kate wiped her tears and abruptly stood, shaking off her self-pity. However Kate looked at it, Marian was a strong and compassionate woman. There was no guessing how she'd react to Mac should she meet him. Marian was a law unto herself.

Kate walked into the kitchen and filled a glass with water. She drank deep and tried to calm her aching heart. Mac needed her help. She would do all she could to support him and protect Marian at the same time.

She refilled her glass as her mind wandered over what she'd learned.

Ball was a common surname, and, at first glance, the number of women named Marian Ball living in southwest England had been overwhelming. There was every possibility Marian's life had only truly begun when she'd come to the Cove; she and Mac had no right to dig up a past best forgotten.

Yet, it still troubled her how anyone could

live close to sixty-five years and leave nothing behind.

Part of her had really wanted to bring something new to the table when he came by, but even her contacts at the housing association and missing persons department hadn't found anything. Thank goodness. The last thing she wanted was to end up blaming Mac for tainting her view of Marian.

She returned to the living room and sadness pressed down on her. If Marian was Mac's grandmother and she'd had a child, did she pine for that child? Think about him? Wonder about his health? Whether he had a family? Was happy?

Kate walked to her patio doors and stared toward the fairground, hating that her friend might have been suffering in silence for years. Kate gripped the balcony railing. She had to protect the woman who'd helped countless people in the Cove, young and old. Marian's heart was bigger than most, and she had a forceful passion for the community and the town itself.

Which led Kate to the only conclusion. If Mac's father was Marian's son, his conception, or maybe his birth, was a long-buried secret Marian had made every effort to ensure was never uncovered.

She wanted to help Mac, but she also knew she trusted people too easily and quickly.

Determined that Marian would come first rose once more. If Mac thought, for even a second, that she'd keep his presence a secret from Marian when she returned from vacation, he was mistaken. Kate owed Marian a lot more loyalty than she did to a man she'd known barely a week.

Her apartment buzzer sounded, and Kate turned toward her door, her resolve back in place. Great kisser or not, Mac was just a man. A stranger—one hell of a sexy stranger, but a stranger all the same.

Putting her glass on the coffee table, she took a deep breath and walked to the intercom. "Hello?"

"It's me."

Mac's rich masculine voice rasped down the line, causing a hitch in her chest and a pull in places that had no business feeling pulled. "Come on up. I'm in apartment ninety-one."

She pressed the buzzer, allowing him access into the apartment block, and unlocked the door, leaving it ajar. She sat back down, pleased that her glass remained steady as she lifted it.

A few moments later, the heavy tread of Mac's biker boots sounded outside the door. "Hello?"

"Hi." She looked up and smiled, her heart beating a little faster at the handsome sight of him as he stepped in. "You found me okay, then?"

"Uh-huh."

"Do you want a drink? Coffee?"

"No, I'm good. Thanks."

The seriousness of his tone and the distraction in his gaze raised Kate's wariness. She thought they'd gotten past their initial push-pull and moved toward something more intimate. He'd opened up to her about his search. Was this where he shut down or shut her out?

Clearing her throat, she waved toward the couch. "Have a seat."

He looked at her, his gaze steady. "I have news."

"About Marian?"

"Yes. I stopped by the bakery again this afternoon, and it seems she's having a great time."

Kate relaxed, the tension leaving her body. She laughed. "Marian doesn't know how *not* to have a great time. That isn't news, Mac. Well, maybe it is to you because you haven't met her, but—"

"That isn't the news."

She stilled. "Oh."

He shrugged out of his jacket, and Kate drew her gaze over his broad chest beneath his dark blue T-shirt, then over his arms. Attraction stirred in her as she stared at the tattoos on his forearms. Black-and-blue ink depicted a raging sea, a crack of lightning. Another showed a face, mouth open and grimacing as though in pain.

She met his eyes, questions freezing on her tongue.

He stared back at her. "They each mean something. The tattoos."

She nodded, unsure how to respond. The tattoos were dark, angry...so like Mac.

He drew an envelope from the inside pocket of his leather jacket and handed it to her. "This is the news."

Curiosity chased away her wariness, but as she moved to take the envelope, he touched her hand. "Before you open it, I need to tell you what I've been doing this afternoon."

She laid the envelope in her lap, and he clenched both his hands on his thighs. His biceps strained against the sleeves of his shirt, illustrating his tension.

He inhaled shakily. "When I got back to the Coast after leaving the bakery, yours and my sister's warnings circled around in my head, mixing with the realization that maybe my determination to find my biological grandmother might be about pain caused by something else."

"Something you want to share with me?"

"Maybe, but I need to tell you something about Marian first."

"Okay."

"I scanned through my father's papers, weighing the pros and cons of continuing my pursuit of Marian and telling her I'm her grandson…and that her son is dead. No matter how much I considered Marian's possible rejection of my claims, or even me, I can't carry on without acknowledging my reasons for contacting her." He searched her face. "I'm not sure you'll like them, but you should know. You also need to know that whatever your feelings, I will be speaking with her."

Her defenses rose. "She's my friend, Mac. I owe it to her to protect her, if necessary. I was right to ask that you to take into account we have no idea of the circumstances surrounding Marian's decision to give up her baby."

"And I appreciate that. When I took another look through my father's research this afternoon, I came across something I'd missed."

"Which was?"

"Marian had placed her name as wanting to be contacted should her biological son look for her at any point in the future."

Kate dropped her shoulders, her stress vanishing. "Well, that changes everything. If she wants to be found—"

"I was thinking of leaving." He looked into her eyes, his focus slowly moving to her mouth. "Only, I'm not sure I can anymore."

Her heart gave a traitorous blip, and she forced a smile. "Why? If you don't want to pursue—"

"I didn't expect to find you, Kate." He met her eyes. "Only a grandmother I've never known."

Kate stilled. "Find me?"

He nodded, his gaze softening. "Yes, you. You seem to be changing every original reason I had for coming here."

Dangerous hope whipped around her heart. "What are you saying?"

"I'm saying, there's more you need to know about me and there's more I need to know about you. I like you, Kate. A lot."

CHAPTER NINE

MAC DRAGGED HIS gaze from Kate's. If he was staying awhile, she deserved his total honesty. "Could I get a glass of water?"

She leaped to her feet. "Water? Yes, of course."

He grimaced as she hurried into the kitchen. He was stalling because he needed the time to get his words straight. His feelings straight. Everything about being in Templeton seemed to have veered off course, and now Kate was another reason to stay.

"Here." She handed him a glass.

"Thanks." He took a drink. "When I said I like you, Kate, I meant it. I don't want to go through with meeting Marian without your advice. Your suspicion of me when I arrived here was justified. I see that now."

"Oh." She sat beside him. "I'm glad, because I can be a real pain in the butt sometimes. It comes from looking after the teenagers at the center. Often they come in resentful and angry, but nine times out of ten, they're hurting." She smiled softly. "Once I saw that you accepted how important Marian is to me, I recognized the same hurt in you."

He nodded, feeling entirely exposed. He still had to finish what he came here to do, even if that meant upsetting Marian Ball.

Exhaling, Mac took her hand. "There's something I need to tell you. About me and my family."

Concern flashed in her eyes and she inhaled. "Okay. Good. The important thing right now is you. You and Marian. Or maybe not Marian, if Marian isn't…" She laughed nervously. "I'll stop talking. Go ahead."

Mac failed to hold back his smile. "Right there. That's why you're messing with my head. You're cute…and sexy."

She raised her eyebrows as her cheeks darkened. "Sexy? You think?"

"Absolutely."

"Thanks." She grinned. "But you need to stop looking at me like that if you want me to concentrate on whatever it is you have to say." She cleared her throat. "Tell me about you and your family."

Mac leaned back. There could be no cowardice, only honesty. She deserved to know his search for his grandmother was tied to his pain over the loss of Jilly and their baby. That loss was an integral part of who he was, and if there was a chance of him and Kate acting on the attraction between them, she deserved to know all about Jilly and the accident.

He didn't know why he trusted Kate so much, or why he wanted to share the most devastating time of his life with her. But the need was there, and life was too short to question such immediate faith in someone.

He drew in a long breath and released it. "I lost my girlfriend and unborn baby in a car accident three years ago. She and I were both twenty-two. Children, really. But Jilly and I were in love and spent as much time together as we could. I wanted her and I wanted our baby." His heart hitched under the weight of his confession and the deep sympathy in Kate's dark brown eyes. "When she died... when *they* died... I thought my life was over."

Further words clogged his throat as memories of the darkest days of his life slammed into his chest.

"Oh, Mac. I'm so sorry." She inched closer, lowering her head on to his shoulder and loosening his fisted hand to intertwine her fingers with his. "I can't imagine how that must've felt or even how you got through it."

Relief that he'd managed to at least tell her about the loss swept through him—even if he couldn't bring himself to confess the truth about the angry, ugly mess he became after his life fell apart.

He forced himself to continue. "I got through it with a lot of support and patience from my mum and sister. Dad pretty much withdrew from the situation. I wasn't the easiest person to be around for a long time."

"Maybe not, but I imagine that's why you're so close to your mum and sister now. Losing someone you loved that way is too awful for words."

"And it's also what led me to wanting to find my grandmother. When Dad died, it was the last death I could take. I wanted to lash out. Hurt someone. Marian Ball became my target. She meant nothing to me. She still doesn't."

She lifted her head and looked deep into his eyes, hurt and disappointment in her gaze. "You haven't met her yet. She's just a name on a piece of paper. But when you meet her—"

"Should I meet her? Now you know my reasons behind finding her..." He shook his head. "I can't promise what I'll be like if she sends me away or isn't at all emotional about Dad. When people find out what happened to Jilly, they immediately ask what happened. When and who was to blame. But you…you understand how what happened sent me into a destructive tailspin." He touched his fingers to her jaw. "I'm not sure I deserve your understanding, Kate. I'm still that angry person you saw when I walked in the bar."

"No, Mac. You're not, and you've promised me no bloodshed, remember? You need to meet Marian. You really do."

"But—"

"Listen to me." She turned his hand and kissed his palm, her eyes shining with unshed tears. "You need to do anything you think will help you to heal. Anything. It wasn't your sister who lost Jilly and your baby. It was you. I think Marian might be just the person you need in your life right now."

The desire to kiss her surged through him along with a strange sense of freedom, which came with the absence of any judgment or condemnation in her gaze. "You're quite something, do you know that?"

She shook her head. "I'm nothing out of the ordinary, believe me." She reached for her water, her face turned from his. "I sometimes think I've suffered, but then I meet teenagers all alone and pregnant or living with depression. Families that are struggling…" She drank. "And now I've met you. I haven't known pain at all. Not really."

"Hey. Pain comes in hundreds of different forms. If something, or someone, hurt you enough that the memory lingers, that's enough to warrant every one of your feelings. You don't have to justify your inability to get over something to anyone. Including me."

She faced him. "You lost a girlfriend, Mac. A baby."

He swallowed. "Yeah, and I also rejected the suggestion of counseling and any comfort or solace my friends and family could offer. I pushed them away and struggled to come to terms with my loss alone. That was stupid and unfair. Even after three long years, I haven't learned anything. Maybe my sister's right and I should be at home. Not here, doing what I'm doing."

"You should be here."

The firmness in her tone surprised him.

"Don't give up on what you've started, Mac. Not now. When we feel strongly about something, we have to see it through to its end. No regrets. No looking back. I try really hard to live by my words and, of course, some days I fail miserably." She gave a wry smile. "But then another day breaks and, with it, another chance to do better. You'll get through this, and you will have your happy ending."

"Maybe."

She squeezed his hand, tears in her eyes. "Definitely." She took his hand, her gaze dropping to their fingers. Slowly, she raised his hand and pressed a soft, lingering kiss to his knuckles. "I'm going to help you, Mac." Her breath whispered over his skin. "I'm going to help you find your closure." Another kiss. She raised her head. "And maybe I'll find mine, too."

He stared at her mouth, its sweet, soft taste tormenting his mind and seeping into his body. He should've asked her what she sought closure for, but all he wanted was to kiss her.

So he did.

She sighed into his mouth, her hands gliding onto his shoulders as he gently grasped her jaw. Their tongues were gentle at first, but as the heat rose, Mac's heart beat faster, and his need for this woman grew. He kissed her harder, deeper, until he was forced to move away for fear of scaring her.

She shook her head, her eyes dark with desire, her mouth pink. "Oh, no. You don't get to do that again."

Fear tiptoed through him. To never kiss her again…the possibility was unbearable. "Don't get to do what?"

She grinned, her eyes glinting with mischief. "You don't get to kiss me like that and walk away again."

He smiled, his heart slowing. "I'm going nowhere, but unless you want me to pick you up and march straight into your bedroom, we need to stop."

"Hmm." She glanced over his shoulder. "The bedroom is just a few feet away." She met his gaze, her eyes slowly sobering. "No. You're right. Too much, too soon. I might want to throw caution to the wind as far as you're concerned, but that pain I spoke about? I won't let it happen to me again."

Her words and the remembered heartbreak that showed in her eyes instantly doused his desire. So it had been a man who hurt her. "What did he do to you?"

Her hands slipped from his shoulders and she shrugged, but as she turned away, Mac caught the flash of humiliation in her pretty eyes. She reached for his glass. "He cheated on me...with my sister."

Anger that any guy would hurt her gripped Mac's gut. "What?"

She looked at him. "It's ancient history. Well, at least it will be when I find my closure. Right?"

He clenched his jaw. "Right."

His anger, his need to find the guy who hurt her and slam him up against a wall, shamed him. Her pain wasn't about him. It was about her. He would be what Kate needed him to be instead of acting on a primal need to protect her. Kate was special. She was brave, generous, funny and beautiful. He couldn't risk sabotaging what was growing between them before they'd even begun to explore it.

He offered her glass to her. She took it, her gaze questioning.

He winked and smiled, picking up his glass, too. "To closure."

She softly laughed. "To closure."

They clinked glasses and drank, their gazes locked above the rims, and Mac wondered if the fiery strength mixed with fear in her eyes was reflected in his.

KATE MOVED INCONSPICUOUSLY along the couch, putting space between her and Mac. Once again, his kiss had set her on fire and pushed desire into every intimate place. Her want of him was as stupid as it was scary, and she could not afford to let it overtake her sanity.

Her lust had led her to Dean, who'd hurt her so deeply, the effects still lingered on her heart. She would not allow a man to hurt her that way again. No matter how sexy, kind or dangerously attractive he might be. Never again would she fall too quickly or too naively. She didn't really know Mac; though she'd learned more about him tonight, the alarm bells ringing in her head and the desire warming her body told her to put on the brakes.

She'd told him about Dean but couldn't imagine finding the courage to tell him about her miscarriage. She understood Mac's determination to find Marian, to find his roots. Family was important to him. Her father, mother and sister mattered to her, too. What would he think of her if he discovered her estrangement from her sister?

Her family was fractured. His was in pain but still so very close.

Putting down her glass, Kate remembered the envelope Mac had given her and picked it up from where it had fallen on the floor. She held it out to him. "Here. You know, I really ought to get some sleep. I have an ultra-early start tomorrow."

Surprise and then concern flashed in his eyes as he took the envelope. "Have I said something wrong?"

"Not at all. I just need to get some shut-eye. Do you mind?"

"No problem." But he didn't get up from the couch.

And she didn't want him to go. She wanted to learn more about him. To like more about him. She swallowed. "How about we meet up somewhere tomorrow night?"

"Sure, but I have one more thing to tell you about Marian before I go."

"Shoot."

"Could you sit down?" He raised his eyebrows. "I don't want to risk a crick in my neck."

She laughed, feeling more than a little foolish, and rejoined him on the couch, concentrating on his face rather than on the sexual thoughts racing through her mind, or the fact her bedroom was only a few feet away. History had proven what a mistake a rash decision could be. "Go ahead."

He leaned over and stuffed the envelope into his leather jacket. "The letter doesn't say much more than what I already told you, but…" He faced her. "Along with the letter there was something else. Something I think my father was ashamed of."

"What?"

"It seems at the time Marian requested to be added to the register, she'd already attempted to find my father. At least three times over three decades."

A mix of pleasure and relief swept through her. "So if the Marian you're looking for is the Cove's Marian, she's already looked for her son in the past? She definitely wanted to find him, then. So why wouldn't your father have come here? It's clear she wanted to meet him."

"I know and that's another reason why the initial anger I had toward her is lessening. I loved my father, Kate, but he was a coward. A man afraid of so damn much, especially emotions. Confrontation. Grief. He knew his mother had looked for him, but he did nothing about it."

He trembled, and Kate drew in a long

breath, covering his hand with hers. His anger was there again, but now it seemed more about his father than Marian. "Mac, listen to me. I'm pretty sure if Marian wanted to contact your dad, she'll welcome you with open arms."

"Maybe, but how will she take the news her son is dead?"

"Oh. Right." She closed her eyes, imagining what the news would do to Marian. She opened her eyes. "You can't just blurt something out like that, can you."

"No, but you accept she needs to know?"

"Yes."

"Good." Looking relieved, he exhaled. "I thought you might try to stop me."

"Maybe I would have, but that was before."

"Before what?"

"Before I got to know you a little better." She looked into his eyes, feeling the attraction between them. "The thing is, you came into town looking dangerous and angry. I jumped to the conclusion you were here to make someone atone for something. I was wrong. Now I know more about you and Marian…" She shook her head, convinced Mac had to see his search through for his sake and Marian's. "I think you have to be certain Marian is your grandmother and then you tell her everything. It could mean as much closure for her as it could for you." She smiled. "Believe me, if Marian is your grandmother, you'll want to know her. She's wonderful. Truly."

"Aren't you basing that advice on who she is since she arrived in Templeton? She gave birth to my dad forty-eight years ago. She was seventeen. The first record of her starting her search for him shows she was around twenty-five or twenty-six. Then again at forty-five and finally at fifty-five. After that, nothing. She stopped and hasn't tried again for the last ten years. Why? What changed to make her give up completely?"

Kate thought. "There must be a link to her arrival in Templeton and her decision to give up her search."

"Exactly. Maybe it has something to do with why she's never had friends or family come to visit. Why no one seems to know anything about her. About her child."

"Maybe."

"We need to find out what happened ten years ago to make Marian Ball, or Cohen, or whatever her name is, finish with the life she had before she came here. It's as though she wanted to forget everything that happened before and start her life over. Why?"

Kate leaned back as sadness for Marian enveloped her. When Dean had hurt her and Ali, Kate would've happily disappeared for months so no one witnessed her humiliation. When she lost her baby, she didn't want anyone to know because she felt like such a failure... so much less of a woman. With time, she realized her feelings were unfounded and irrational, but it had done nothing to alleviate her loss. Did Marian's decision to give up her baby haunt her in the same way?

"We have to talk to her." Kate held Mac's gaze. "Maybe she's never gotten over giving up your father. When Jilly died, did you feel like running away, starting over somewhere new?"

His jaw tightened. "Running away was the last thing I wanted. I cherish my memories of Jilly. I cherish the time we spent together. I wouldn't change that for anything. Her death..." He swallowed. "Her death nearly killed me, but it didn't taint the good times we had."

Regret swept through her, and Kate's eyes stung with shame. "I'm sorry. I wasn't thinking. I only asked because when Dean cheated on me, I wanted to forget the entire year I was with him. For me, there were no good times to hold on to, just the glaring memory of finding him in my bed with my sister."

The pain left his eyes and was replaced with empathy. "I get that, too. You've got nothing to apologize for, remember?"

She nodded, her thoughts turning to Marian once more. "You know, Marian's back the day after tomorrow, and there's only one other person who could possibly know what happened ten years ago."

"Who?"

"Her husband. George."

He frowned. "But we can't ask him without him alerting his wife. Especially if they're as close as you've said they are."

"You certainly couldn't ask him, but I could." She inched closer to him. "If you lie low for a couple of days, I'll try to test the waters with George and gauge what Marian's reaction to you will be."

He studied her uncertainly. "I'm not sure that's such a good idea."

"Mac, trust me." She smiled. "George is kind, lovely and a complete softie with the ladies. If there's anything to find out, I'll find it without raising his suspicions. I'm good with people. Surely you know that much about me. I can do this and arm us with something to at least approach Marian with when you're ready. What do you say?"

He took a long breath, a hint of a smile on his lips. "I can't speak for a man I've never met, but if you look at George the way you're looking at me right now, he'll be putty in your hands."

She grinned. "Is that a yes?"

"It's a yes."

Kate leaned forward and kissed him before slowly drawing back. "Great. Then leave everything to me."

CHAPTER TEN

"THAT'S GREAT, Iz." Kate marched into the ladies' bathroom at the Teenage Support center, her phone to her ear. "If Jay's confirmed George is there, I can go see him this morning. Jay won't be there, right?"

"Right." Izzy sighed. "But I still don't see what you're trying to achieve by going to see George. You know how he and Marian feel about each other. I can't imagine George easily talking about her past with you. He won't betray her trust for anyone."

"He won't have to." Kate pushed a couple of the stall doors open. The last thing she wanted was anyone overhearing this conversation. Satisfied she was alone, she leaned against one of the sinks. "I just want to test the waters a little before she meets the grandson she didn't know she had. Then I'll do what I can to support Mac, but the rest will be up to him, not me."

"You seem to really like this guy…and I'm

happy for you, but don't you think you're getting a little too involved?"

Ignoring the way her thoughts echoed her friend's, Kate pushed her hair back from her face. "He's hurting, Iz. That tough exterior hides a good man with a good heart."

"So, what's happened to change your mind about him?"

Everything. Kate forced some breeziness into her voice. "Oh, you know. I just know him a little better, I guess. I understand his need to get closure for himself and his family. It's important he gets that, Iz. Trust me. I know what it's like when people are left flailing after a tragedy."

"Mac's had a tragedy?"

"Yes, but it's not my place to talk about it. Will you just trust I'm doing the right thing by him?"

"And Marian? Are you doing the right thing by her?"

"Yes, which is exactly why I want an idea of her reaction before Mac talks to her. We're doing this as a team. I speak with people who are emotional or grieving all the time. I can help ease the shock for Marian and help Mac speak with her."

"But it isn't your place to do either of those things. You know that."

Even though Kate would never get her baby back, she could at least help Marian reunite with her grandson and his family. But how could she explain that to Izzy? "Mac asked for my help. I didn't thrust myself on him…" She tried to lighten her tone. "Not that I don't want to thrust myself on him in other ways."

"Hmm. And how are those other ways going? Have you slept with him yet?"

"Of course not. I'm playing it nice and cool. I'm in the driver's seat, believe me. We've kissed, but that's it."

"And why are you so sure you're in the driver's seat and not Mac?"

"Because, ye of such little faith, I could've easily led him into my bedroom the other night and I didn't. See? Driver's seat."

"Well, you must really like this guy if you're willing to risk Marian's wrath. Once she finds out you knew about her grandson way before she did, she's going to go mad, and rightly so."

Despite her bravado, trepidation gripped Kate's stomach. She waved her hand. "She'll be fine. Once she meets Mac and they've talked a while, she'll thank me for greasing the wheels a little. Look, I appreciate you letting me know George is at Jay's. I'll let you know how things go."

"Sure, if you're alive the next time I see you."

The line went dead, and Kate glared at her phone. "I'll show you, Izzy Cooper. I'll show you good and proper."

Kate stalked to her desk and grabbed her purse, along with a couple of envelopes that needed to be mailed. She glanced at Nancy, who worked at the opposite desk. "I need to run a couple of errands. I should only be an hour or so, but I have my phone if there are any emergencies."

Nancy waved distractedly. "Sure. See you later."

Glad of the easy escape, Kate hurried into the street and to her car. *Clover Point, here I come.*

George Cohen had worked as a handyman for Jay Garrett, the Cove's millionaire entrepreneur, for years and many more for Jay's father before him. Izzy had not only confirmed George would be working at Jay's log cabin–style mansion at the top of Clover Point, but also that Jay was away for a few nights with his wife and little girl. Kate gripped the wheel. There was no reason why she and George should be interrupted, and she was confident now about how to approach him.

Her sole mission was to establish Marian's acceptance of Mac while also ensuring the safety of her dear friend's heart. If she kept her exploratory questions to a minimum, there was no reason George should go racing to Marian. She exhaled shakily. She just needed to stay calm and not blow her subterfuge sky-high.

Marian's past wasn't Kate's to uncover, but she understood Mac's desire to learn about his roots. She would do all she could to help him puzzle out his ancestry.

Fifteen minutes later, Kate pulled into Jay's mammoth gravel driveway and parked next to George's car out front. She sat back and drew her gaze over the front of the huge log cabin. Its golden-brown exterior stretched to God only knew how many feet, its many windows glinting in the sunshine, and two chimneys released columns of puffy gray-white smoke, making the mansion look like something from a fairy tale.

Taking a deep breath, she got out of the car and strode to the front door, lifting the knocker and stepping back as sudden nerves somersaulted in her stomach.

The door swung open.

George's mouth broke into a wide smile. "Kate! Fancy seeing you here."

She smiled, her shoulders immediately relaxing. "Hi, George. How was the holiday?"

"Oh, fabulous. Just fabulous. You know my Marian, up to one thing after another. Jay isn't here right now, but is there something I can do for you?"

She grimaced, hating the way she was deceiving him. "Oh, that's a shame. I came to thank him for his generous donation to the fund-raiser the other weekend and to give him news of the grand total."

"I'm sure he'd love to hear all about it when he gets back. He'll be gone another couple of days."

She battled the weight of her pretense. "I can always catch up with him then. I, um… would love to hear more about your holiday if you have time for a quick cup of tea?"

He grinned. "Well, that sounds like a great idea. I was thinking of putting the kettle on." He opened the door wide. "Come on in."

Kate stepped over the threshold and basked in the glory of a millionaire's hallway. It wasn't the first time she'd been in the Garretts' home, thanks to Jay's generosity to the center and his wife's role as the town's detective inspector. Kate's work meant the three of them had come in contact often enough that they were on a first-name basis, but that didn't lessen the awesomeness of the Garretts' home.

"Let's go through to the kitchen." George ambled along the hallway. "Marian sent me off with some fresh muffins this morning, so we can have one with our tea."

"Great." Kate followed him toward the open kitchen door. "So, she's back to the bakery?"

"Oh, yes. She couldn't wait to get to work as soon as we got back from the airport. I managed to persuade her there was no sense going in yesterday, but she was there bright and early this morning."

"I've yet to learn of anything slowing Marian down." Kate laid her purse on the black granite top of the enormous central island and slid on to one of the chrome breakfast stools. "Did she run you ragged while you were away? I hope you found some time to relax."

"We sure did." He filled the kettle and

chuckled as he put it on top of the stove. Taking some matches from the shelf beside him, he lit the burner. "We swam, ate, shopped and found plenty of time for a few rounds of golf, too. Pure bliss."

Kate raised her eyebrows. "Marian plays golf? I had no idea."

He turned and smiled, tapping the side of his nose. "There are a lot of things you don't know about my Marian. She's a dark horse, but she's my horse."

Her stomach knotted with anticipation. What might he reveal about the woman Kate wasn't sure she knew anymore? "What do you mean a dark horse? Marian's one of the most open people in the Cove."

"Ah, but also one who knows how to keep a secret. When have you known her to blab about someone else's business? She takes on the problems of the whole community and would never betray a soul. Not one."

Shame pressed down on Kate, warming her cheeks. "You're right. She's a rock to a lot of people in the Cove. Most of all to me."

"Hey, now." George frowned. "None of that, Kate Harrington. Me and Marian were just supporters in your time of need. The hard stuff you handled yourself." He smiled. "And look at you now. You're a strong, beautiful girl and we're very proud of you." He walked to a side cupboard and removed a couple of mugs. "Sugar?"

Humbled, Kate released a shaky breath. "No, thanks."

She stared around the peach-and-cream kitchen, her mind racing. George had so firmly, if unwittingly, reminded her of Marian's love and devotion, not only to Kate, but many others in the Cove, too. She just needed to be sure news of Mac wouldn't damage her friend irreparably. If Kate suspected for one minute Mac's arrival would distress Marian, she would make Mac leave…regardless of her growing feelings for him. After everything Marian had done for her, Kate could at least protect her.

George slid a cup of tea toward her along with a blueberry muffin on a small plate. "Here we go."

Kate smiled. "Yum."

"Yum, indeed. I was the most blessed man on God's earth when that woman agreed to marry me. I thank my lucky stars no one snapped her up first."

Kate sipped her tea, a way into her questioning unexpectedly landing in her lap. "She wasn't married before? You're her one and only husband."

"The one and only."

She took a sip of tea, carefully watching him from beneath her lowered lashes. "Doesn't she ever wish she'd had kids? She'd make a wonderful mum."

Melancholy glazed his eyes. "Oh, of course she would have, but she didn't meet me until it was too late, did she?" His eyes twinkled with fondness. "That woman loves kids, you know that, but she's also passionate about them having a stable and loving home, parents who love one another."

"And she only found that love in you." Her heart squeezed. "I love you both so much, you know."

"And we love you." His focus drifted to the window. "And I wish I could've given her the family she deserves."

Her heart pounding, Kate picked up her muffin and slowly peeled back its wrapper. "Maybe her family is already here. In the Cove."

He met her eyes. "In Templeton's community, you mean? Yes, I suppose it is, but she would love to have some blood family, too. Not that she'd ever admit it."

Hope twisted inside Kate, and she touched his hand. "She loves you so much, George. You know that, right?"

He smiled softly. "Of course I do. I just never want to be without her."

"You won't be."

As he turned away and lifted his mug to his lips, Kate stared at his profile. An undeniable sorrow permeated the room, caused by one man's deep, unwavering love for a woman. A woman, Kate surmised, who must have been incredibly unhappy before her knight in shining armor rescued her and brought her to live in the most beautiful cove in the whole of southwest England.

She took a bite of her muffin distractedly. George hummed as he stared into the depths of his tea and Kate watched him, wondering what he was thinking.

He looked up and smiled. "Yep, no one on earth like my Marian."

"We all love her, George."

"Aye, I know you do. That's why I've never got to worry about my beautiful lady being upset. Certainly not by anyone around here."

Kate took a sip of her tea…her part in what could unfold, heavier than ever, mixing with the worry that George was wily enough that he had seen straight through her ruse and guessed she was there fishing for information about the woman he loved.

MAC NARROWED HIS eyes and studied Marian, who stood behind the bakery counter. She was plumper than he'd imagined, with steel-gray curls that peeked from beneath a white trilby hat, and her hands routinely left the counter to slap her apron-covered bosom as she chatted and laughed with customers. He couldn't deny the speed and efficiency with which she worked, nor her popularity.

Customers didn't just place their orders and leave. They seemed to linger, as though talking with Marian was the only thing they had to look forward to that day.

Dragging his study from her, Mac stared into his half-empty cup of coffee, indecision and doubt swirling deep in his gut. Kate's insistence that her first priority was Marian's well-being, no matter the circumstances, prodded at his conscience. Now he'd seen his grandmother, his impatience to introduce himself grew stronger with each passing minute.

Despite Mac's need to move past the pain that continued to darken his heart, Marian

Ball was still the woman who'd given up his father for adoption. Sure, people gave up their children for a better life than they could provide, but didn't Marian know how lucky she'd been to have the chance to be a parent?

His jaw tightened. Whereas his chance to be a father had been ripped away from him.

Glancing at Marian again, his heart stumbled.

Her curious gaze zeroed in on him as she stepped out from behind the counter, and panic gripped him. Slowly, her eyes softened, and her round face lit with her magnetic smile as she came toward him, an empty tray in her hand.

His mouth dried and his hands turned clammy.

"Well, good afternoon to you, young man." She thrust her hand toward him. "Marian Cohen. Nice to meet you."

Mac stared into eyes as kind as his father's, the same shade of brown and the same crinkles at the sides when she smiled. His heart slowed as his confidence returned. He clasped her warm hand in his. "Mac Orman."

"Now that's a proper man's name. Mac Orman." She rolled his name around her tongue as though savoring it. She released his hand and frowned. "You're not the musician I heard stood in and saved the day at the fund-raiser last week, by any chance?"

Mac lifted his coffee cup. "Yep. That was me."

"Glad to hear it. I admire anyone willing to do what they can for charity. There's always a time when any of us might need a helping hand. Pay your dues while you can, and you'll get back what you deserve. That's my motto, anyway." She grinned, her eyes glinting mischievously. "Mind you, I do have more than one. A lot more." She nodded toward his coffee cup. "Can I get you another?"

Questions burned on his tongue, and Mac abruptly stood, forcing her to take a step back. "Thanks, but I've got to go." He slipped a five-pound note from his wallet and put it on to the table. "Keep the change."

He moved to brush past her, and she gently touched his arm. "Are you all right?" Her brown eyes filled with concern. "I won't bother you if you want to be left alone."

Slowly easing his arm from her gentle grasp, Mac shook his head. "I just have somewhere I need to be. Excuse me."

He walked toward the door, feeling her gaze burning into his back right along with the curious stares of others as he passed them. As soon as he was outside, Mac breathed deep. God, he'd just spoken with his grandmother. Turning left, he marched along the street, willing the tightness from his chest.

"Mac, wait up. Mac!"

Kate. He squeezed his eyes shut and halted but didn't turn around. Tipping his head back, he tried to get a hold of the torment rising inside him like a gathering storm.

"Mac?" Her breathing was heavy as she came to stand behind him, her hand on his upper arm. "Did I just see you come out of the bakery?"

Slowly, he turned. "Yeah. And?"

She slid her hand from his arm and stepped back, her cheeks turning pink. "Whoa." She raised her hands. "Don't shoot me, will you?"

He clenched his jaw and looked past her toward the bakery. "I spoke to her."

"Marian? Oh, no."

He faced her. She stared at him as the color drained from her cheeks, and her deep brown eyes widened with worry. "What did you say to her? Please tell me she doesn't know who you are. You didn't just lay it on her without warning, did you?" She pushed the curls from her face. "She doesn't deserve that, Mac. I asked you to wait for me to speak to George."

"And did you?"

"Yes, but—"

"He doesn't know she had a son, does he?"

"I don't know, but I do know she would love a family of her own, which means something clearly wasn't right when she fell pregnant with your dad. Did you tell her who you are?"

He shook his head, confusion burning hot in his gut. "No, but I should have."

"Why?" Anger burned in her eyes. "Do you think shocking her, hurting her in front of all those people, will make her welcome you with open arms?"

He met her glare as further words stuck in his throat.

"I owe her my protection, Mac. I can't let her down. Not with something as life-changing as this. I agree she needs to know, but we need to figure out how you can tell her in a way that will cause her the least pain. I care about Marian and I care about George. I don't want you to just barrel into the bakery and—"

"Pierce a hole in her newfound, happy, bouncy life where the sky is always blue, the sand always golden and the coffee just the right shade of brown? She might have looked for Dad in the past, but clearly once she found her nice little life, she no longer gave a crap. I've watched her. She's living as though she's never done a thing wrong in her life. Why shouldn't I *barrel* in there and tell her a few hard truths?"

She planted her hands on her hips. "Because you'll have to get past me first. How dare you? I've told you how I feel about her."

"Yes, but you haven't told me why."

She flinched as though he'd struck her, and all the fight left him. "Sorry. It's none of my business."

She glared, but Mac saw the sadness in her eyes. "Maybe not, and if you weren't so damn angry, I might have come to tell you, in time. But right now, with you acting this way, there's little chance of that happening any time soon. You have no right to say I have no idea, Mac. You don't know me."

He swiped his hand over his face and squeezed his eyes shut. "This is such a mess and not knowing how to talk to her is making me act like a jerk." He opened his eyes. "I don't want her upset any more than you do. She looks…kind of cool."

"She is. Really cool." She glanced toward

the bakery. "Which is why you can't turn her world upside down with all the tact of a stampeding herd of elephants. She gave your father up for adoption in the kindest and safest way possible. Others…"

He frowned. "Others what?"

"Other women—" her cheeks reddened "—don't get to even consider that option." Her gaze turned angry once more. "If you're mad at Marian, at anyone, because of all the terrible suffering you've experienced, you need to leave. Now."

"Leave?"

She nodded and defiantly lifted her chin. "Leave Templeton. Just go. You've found your paternal grandmother, but I wonder if you have no intention of listening to her and finding out the truth. If you'd rather believe in your assumptions, then you aren't welcome here. Okay?"

He glared, every fiber in his body trembling with frustration as he gripped her hand. "Now you've had your say, here's mine. I'm going nowhere, Kate. I'm not leaving town, and I'll definitely be speaking to Marian Cohen now I know for certain who she is. My father wanted her to know he had a family, even if he didn't do anything about it. I'm part of that family, and I'll make damn sure she knows who I am. You don't get to tell me what to do here."

He released her, and she stumbled backward, tears glinting in her livid gaze.

Regret dropped like lead into Mac's gut, but he couldn't let her see his weakness. Couldn't let her see how distraught meeting Marian had made him, seeing how easily she could be liked or loved. He needed time to brood and drink. So he left Kate staring after him as he marched along the street toward the Coast.

CHAPTER ELEVEN

TREMBLING, KATE STARED after Mac, her feet refusing to move. She wanted to stroll in the opposite direction as though she didn't care that they'd argued. The anger in his eyes and the tremor in his voice had raised something ugly inside her, that feeling of failure and inadequacy she so often fought around her mother, which suffocated her usual empathy.

Mac's clear lack of trust in Kate's methods showed that he, too, thought she was inept. Even though she'd proven her worth over and again at the center, the harsh truth remained that, all too often, the people she longed to care for, and have care for her, thought her useless.

Except Marian. Tears burned. Kate owed her so much, including her loyalty…and heart.

Pain struck deep in her chest, and she sucked in a breath. Damn him. Damn her mother and damn Dean. What did any of them matter? It was Marian she had to look out for right now.

And, God knew, she was all too aware of the haunting pain of never knowing the child that should've been a woman's to raise.

Swiping at her damp cheeks, Kate pulled back her shoulders and headed for the bakery. She needed to at least check Marian was okay. She had no idea what Mac might have said to her.

She pushed open the bakery door and scanned the many smiling faces, her shoulders lowering. He couldn't have had a fit of temper in here like he had outside, for surely the aftermath of such an outburst would be hovering amongst these customers if Mac had shown his true colors.

True colors she was glad she had seen before acting any further on her previous attraction. Bad boys were bad news. She should've listened to her instincts from the very first moment she met him. Instead, she'd kissed him, wanted him and, more than anything else, wanted to help ease a little of his pain at having lost his girlfriend and baby.

She joined the line to the counter. What could she say to Marian? How could it be that she, Kate and Mac had all lost a child?

Albeit under vastly different circumstances. Regardless of how their losses occurred, it was clear each of them had suffered the loss of their own baby, their own flesh and blood.

Surreptitiously, she watched Marian walk back and forth, her mood as buoyant as ever. Kate released a slow breath as she fought to get the quickened beat of her heart under control. Thank goodness Mac had shown a little restraint here.

She reached the counter and Marian beamed. "Hello, lovely. What can I get you?"

Kate forced a wide smile. "Just a latte, please."

"Coming right up. Are you grabbing a table?"

Kate glanced over her shoulder for a table where she might be able to grab a discreet word or two with Marian. "Sure. Why not? I'm supposed to be heading back to work, but another half an hour won't hurt."

Plus, she needed to calm down before her temper showed to Nancy or anyone else she worked with.

"Then I'll bring it over. If you're in the mood for some company, I'll join you."

"Great." Kate's smile faltered. Would George tell Marian that Kate had stopped by Jay's earlier? That he thought she'd acted strangely? If he did, there wasn't a lot she could do about it. "It will give you a chance to tell me about your holiday."

"It will…as well as telling you about a very interesting introduction I had to the young man I believe helped you out at the fundraiser last weekend. Mac Orman?"

Dread twisted Kate's stomach. "Sure. I know Mac."

"Where's he come from?"

"I'm not sure. I think he's staying at the Coast while he's here."

"And what is he in town for?"

Hating the way the ensuing mistruths half clogged her throat, Kate coughed and silently blamed Mac for putting her in this position. Or was Izzy right and it was Kate's own fault for having to face Marian while carrying such a mammoth secret? "I think he's…um… I'm not sure."

Marian's wily gaze burned into Kate's, and she nodded slowly. "I see. Well, grab a seat, and I'll be straight over with our coffees."

Kate turned robotically, her conscience screaming. What was she supposed to do, or say, when Marian had her cornered in her own territory? Marian could have Kate trussed up like a Christmas turkey within ten minutes. She glanced toward the door as indecision messed with her conscience. Could she make a run for it?

Coward. No, she wouldn't do that. If she did, Marian would only chase her down and rugby-tackle her to the pavement, regardless of any nearby pedestrians.

Kate slid into one of the booths and looked through the window toward the main promenade. It was a crisp and cold February day, but the Cove shone beautifully beneath the hazy sunshine. For the most part, Templeton was peaceful. Of course, they'd had times of trouble and spats of crime the same as any other town, but Kate loved it here. No one, including her mother, could ever make her leave. Even if Dean came back—which undoubtedly he would one day, considering his mum and dad lived in the Cove—his presence wouldn't change the life she'd built here.

The consequences of her sister's three-week visit two years ago—and her subsequent betrayal with Dean—had obliterated Kate's previous contentment in the town. Unable to listen to her sister's feeble explanations about Dean's charm, money or other temptations, Kate's estrangement from her sister had been immediate.

But now, Ali was getting married. Kate swallowed. Did she really want to miss being a part of that? Could her mother actually be right that it was time for her and Ali to reconcile? To move on?

Despite the struggle and heartbreak, Kate was almost back to the person she was before Dean. She was even beginning to believe she had as much right to happiness as anyone.

"Here you go, sweetheart."

At the sound of Marian's voice, Kate swiped at her damp cheeks and turned.

"One latte. And I threw in a cinnamon roll for good measure." Marian lifted her gaze to Kate's, and her smile faltered as she slid into the opposite seat. "Are you all right?"

"Of course." She blew across the top of her latte. "Just a little tired."

Marian's gaze bored into Kate's, and she held herself still.

Finally, the older woman relaxed against her seat. "Phew, I'm bushed. People are so nice to say they missed me while George and I were away, but you'd think we'd been gone a year, rather than a fortnight." She chuckled, her eyes never leaving Kate's. "So, tell me about the fund-raiser. I gather it went well?"

Kate prayed Marian let go of her concern over Kate's emotions. "Really well. We surpassed expectations. Not bad for one day and night."

"And the Moon Shadows? Did they go down as well as I thought they would?"

"Sure. They've got a lot of fans in the Cove."

"They do. Apparently, this Mac Orman stepped in and saved the day. Played the guitar, even sang a little, I heard."

Kate cleared her throat. "He was a lifesaver."

"Uh-huh."

Marian's gaze once more held Kate's, and she fought the need to squirm. Instead, she arched her eyebrow, hoping to feign nonchalance. "What?"

"Who is he, and why are you being so secretive about him? Don't tell me you haven't spent some time with him."

"I have. On and off."

"And?"

Kate shrugged. "And nothing."

"Nothing, my backside." Marian grinned. "I understand the Moon Shadows are a big deal, but why would anyone, a stranger no less, step up the way Mac did unless he wanted to impress somebody? Or at least do something to make sure she knows he exists." Her tone was teasing. "I don't need to show you my saggy bottom and droopy bosom to prove I wasn't born yesterday."

Kate laughed, despite her friend's astute observations.

Marian grinned. "So, who is he? A new boyfriend? God knows, I'd like to see you've moved on from the good-for-nothing last one."

Caught between fear and further laughter, Kate's shoulders slumped. A girl knew when she was beaten. "Mac's in town for a while, but his plans are his own. I just hope when he puts them into motion, he does so with a little diplomacy."

Marian frowned, her humor dissolving. "Diplomacy? That sounds ominous."

Nausea rose bitter in Kate's throat, and she sipped her latte before slowly returning the oversized cup to its saucer. "His situation is…complicated, but he's an okay guy who's known some pretty awful heartbreak. Just go easy on him."

"Go easy on him?" Marian laughed. "You're talking as though I might have reason to roll him around in a muddy puddle. Stop your overprotecting, Kate Harrington. A man like that, can presumably handle a little old lady like me."

"Maybe."

"There's no maybe about it. You know I just like to get to know everyone who comes to town, whether they're here briefly or long-term. Plus—" she wiggled her eyebrows "—he seems just your type. Why don't you flutter those beautiful eyelashes of yours and see if he takes the bait?" She glanced toward the lengthening line at the counter. "I'd better get back to work. Just let yourself have some fun with this boy. He looks as though he could use it as much as you."

As Marian levered herself out of the booth, Kate opened her mouth to...warn her? Ask her not to bother Mac? Tell her he was her grandson? She snapped her mouth closed. The truth of his and Marian's relationship wasn't Kate's to tell. She just hoped to God Mac got the telling of it right because bad words, misjudged assumptions and a past full of regret often caused disastrous results.

She watched Marian as she marched behind the counter, her expression as happy and carefree as always. Kate had seen buried secrets revealed enough times through her work at the center and in her own life to know that sometimes honesty was far from welcomed. Mac acted as though he was the one calling the shots, but once he told Marian who he was, Kate didn't doubt for one second Marian would take charge.

Kate left the bakery. Turning toward the Teenage Support center, she pulled her phone from her bag and typed a text to Mac.

Please don't say anything to Marian until we've spoken. I didn't mean it when I said you should leave. I want you to stay. Everything will work out… She hesitated, took a deep breath and resumed typing. Promise. X.

Dropping her phone into her bag, Kate lifted her chin and focused on work, the one thing she could do well…even if it took a while to convince certain people of her abilities.

MAC PICKED UP his phone from the bar at the Coast and opened the new text. His stomach knotted at Kate's name. He didn't think she'd speak to him again after his obnoxious speech…yet she offered an olive branch. One he didn't deserve.

He put the phone on the bar and nudged it

away from him before picking up his second bottle of beer. He drank deep as though the liquid could dissolve his self-disgust.

The more time he spent with Kate, the more he felt like the man he was before he lost Jilly. Now, after his outburst, he felt waist deep in the man he'd become *after* Jilly. He took another drink. God, he so wanted to be the old him. The man who listened, cared, helped and supported.

"What's up, Mac?"

Mac shifted his gaze to Dave, where he stood a foot or so away, wiping glasses with a dish towel. Mac drained his bottle. "Nothing. Can I get another?"

"Sure, if you think drinking in the afternoon is going to help whatever it is bothering you." Dave opened the fridge behind him and pulled out a beer. He snapped off the top and slid it on to the bar. "What's her name? Wouldn't be Kate, by any chance?"

Mac scowled. Was the woman's name tattooed on his forehead? "No, not Kate."

Dave smirked and came closer, leaning his hands on the bar. "Look, my wife talks...a lot...and she isn't backward in coming forward. When she says there's something between you and Kate Harrington, I'm leaning toward believing her, unless you can prove her wrong. Bartenders are good listeners. That's all I'm saying."

Mac took a slug of his beer. "Well, musicians aren't great talkers."

"Is that so?"

"Yep."

"Well, if you're not going to use the tongue God gave you, how about you use your ears? I know Kate well enough to say she doesn't let people in easily. Oh, she'd love to be everything to everyone, but, through her job at the center, she's learned to help whoever she can as much as humanly possible, while maintaining some emotional restraint."

Disappointment squeezed at Mac's chest. Was Kate successfully managing emotional restraint with him? Because if she was, he was in deeper trouble than he thought. His emotions weren't restrained in the slightest as far as she was concerned. He really liked the woman. She had gotten deep under his skin.

And it felt as though there was nothing he could do to halt his feelings for her.

"If Kate's spending time with you, listening to you or helping you in any way, then you'd be a fool to reject what she's offering. That girl is a diamond. She's had a rough time of it, but she's doing her best to brush herself off and start over."

Mac's heart quickened at the need to know more about the bastard who'd hurt her. "Would that be after this ex-boyfriend?"

"Maybe." Dave looked across the bar, his unwillingness to share more as obvious as the nose on his face. He met Mac's gaze. "Look, I don't know why you're in town, and I'm not going to ask, but, to my mind, if you plan on staying a while, you'll be needing some work. Am I right?"

Mac frowned, a little of his defensiveness diminishing as it became clear Dave wasn't going to poke into affairs unless invited. "Possibly."

"Then how about we help each other out? I've been thinking about having a resident singer in the bar. A soloist. I can't afford to keep paying a four- or five-piece band on a regular basis. How about you give it a shot? Starting tonight."

"A resident singer?" Mac shook his head and smiled wryly, lifting his bottle to his lips. "I don't plan on hanging around long enough to become a resident anything."

He was leaving…just as soon as he'd spoken to Marian Ball, or Cohen, or whatever the hell her name was. Mac sipped his beer. "As much as I can see how people look out for one another around here, I'm a city boy and have every intention of staying that way. I won't be in the Cove much longer."

"Which city?"

"The best. London."

Dave nodded and protruded his bottom lip, his gaze steady on Mac's.

Mac frowned. "What?"

Dave shrugged. "You just don't seem the type."

"What type?"

"The type who's happy to live alone in a big, flashy city." Dave frowned. "Despite the giant chip on your shoulder, and an attitude that could use some serious work, you stepped in at the fund-raiser, and I've seen you carrying stuff back and forth for Vanessa."

"So?"

"So, you don't seem the guy who goes to work, comes home or goes to a bar where no one knows your name. Whether you realize it or not, you like people."

"I do, and people in the city aren't any less friendly than they are here."

Mac took a sip of his beer, uneasy that people might have tried to get to know him back home, but since the accident he'd brushed off any indication of friendship. He hadn't been the solitary type before Jilly died, but he'd imposed a more lonesome way of life on purpose ever since…self-protection was key.

Shifting on his stool, Mac glanced around the bar. A few guys stood around the pool table, drinks or cues in their hands, ribbing one another. A trio of girls in their late teens hovered by the old-fashioned jukebox, checking out the guys at the pool table. "Look, I'm okay in my own company. That's all you need to know."

"Maybe it is, but I can't help thinking you're trying to convince yourself of that, rather than me."

Wanting the focus shifted from him to Dave, Mac leaned back on his stool. "How long have you lived here? I'm guessing your whole life, right?"

"Nope. Vanessa and I moved here about twenty years ago and never looked back."

"Twenty years? What are you? Forty-four? Forty-five?"

"Forty-six."

"So you came to Templeton in your mid-twenties with a wife in tow and settled just like that?"

"Yep."

"From where?"

"Bristol. Best thing I ever did. Vanessa used to come to the Cove on holiday as a kid. Loved the place so much she set her mind on living here when she was grown. If I wanted the girl, I wanted her dreams, too. As soon as she asked me to move to Templeton, I agreed. End of conversation."

"You have kids?"

"Two. Boy and a girl. Paul's in his last year studying criminology at uni. And hoping there will be a place for him working with DI Garrett right here in the Cove when he's done." He smiled. "Jenny's at drama college with dreams of living in your home city and never leaving the West End."

The man's eyes were lit with a deep pride, his smile wide and his cheeks full of color. It was clear the bar and Dave's day-to-day existence were a means to an end, nowhere near as important to him as his family. His wife and kids were all that really mattered to him.

A tug of loss pulled at Mac's chest, and he quickly picked up his beer and took a long drink. "Yeah, well, I don't see a family on my horizon anytime soon, so for now the city life suits me just fine."

Dave whipped the dish towel from his shoulder and wiped it in circles over the bar. "A family comes in many forms. If you're a family man deep in your heart, you'll have your family. It just takes finding the right place to search for them. That's what comes first. How old are you?"

"Twenty-five."

"Right."

Mac frowned. "Now what?"

"Not many people get to your age without falling in love, my friend. That whole broody I-don't-give-a-crap-about-anything-or-anyone attitude you think you've got going on isn't fooling me, and I'll bet it's not fooling Kate either."

Mac dropped his gaze, his fingers trembling as he pulled at the label on his beer bottle.

"So, who did you fall in love with?"

Mac snatched his gaze to Dave. "What?"

"What was her name? The girl who stole that black heart of yours."

He looked past Dave to the fridges behind him. "Jilly." He clenched his jaw. "She died."

The seconds beat in time with his heart, and Mac tightened his grip around his beer bottle as he waited for whatever Dave said next.

"Hey."

Mac met Dave's gaze. "What?"

"I'm sorry."

Mac nodded. "Thanks."

"How long has she been gone?"

"Three years."

"Three years?" Dave shook his head, his gaze steady. "Then that's long enough, man."

"Long enough for what?"

"Long enough for you to be alone. Long enough for you to stop thinking you'll always be alone. Now, if you take my advice, you'll accept my offer of a gig or two, or for however long you're here. Then you'll pick up the phone and invite Kate to watch you play tonight. And finally…"

Mac lifted his eyebrows, disbelief at the guy's arrogance tensing his shoulders. "Finally?"

"You'll determine what's really stopping you from moving forward. Stopping you from searching for a new woman, a new love, and you'll damn well do something about it."

Mac glared at Dave's back as the man wandered to another customer at the other end of the bar. Who the hell did the guy think he was? His damned dad? Then again, giving advice about love and taking risks was the last thing Dan Orman would've done.

He closed his eyes, and Kate's face appeared behind his lids. He'd grown to like her with more speed and depth than he had any of the other women he'd been with since Jilly. He cared about Kate. Cared what she thought and felt…which made it all the harder for him to leave this stupid town without speaking with her first.

Opening his eyes, he drained his beer and pushed to his feet. Shooting a final glare at Dave's back, Mac snatched up his phone and stabbed in Kate's number.

She picked up almost immediately. "Mac? Look, I'm sor—"

"Stop." He massaged his brow. "I'm the one who's sorry. Sorry for shouting at you… sorry for everything." He opened his eyes and slid his hand into his hair as he made his way to the stairs leading to the rented rooms. "I'm playing at the Coast tonight. I'd really like it if you came along. We could talk after I'm done."

"Talk?"

He inhaled. "If you still want to speak to me, that is."

"Of course I do. I'll be there by eight. See you then."

He released his breath. "See you then."

Pulling his keys from his pocket, Mac opened his door and walked inside. He had a second chance to do something about moving forward.

Dave was right. It was time Mac got back into the game...back into life.

CHAPTER TWELVE

KATE GRIPPED IZZY'S arm and pulled her to a stop outside the Coast. "Wait."

"What is it?" her friend frowned. "Have you changed your mind about seeing Mac?"

"No. We need to go in there. It's just…"

"Just what?"

"I don't know." Kate pressed her hand to her stomach to calm her nerves as she looked through the window. "The place is packed, and I can hear him playing."

"And? Aren't we here to see him play? Come on, Kate. I want to meet the guy. Besides…" Izzy tossed her long, blond hair over her shoulders, her gaze dancing with mischief. "If he's half as good-looking and charming as you say he is, I'll want him to know he has your best friend looking out for you and he'd better treat you right."

"Hmm."

Izzy frowned, her shoulders dropping. "What?"

"The last time Mac and I saw one another, we kind of argued. How do I know he didn't ask me here to continue that argument? Maybe we should leave. The Coast is not the place I want to be talking with him about Marian."

"Look—" Izzy slipped her arm around Kate's waist "—we'll get a drink and see what happens. You asked me here to act as a buffer between you, right?"

Kate shrugged, feeling like a child being taken care of by a grown-up. "Maybe."

Izzy squeezed Kate closer. "Maybe nothing. I'm here, and I'll make sure nothing happens that you don't want to happen, okay? You like Mac, right?"

Kate shrugged a second time.

"Oh, for the love of…" Izzy rolled her eyes and released Kate. "Come on. We're going in."

Kate kept her feet planted on the asphalt as Izzy strode a few paces toward the door. What would happen once they entered the bar was anyone's guess, and the dread that tensed Kate's body warned her the outcome wouldn't be pretty. Or sexy. Or romantic. Or any of the things she'd kept hoping for since she and Mac had parted ways.

She blew out a breath. "Iz, wait up."

Her friend halted and turned.

Slowly, Kate walked forward and took Izzy's hand. "Don't let me do anything stupid."

"Like what?"

"Like telling him how he's been in and out of my thoughts all damn day. Like the fact I'm less pissed and more pained that he would get so upset with me when I'm starting to like him way too much. That sort of thing."

Izzy nodded. "Got it. Now, come on."

Izzy dragged her to the door and none-too-gently nudged her inside. Mac's deep, smooth voice filled the bar, the sound of his acoustic guitar coming in second place to the blatant sex appeal of his husky, heartfelt singing. Kate drew on her invisible armor and strode toward Dave, who stood behind the bar.

She couldn't look at Mac. Not yet. It was Friday night, and tomorrow was her day off. Liquid courage in the form of Ms. Sauvignon Blanc was needed...and lots of it.

Slapping her purse on the bar, she forced a wide smile. "Two glasses of dry white wine when you're ready, Dave."

He arched an eyebrow. "The usual?"

"Yes, please."

Dave nodded and pulled a bottle from one of the fridges, filling two glasses and sliding them on to the bar. "You girls planning to stay all night? Mac's going over really well." He nodded toward the stage over Kate's shoulder. "A real ladies' man, it seems."

Kate huffed a laugh and held out a ten-pound note. "Is that so?"

"Yep." Dave took the money, his gray gaze amused. "Why don't you turn around and see for yourself?"

"No, thanks."

Izzy prodded Kate's arm. "Good God, woman. You weren't joking about him, were you? That is one hell of a man. Look at his biceps, for crying out loud. Not to mention that chest." Izzy gave a low whistle. "He could give my Trent a serious run for his money."

Lifting one of the glasses of wine, Kate squeezed her eyes shut. *God, give me strength.* She opened them. Dave grinned and slipped some coins across the bar. "Your change... scaredy-cat."

"Scare..." Kate narrowed her eyes. "I'm not scared of anyone or anything. Including Mac bloody Orman."

She dropped the coins into her purse and turned. Her heart stumbled. He wore faded blue jeans that had a stupid rip across one thigh, paired with a white T-shirt that seemed to scream for mercy it was so tightly stretched over his damn pecs and flat stomach. Kate consciously breathed in. "Tattoos."

"What?" Izzy turned and picked up her wineglass, jigging in time with Mac's singing. "Tat what?"

Kate snatched her glare to Izzy. "Tattoos. *Tattoos.*"

Izzy grinned as she wiggled her eyebrows. "I know. I can see them." She sipped her drink and tilted her head in Mac's direction. "Why don't we get closer? Let him know we're here?"

Kate stilled as her gaze locked with Mac's. "Too late. He knows."

As Izzy turned to the stage, Kate took a long breath and slowly released it. She wouldn't look away, no matter that her entire body had heated in one fiery rush as soon as the man glanced in her direction. She swallowed and lifted her glass in greeting.

He accompanied a wink with a flash of his white-toothed, curled-lip, stupidly sexy smile. Her center pulled, and she snapped her gaze to Izzy. "The man is full of himself."

"Why wouldn't he be? He's clearly in his

element and very talented." She bopped on the spot. "I think he's great. Really great... and handsome as hell."

Kate gripped Izzy's arm and scowled. "Will you stop dancing around? We're not here to enjoy ourselves, remember?"

"Why are we here then? Because you seem to be doing a whole lot of nothing. Let's grab a table near the stage. That way once he's finished his set, he's either got to walk straight past us or join us."

"I'm not ready."

"Why not?"

"Because..."

Izzy's gaze instantly turned triumphant. "Because deep down you know getting involved with Mac's mission here is not a good idea. Because deep down you know that sooner or later Marian is going to find out you knew her grandson was here and you never said a word to her. Don't you think you are all too aware that you don't really know the guy and he could be playing you?"

"Fine. You're right." Izzy glared. "I don't know him. He could be another Dean. He could be a man intent on upsetting Marian. God damn it..." She glanced toward the stage as Mac moved into his next song. "He could have every intention of moving forward without me, and he has every right to do so."

"Hey." Izzy's eyes filled with concern, and she put her glass on the bar before taking Kate's hand. "Are you trying not to cry?"

"Of course not." Kate blinked, hating the tightness in her chest, which proved how badly she wanted to be involved with Mac's quest...with Mac. "He's gotten to me, Iz. I care about him. I care about his connection to Marian. Worse, I fancy him so damn much, and that's making me want to help heal all the pain he's carrying around like a boulder on his broad shoulders. How can I be sure I'm not going to get hurt again? He's a stranger. One who's going to up and leave the Cove, possibly in a matter of days."

"Okay. Come on."

Kate stiffened. "What? Where are we going?"

"We're getting out of here. If you really like him, he can meet you halfway. On your terms." Izzy released her hand and took a hefty gulp of wine before setting the half-empty glass on the bar. "Not like this. Not when he looks so comfortable up there. It's not a fair playing field. If he wants to speak with you…or more…he can see you somewhere nice and neutral."

"Like where?" Kate took a sip of wine, warming to her friend's thinking. "Somewhere like a restaurant? A date?"

Izzy smiled. "At last. The girl starts to see how men need a little coaching sometimes. Coaching in the form of meeting us halfway."

Kate took another sip of her drink and glanced toward the stage. Once again, Mac's gaze locked on hers…but this time it was *her* who tipped him a wink.

And then, arm in arm, she and Izzy left the bar.

MAC WALKED UPSTAIRS to his room. Slowly closing the door behind him, he leaned his guitar against the wall.

Kate had left over an hour ago, just walked out without speaking with him. God only knew how he'd managed to get through his second set without abandoning the packed bar and chasing after her. His mouth had dried just looking at her. She was so damn beautiful in skinny white jeans, a black top and blazer. The looks she'd sent him and the way she clearly grappled over something with her friend didn't bode well for his eventual talk with Marian—or even how Kate felt about him.

He dropped backward on to the bed and closed his eyes.

It was around ten and still early enough to call her, but what could he say? His confusion over meeting Marian, and realizing what a vibrant person she was, had somewhat cooled, and now he felt like a class-A idiot for the way he'd spoken to Kate. He needed to make amends, but how was he to do that if she didn't want to speak to him?

He had to call her.

Taking a deep breath, he reached for his phone on the bedside cabinet and scrolled through, then dialed her number.

She picked up. "Hello, Mac."

He winced at the stiffness in her voice, his heart thumping "How are you doing?"

"Good. You?"

"Good." He smiled, trying to keep his tone light. "Was my playing so bad that you and your friend had to leave?"

"Not at all. You play well. You sing even better."

Relief steadied him, and he blew out a breath. "Then why did you go? I was hoping to talk to you."

"I…had an epiphany."

"An epiphany?"

"About you…about us."

He grimaced. "And?"

"And you need to meet me halfway with Marian and with us. I'm not the type of woman to be ordered around. I've told you about my ex, and I told you how much he hurt me. I won't stand for any man talking to me the way you did earlier. Not anymore."

He squeezed his eyes closed as shame poured over him. "I shouldn't have spoken to you like that. I'm sorry. I was in shock after speaking with Marian, and I took my confusion out on you. It won't happen again. Getting angry…" He opened his eyes, the vulnerability he felt since the accident gripping his chest. "It's who I've been since I lost Jilly, but it's not who I am, Kate, not really."

His heart beat out the seconds as the silence stretched.

Finally, she cleared her throat. "Okay then. Well, now we've sorted that out, we need to decide what happens next."

"With Marian or with us?"

Another beat of silence.

She sighed. "Both. But let's start with Marian. I spoke to a friend of mine after I saw you at the bakery."

"The one at the bar?"

"No. That was Izzy. This friend works for a private investigator and has picked up quite a few strategies through her work."

Mac sat up, dropping his feet to the floor. "I don't need a private investigator. I've found my grandmother."

"I know you have, but just hear me out."

He held his head in his hand. "Go ahead."

"She said it's an extremely positive sign that Marian has tried to make contact with your dad in the past, but…" She exhaled. "Because she hasn't reached out in over ten years, once you have told her who you are, you need to respect her wishes and walk away if that's what she wants. Quietly. I need you to promise me you'll do that. If you won't, I'll call Marian right now and tell her who you are and why you're here."

Mac pushed to his feet and walked to the window. Light wisps of snow fell to the ground, the cars below slowly turning white in the darkness. "I'm not going to harass her. I realize now just how big a thing it is that she looked for Dad. I've no right to question her reason for stopping, but I hope, one day, she'll tell me. For now though, I just want her to know who I am, who Dad was, and then the rest will be up to her."

"Good, because your outburst at the bakery scared me, Mac. Marian's happy. She's married to one of the gentlest and loveliest men on the planet. I have no idea whether George knows about the adoption, but I do know he'll support her once the pair of you meet."

"I want to do this the best way possible, and cause the minimum amount of distress to everyone." He paced the room. "The trouble is, I've got no idea how."

"Then it's just as well I'm here to smooth the way a little…if you still want me to, that is."

Relieved, Mac smiled. "I do. So, what's your plan? I'm assuming you have one?"

"Not as such." She exhaled. "First, I need to be absolutely sure of something."

"What?"

"That you finding Marian and speaking with her is about you gaining closure. That you have no other agenda. Not anymore."

He hated that she still doubted him. "My anger's gone, Kate. So is my resentment. Jilly dying was an accident. A horrible, soul-destroying accident, but it's time I let it…

let her go…and do all I can to live the life she would've wanted for me." He pushed the hair back from his face. "I think I've been trying to find something or someone to pull me out."

Her tone was soft. "Pull you out of what?"

"Out of my loneliness." Mac moved to the bed and sat, his chest aching and his shame heavy. "Maybe part of me even hoped if I found my dad's mum, she might be what I needed to hang on to for a while until I feel more like the old me."

"Marian could be that person, you know. She really is amazing."

"So are you." Heat warmed his face. "I mean, who's to say it's Marian and not someone else entirely that I've been looking for?"

Her breathing grew just a little quicker, and Mac gripped the phone. "There's no pressure, okay? I'm just saying I like you, Kate. You're kind and funny, beautiful and sexy." He huffed a laugh. "There's very little about you not to like."

She chuckled. "Charmer."

"I'm only telling the truth. We have something. You feel it too, don't you?" Hope rose inside him. Finally, after three lonely years, he wanted to reach out a little and explore a maybe, if not a certainty. "Kate?"

"I'm scared, Mac. I don't want to get hurt again, and the truth is, somehow, you've managed to occupy my thoughts for much of the day and night. I'm willing to try, to see what happens, but…"

"You're wary. Good, because so am I."

She exhaled. "Okay then, even playing field."

"What?"

"Nothing. Look, let's tackle your conversation with Marian first and then move on to us afterward? You may want to flee Templeton immediately after you speak with her. Why don't we meet at the bakery tomorrow afternoon? We can gauge her mood, and then maybe you'll be able to judge how, when and where you want to tell her you're her grandson."

Mac closed his eyes and massaged his temple. "Okay. That's sounds as good a start as any. Shall we say two-ish?"

"Perfect. I'll see you there, okay?"

"Okay. 'Night, Kate."

"'Night."

There was a moment's hesitation before the line went dead. Mac tossed the phone on to the bed. Tomorrow he'd move forward both in his mission and in another area, one he'd thought impossible when he came to the Cove.

The possibility of a new relationship.

CHAPTER THIRTEEN

MAC CARRIED HIS cup of coffee to one of the booths in Marian's Bonniest Bakery, but bonny was the last thing he felt. Shrugging off his rain-soaked leather jacket, he hung it over the edge of the seat and pushed his damp hair back from his face. He sat and stared through the window on to the street, searching through the gloom for Kate. Although, considering he'd arrived three-quarters of an hour earlier than their agreed-upon time, he hardly expected to see her.

He leaned back and picked up his coffee, glancing toward Marian as she cleared cups and plates, chatting with a young couple and their little girl sitting at one of the tables. With her steel-gray curls, rosy cheeks, bright smile and almost comedically buxom bosom, it was hard not to warm to the woman. Once a person heard her voice and her laughter and witnessed her care for the community, it was darn near impossible.

Not to mention how Kate felt about her. He couldn't think of anyone who had Kate's instinct about people. She'd had him pretty much spot-on within ten minutes of meeting him.

Marian waved the couple and their daughter off before her focus landed on Mac. He quickly redirected his gaze to the window. The comforting smells of sugar and cinnamon preceded Marian to his table.

Mac took a deep breath and turned. "Hi."

She beamed and put the loaded tray she carried on to his table. "Hi, yourself. Can I tempt you with something to eat with your coffee?"

"No, thanks."

"I make a mean brie and cranberry panini. Great comfort food for a wet and windy day like today."

He lifted his coffee cup and tried to ignore the sharp pang of remembrance that jabbed at his gut as he noted the crinkles identical to his father's at the corners of her eyes. "Coffee's good."

"Mind if I sit down?" Her smile faltered, and her eyes shone with curiosity. "I didn't feel we had time to get properly acquainted the other day."

He struggled for an excuse to stop her sitting with him. He wasn't ready for more than a casual hello. "I'm kind of waiting for someone so…"

"So I won't sit with you for long." She sat and pushed the tray to the side. Leaning her forearms on the table, she clasped her hands together. "I understand from Kate that you were quite the lifesaver at her fund-raiser the other night."

Deciding to play dumb in the hope it would deter any questions about him and Kate, Mac frowned. "Kate?"

She laughed, her soft brown eyes twinkling. "Harrington. You can't kid a kidder, Mr. Orman. A man would have to be half-blind to not notice a girl like her. As it is, you appear to have two working eyes, so don't go acting the innocent with me. I won't buy it."

A smile tugged at his lips even as his gut knotted. His father had used the exact same "you can't kid a kidder" line whenever he wanted the truth out of Mac or Dana. Mac leaned back and crossed his arms. Now alone and face-to-face with Marian, why waste the opportunity to dig a little deeper?

"So, what do you want to know about me?" He raised his eyebrows. "I get the impression you're fond of knowing something about everyone around here."

"Ah, the observant type. Do you write?"

"What?" Mac frowned, completely thrown by her unexpected question.

"In my experience, the observers of this world are prone to pick up a pen or play at the keyboard. So, do you write, Mr. Orman?"

"It's Mac."

She smiled. "Mac."

He looked away from her soft, attentive gaze. "Songs. I write songs."

"I knew it." She chuckled. "A comrade-in-arms then."

He returned his gaze to hers. "Pardon?"

"When I was around about your age, maybe a little older, I wrote songs. Swapped songs for a diary as I got older, but I consider myself a writer all the same. I use my diary to remember the good times. The bad times. The pain." Her expression grew shadowed before she blinked and smiled again. "But especially the good times. That's what is important."

Mac's heart thumped as he tried and failed to not be moved by her words and the knowledge his grandmother had written out her miseries and elations through music, just as he did. He took a sip of his coffee. "I gather you had some fun and games on your holiday."

She laughed. "You heard about that, did you?"

He smiled, unable to resist her homey charm. "I was in here the other day when your shop girl was chatting with you on the phone."

She grinned. "Ah, George's swimming trunks." Her eyes glistened with tears. "I laughed so hard, I nearly busted my bra strap. Oh, lordy! What an eyeful those poor holiday-makers lying around the pool would've had if my bikini had let me down that day."

Bikini? This woman wore a bikini? Mac stared, all too aware his eyes were wide.

She slapped her hand on the table, her body shaking with her laughter. "Look at your face! Hey, I may be the wrong side of sixty, but my George likes nothing more than to see a bit of flesh. Who says we have to stop wearing bikinis at a certain age or size? No one will ever tell me what to do. Not anymore."

Curiosity shot through him, and Mac leaned forward. "Not anymore?"

She stared at him, consideration clear in her eyes. "Another time, maybe." She stood and held out her hand. "It was nice talking to you, Mr... Mac."

He hesitated. Skin to skin contact was dangerous. This was his father's mother. His grandmother. Lifting his hand, he reached for hers.

"Mac! At last. This town might be small but, my God, I thought I was never going to find you."

With his hand in midair, Mac turned and the breath left his lungs. "Dana? What the—"

Marian stepped forward, her arms outstretched. "Oh, my word. And who are these adorable babies?"

Mac watched in slow-motion horror as Marian stepped forward and clasped his five-year-old niece by the hand. "You're as pretty as a picture. What's your name, sweetheart?"

The little girl beamed. "I'm Lily, and this is my little brother, Mac. The same as Uncle Mac."

"Well, aren't you two the cutest pair of buttons I've ever seen?" She looked to Dana. "I assume these beauties belong to you?"

Dana arched an eyebrow at Mac before planting on a smile and facing Marian. "They certainly do. These are my children. Mac's niece and nephew."

"You're his sister? Well, that's lovely. Welcome to the Cove. How about I leave you two alone for a moment and take these two angels to choose an iced bun each?" She looked to Lily and little Mac. "Does that sound good?"

Mac's stomach clenched with bitter nausea. "I really don't think Dana is staying—"

Dana clasped his shoulder, her nails digging through his T-shirt. "That would be lovely. Thank you."

"Mum says yes!" Marian leaned down and expertly lifted little Mac on to one ample hip before taking Lily's hand again. "Come on then, let's see what I can find for you, shall we?"

Mac stared in shock as Marian walked away with her great-grandchildren as though she was already their proud Nana who saw them every day. Slowly, he turned to look at Dana. "You have no idea what you've done."

"What do you mean?"

"We need to leave. Now."

Dana frowned and looked from Marian and her kids standing at the glass display counter to Mac and back again. "What's the problem? She's great."

"Yeah. She's just terrific." Mac swiveled and pulled his jacket from the back of the booth. "We're getting out of here. What possessed you to turn up here without warning? Why didn't you call first?"

Dana slid into the booth opposite him and glared. "Because I can't believe what you're up to, that's why. Mum's staying with Aunt Beverly for a few nights, so I packed up the kids and brought them here to try and talk some sense into you. You cannot keep up this futile search, Mac. It's not fair to Mum, and it's not fair to us."

He looked back at Marian, who had sat Lily and little Mac on the counter, crooning and fussing over them as if she knew they were family. Things had just gotten way out of his control.

He faced Dana and tilted his head toward the door. "Let's go. Now."

She gripped his arm. "Not until you tell me I'm not too late. That you haven't already done something you can't undo."

"Me? You've just managed to jump ahead at least one Christmas, if not two," he hissed. "Why here, Dana? Why the hell did you have to find me here?"

She frowned. "What are you talking about? I got off the train, the kids were hungry, and when I spotted this bakery—"

"Did you spot the name of this bakery?"

"No. Why?"

He swiped a printed napkin from the metal holder beside him and slapped it in front of Dana. "There."

She dropped her gaze to the napkin. Slowly, her eyes widened. "Marian? As in Marian Ball?"

"The one and only."

"Oh, my God." She turned around and stared at Marian, currently stabbing straws into the lids of two cartons of juice. "That's her? That's our grandmother?"

Mac blew out a breath. "Yes. Now can we leave?" He stood and swept from the booth. As he strode toward the counter, he forced a smile and pulled his wallet from his back pocket. He addressed Marian's turned back. "Um, we're leaving. Could you tell me how much my bill is, please?"

Marian turned, her eyes shining with happiness. "So soon? Your sister only just arrived. Why not take your time? I can make you a sandwich, or I have cake or pies. I bet a man like you loves a good steak and ale pie."

"Sorry. Things to do. Places to be. If I had my way my sister wouldn't be here."

"Is that so?"

"Yes."

"I see. Well, I hope to see you in here again sometime soon. Be even nicer if you saw to it that a certain Miss Harrington accompanied you next time. Don't you think?"

Mac froze. Kate. How could he have forgotten? "Um, if Kate arrives, can you tell her something came up and I had to leave?"

Marian beamed. "So you were waiting for Kate? Not your sister? Well, that is good news."

"Uh-huh. The bill?"

"I'm sure Kate would love to meet your family."

"Maybe, but if I've got anything to do with it, my sister will be on the next train out of here"

She let her gaze roam languidly over his face. "It's on me this time." She lifted Lily and then little Mac from the counter. The moment they were on solid ground, they raced to Dana, holding their treats. "You know something, Mac? You really need to work on that attitude of yours. Family's important. Family should be cherished. Not disregarded, nor taken for granted. Not ever."

She brushed past him, and Mac swallowed back his retort. Family? What did Marian

Ball know about the meaning of family? Hackles raised, and fear his very shaky plan to speak with Marian on his own terms could be upended by Dana's arrival, he slapped a ten-pound note on the counter. "Keep the change."

Turning, he held out his hand to Lily as he reached the table where Dana and the kids waited. "Let's go."

KATE PUSHED OPEN the door of the bakery and shook off her umbrella before stepping inside. She put her umbrella in the stand by the door and glanced around as she unbuttoned her coat. She frowned. She was running a little late, sure, but fifteen minutes past their agreed time and he'd already left?

She walked to the counter. Maybe he was running late, too.

"Hi, Marian." She smiled at the older woman. "Could I get a latte?"

"Sure."

Kate slid some coins on to the counter and looked around the bakery again. Nope, he definitely wasn't here.

"If you're looking for Mac, he bolted."

"What?"

"Mac. He was in here a few minutes ago."

Marian raised her eyebrows, her mouth briefly pursing with disapproval. "Are you sure you want to go down that road with a man who runs as easily as he seems prone to do?"

"Wait, Mac was here, but he left?"

"Yep."

"Why? Did he...did you two have words?"

"Us?" Marian picked up Kate's money and turned to the espresso machine. "Why would we have words? His disappearing had nothing to do with me. When his sister walked in here—"

"His sister?" Kate froze. "His sister was here?"

Marian turned, her gaze turning misty. "With the most gorgeous little girl and boy. Mac's niece and nephew, apparently. Did he tell you he has such a beautiful family?"

Kate's heart beat fast. "Oh, no. This can't be good."

Marian's smile vanished as she pushed Kate's coffee toward her. "What can't be good? His family seemed thrilled to see him...although I can't say he seemed in any way pleased to see them. Is something wrong?"

"No." Kate's cheeks burned. "Nothing's wrong."

"Kate Harrington…" Marian glared, her fingers busy at the cash register as she rang up Kate's order and dropped her payment into the drawer. "Since when did you start telling me mistruths? Why wouldn't Mac want his family here?"

Kate opened her mouth. Closed it. Opened it again. "He's…she's…" She sighed. "It's complicated."

"Hmm." Marian glanced over Kate's shoulder. "I've got customers coming through the door, but this isn't finished, my girl."

Kate swallowed. "Do you know when his family got here?"

"Just a while ago, I think. They had their bags with them, so I assume the bakery was their first stop. You know, I get the distinct feeling that man has something he wants to say to me. You wouldn't have any idea about that, would you?"

"Me?" Kate huffed a laugh. "Why would I?"

"Because I know you and you're looking mighty on edge about something."

Dread unfurled in Kate's stomach. "What makes you think Mac has something to say to you? He barely knows you."

"Well, for one, every time I've seen him in

here, he's glancing my way. Now why would a man on his own, a sexy singer, no less, want to spend his time sitting in a bakery, studying its aged owner over and over when he thinks she's not looking? So, you tell him to either ask me what it is he wants to know or quit coming in here and then fleeing every time I speak to him." She nudged Kate's coffee forward and looked past her to the next customer. "Hello, lovely. What can I get you?"

Feeling numb, Kate picked up her coffee and took a seat at one of the pine tables in the middle of the bakery. Her mind raced with what-ifs and maybes. What was she supposed to do now? Mac's sister and her kids were in town? The last thing she wanted was to be prematurely introduced to the family of a man she really liked, especially when it was anyone's guess how things would pan out between them.

A niece and nephew? Her heart kicked.

Her phone beeped from inside her bag, and she quickly retrieved it. Mac.

Dana has turned up with my niece and nephew. I'm going to do my best to get them on the next train out of here, but God only knows if she'll cooperate. I shared a few words with Marian and she said some things to make me realize there's every chance things could end up a lot different than you and I hoped. I'll be in touch. I'm sorry x

Kate stared at the kiss, and trepidation whispered through her.

There's every chance things could end up a lot different than you and I hoped.

Her heart raced as she glanced toward Marian. What did Mac mean by that? Did he intend saying something that could upset Marian, after all? Kate glared She'd warned him. She'd told him if she couldn't trust him with Marian's feelings, Kate would speak to Marian herself.

Did he think she'd lied? Not brave enough? She narrowed her eyes.

Could she really trust him to do right by her friend? The disconnection between Kate and her family made it extra difficult to watch anyone go through the same thing...though Mac's situation was entirely different than hers. That didn't mean she'd stand by and let him poison her beautiful friend.

Frustration coursed through her.

Had he been lying to her when he'd admitted he'd hoped Marian might pull him out of his sadness? Was Mac a fraud? Another Dean?

She had to think about Marian…and herself.

Kate glanced at Marian again. The bakery was filling up. She couldn't speak to her now.

Kate felt entirely alone, and suddenly her sister drifted into her mind. She and Ali had been so very close once.

Could she try to rebuild her relationship with her sister? Kate stared through the window. How much longer could she deny how much she missed not having Ali to talk things over with? Having them share their problems with each other again might take time and a whole lot of healing, but she needed to at least try to reconnect with Ali. She had to be there for her only sister on her wedding day. Had to try to get past what Ali had done with Dean. Maybe Mac hadn't been sincere in wanting to move on, but Kate was.

How could she ever really give herself to anyone again if she continued to wallow in the hurt her sister and ex had caused? How could she hope for a happy life when she continued to feel guilt and remorse that her body hadn't kept her child safe?

Pain rolled through her. To think she'd even

considered telling Mac about that part of her life. But she'd wanted to.

Tears burned and she quickly typed a reply to Mac.

I'll never forgive you if you hurt her.

She pressed Send and stood.

Maybe she couldn't do anything about the baby she'd lost, but she could do something about Ali. One step at a time. Kate picked up her phone, stomach twisting.

Meeting Mac, seeing his anger and resentment and how hard it had gripped him, had shown her that these things affect the person suffering far more that the person you were angry with.

Ali had moved on…was getting married. Kate took a deep breath. And she wanted to be a part of that. Ali was her sister. How could she not be a part of her happiness? Did she really want to have another regret added to her already overwhelming pile?

She quickly dialed Ali's number. It went straight to voice mail, and Kate slowly exhaled. "Ali, it's me. Mum visited a few days ago. I am so happy you've decided on a date for the wedding. You must be so excited and I want to be there for you. I want to help make your day as wonderful as possible. Anyway, hope to hear from you soon."

There was nothing else she could do now but wait for Ali's call…if it ever came.

She glanced around at the people milling around the bakery, taking coffees to go or sitting at tables. Templeton was where she belonged, but every now and then, she got tired of having no family here, having no one who'd known her a long time to confide in. She had Marian and Izzy, of course, but the older Kate got, the more she wanted something more. *Someone more.*

Mac's face filled her mind's eye.

She felt a strong connection to him, no doubt due to their mutual difficulties with their families, but she didn't want to be with someone who couldn't control his anguish. She'd dealt with kids in despair, and they'd shown more forgiveness to those who'd hurt them than Mac had.

Abandoning her coffee, she put on her coat and made for the door. The rain still came down, and the clouds had grown darker and more ominous. She grabbed her umbrella from the stand and ducked outside, then hurried along the street to her apartment block.

Once there, she let herself in just as her phone rang in her bag. She dumped her rain-drenched umbrella in the sink and quickly pulled out her phone. "Hello?"

"Kate? It's Ali."

Kate gripped the counter. "Hi. How are you?"

"Good. Happy. Excited. You name it, that's me."

"Great." Kate's eyes burned with tears. Ali sounded so happy and open to speaking with her. Kate blinked. She'd been a fool to let things stew between them for so long. "So the wedding date's set, huh?"

"Yes, June seventh. I'm so happy you want to be there. I wasn't sure with what happened between me and...well, that's all in the past now, right? We can move forward and try to get back to the way we were before."

"Dean. His name was Dean." Kate inhaled and slowly released her breath. "I think we need to clear the air before we try to do any-thing else, Ali. What happened, happened, and you hurt me. Deeply."

"I know, and I'm sorry. Truly. I was a dif-ferent person back then. Denny's changed so much in me, Kate. He makes me...me. Does that make sense? I don't have to try harder or be better when I'm with him. I just have to be."

Longing squeezed at Kate's heart, and she swallowed. "Well, that sounds pretty amazing."

"It is. And I want the same for you."

"Believe me, I'm trying to find it."

"Only trying?"

"What else is there? I need to get past the hurt, Ali. Past the lack of trust I now feel. About guys in particular. I wasn't that way before you and Dean, and I'm tired of it. I thought I'd met this really great man—"

"But that's great. What's his name?"

"His name doesn't matter. The point is, I wanted to try with this guy. I really did. So…" She took a deep breath. "I'm going to do all I can to rid myself of this horrible distrust I have. This horrible reluctance to move toward anything intimate. I figure the way to start that process is to be fully on board with your wedding…and with you."

"Oh, Kate." Ali's breath caught. "You have no idea how happy that makes me. Shall I come to the Cove?"

"Not yet." Kate closed her eyes. She might be trying to move forward, but the prospect of Ali meeting Mac was too much too soon, even if her relationship with him was doomed. She didn't want Ali discovering how close Kate had come to falling in love with another self-serving man. Her sister's pity wouldn't fix anything.

She opened her eyes. "I have a lot of work on right now, but why don't I come to you one weekend? I could stay for a couple of nights."

"Oh, my God, that would be fantastic. I can't wait for you to meet Denny. He's the greatest guy. You're going to love him."

Kate swallowed. For Ali, the business with Dean was over. For Kate, it still stung. Maybe not as cruelly as it once did, but hurt still lingered like an unhealed wound. "I'm sure I will. Give me a call next week, and if there's anything you want me to do online for the wedding in between, let me know."

"I will. It's so great to hear your voice. I'll speak to you soon. Okay?"

"Sure. Speak soon."

Kate hung up. Progress had been made. Now she just needed to speak with Marian before Mac did.

CHAPTER FOURTEEN

MAC SAT ON one of the mini stools in the Coast's kiddie play area situated through an archway at the back of the bar. He faced his sister, trying hard to ignore the fact his knees almost touched his chest. "You're not listening to me, Dana. I *have* to do this. It isn't about choice. Marian said that family matters. That it should be cherished. There's every chance she would've wanted to have known Dad."

She sipped her orange juice. "Okay, but…" She glanced toward Lily and little Mac as they tumbled over one another in the soft play area. "Dad's gone, Mac. What's the use in going over old ground?" Her eyes were glassy with tears. "God knows we all miss him, but shouldn't you be concentrating on the family you still have? The last thing Mum wants is you continuing something she wished Dad never started."

"But why does she wish that? Does she

know the circumstances surrounding his adoption?"

"I don't think so, but if she was worried, don't you think we should respect that, now Dad's gone and he never told us he was looking for his mum? We might be curious about this woman, but I don't think you're coming to this from the right place."

Mac raised his coffee cup to his lips. "Who cares where I'm coming from as long as Marian Ball knows we exist. That she has a family."

"That might sound good, Mac, but you're not doing this out of love, are you?"

Mac put down his coffee and scowled toward the play area, wishing he could lessen his pain. His thoughts turned to Kate and the disappointment and coldness in her text.

I'll never forgive you if you hurt her...

He clenched his jaw. On top of everything else he might or might not being doing the wrong way, and for the wrong reasons, he'd alienated the best person who had come into his life for a long time.

Swiping his hand over his face, he blew out a breath. "I can't stop this now, Dana. I'm sorry."

"Mac—"

"Look, I understand what you're saying, but having Marian know we exist is important to me."

"Why?"

Mac fought the need to explain. Since coming to Templeton, his anguish had begun to disintegrate. Looking for Marian had given him a focus. A steady way to regain some control, to make things happen, rather than waiting around for something to shake up his life again.

But hadn't Kate done exactly that?

He took a sip of his coffee. "You need to go home."

"What?"

He met his sister's steady gaze. "I'm not going to do or say anything cruel to Marian, but I am going to tell her who I am. I'll make it clear there's no expectation, that I'm just finishing off what Dad started. The rest is up to her."

"And you think telling her who you are might not be cruel? Mac, this is serious. Once you say something like that to her, you can't take it back. You have no idea who this woman is or how she might react. What if she wants to talk to Mum? Asks questions that none of us are comfortable with? This isn't a one-way street."

Frustration coursed through him. "What could she ask that you're not willing to answer, huh? We're good people who've led good lives. We've nothing to hide, nor did Dad. She can bring on her questions, for all I care. Don't you think she'll be more concerned about what we're going to ask her?"

She held his gaze for a moment before looking across at her children. "I suppose. God knows I couldn't imagine having to give up those two and not hope to have them come look for me one day."

"Then isn't it right we allow Marian the chance to explain her decision? It's better than me being hung up on my suspicions. When I arrived in Templeton, I was intent on venting my anger, making Marian hurt how I hurt. But now…" He shook his head, looked at his niece and nephew as a strange and unexpected shift occurred inside him. "I realize family gets fractured for all kinds of reasons, but nothing that can't be overcome if the people involved put themselves out there. I want to put myself out there, Dana. I have to."

She looked at him. "Okay."

"Okay?"

"I'll go home, but I want you to call Mum. Tell her where you are and what you're doing. You're a grown-up. She can't stop you from speaking with Marian, but Mum does deserve to know what you're doing. Can you at least do that? For me?"

If his mum voiced her fears, he might lose his determination. Now, more than ever before, he wanted to see his quest through and have Marian know about her son and his family.

He took a deep breath. "Okay. I'll call her."

"Good. And there's no time like the present."

"Now?"

"Now. I'm not kidding, Mac. I refuse to go home and explain to Mum what you're up to. If you're okay about doing this, you have to explain your feelings to her." She squeezed his hand, her gaze softening. "I love that something has gotten you fired up again. It's good to see a little of the old you back. This particular scenario is crazy, of course, but the fact you're doing something other than gigging, working or chatting up a girl you have zero intention of having a relationship with... well, to me, that's all good. Call Mum, and I'll get out of your hair. Promise."

He nodded, feeling a little sick. But backing out of speaking with Marian was no longer an option. He had to believe finding her was what his father would've wanted…even if he hadn't had the courage to come to Templeton himself. And he had to believe his own reasons weren't entirely self-serving. He put down his drink and stood. "I'll call her outside."

Dana raised her eyebrows, her gaze suspicious. "But you will call her?"

"Yes. Just wait here."

She raised her hands in surrender, and Mac strode from the kiddie area, through the bar and outside into the chilly February air. He ducked under a canopy that acted as a motorbike parking area and pulled his phone from his pocket.

Leaning against the wall, he quickly dialed his mum's number.

"Hello?"

"Mum? It's Mac."

"Oh, thank God. Do you know how worried I've been? Would it be asking the earth to have you call me now and then?"

"Sorry. I'm okay. I'm with Dana and the kids."

"Dana? But she said she was staying with a

friend this weekend. What is it with my children? Why do you both feel the need to keep me in the dark?"

"We don't."

"But that's exactly what you're doing."

"We're not keeping you in the dark."

"Then what are you doing? You took off with barely an explanation."

He closed his eyes. "I'm in Templeton Cove."

"Templeton Cove? I knew it. You're trying to find Dad's birth mother, aren't you?"

"I've found her, Mum."

Mac opened his eyes and stared blindly ahead. Guilt, hope and trepidation hovered above him like a suspended weight.

She drew in a breath. "You've found her?"

He nodded. "Yes. She has a bakery here. She's…" He exhaled. "Popular with everyone. Happy. Kind. Funny. She's…pretty cool."

"Cool?"

He huffed a laugh. "Eccentric. Tiny bit mad, if I'm honest. But, yeah, cool."

"There was a time searching for his mother ate your father up from the inside out. He could barely think of anything else."

Mac pushed his hand into his hair and held it back from his face, picturing his father's notes and diary. "Maybe he did, but he didn't do anything about it. Don't you think that was a little cowardly on his part? Something that he could've lived to regret?"

"How can you say that? You didn't know anything about it until after he was gone." Her voice cracked. "He couldn't find her."

"Is that what he told you?"

"Yes."

"He lied."

"What?"

"He found her, Mum. I've read his diary. He'd found her but couldn't find it in himself to risk a second rejection from her even though he knew she'd looked for him in the past. That's what it was all about for Dad. Rejection. Abandonment. Whereas I'm fully prepared for either of those things from a woman I don't know."

She sighed. "He was happy with us, Mac. Maybe he didn't feel the need to meet her as you do."

Bile rose bitter in Mac's throat, and he swallowed. Was he floundering in a way his father hadn't been? Or had his father been looking for a place—a constant—that he couldn't find at home? Wasn't that something any number of people felt?

Mac blew out a slow breath as he thought of Marian and how she'd stopped looking for her son once she'd found her husband. How Mac had been looking for something since he'd lost Jilly and the baby. How Kate seemed to be looking for something since her sister's betrayal.

He sighed. "I suspect Dad was no different than anyone else. Let me do this. Let me speak to Marian and tell her who I am…who we are. She seems a good person, Mum. She might be the best person to get us through the grief of losing him."

The seconds ticked by until his mother's heavy exhalation rasped down the line. "Fine. Do what you have to do. Is Dana coming home?"

"Yes. She wanted me to call you first and tell you what I've been doing."

"Okay. Fine. Talk to this woman. But for goodness' sake, Mac, make sure you're prepared for whatever happens next."

"I will be."

"Good. I love you."

"Love you, too."

Mac ended the call, before he called up his texts. He reread Kate's text, and a burning need to be with her rose inside him. Once he'd spoken to Kate and restored her confidence that he wanted to welcome Marian into his family—if she wanted that—he hoped Kate would see the real him. Not the angry, resentful man he'd been for far too long.

He pressed the reply button and texted Kate back.

I know you probably don't trust me right now, but I need to see you. I haven't spoken to Marian. At least, not yet. Will you meet me in the Coast around seven? I really want to work things out between us, Kate. I won't do anything to hurt you or Marian. Promise x

KATE WALKED INTO the Coast and scanned the packed bar, her nerves jumping. She really shouldn't be here. She should be talking with Marian. Yet, deep in her heart, she believed it was Mac's place to tell his grandmother who he was. There would be a far better chance of a happy family reunion if the connection came from Mac, not Kate. How could Marian be anything but hurt if Kate relayed a story that wasn't hers to tell? If Marian learned her personal business had been dissected, without her knowledge? Kate feared her dear friend might hate her for being involved. That was what had forced her inside the bar to hear what Mac had to say.

It was Saturday night, and the Coast was filled with couples and friends. When she spotted Mac at the bar, she shouldered her way closer, smiling hellos and exchanging a few words with familiar people. At last, she reached him. His dark hair had fallen over the side of his face, hiding his expression as he stared at the label on his beer bottle. Judging from the stiff hunch of his shoulders and the way he repeatedly tapped his foot against the bar, his day had been considerably worse than hers.

Shaking off her guilt, she gently tapped his shoulder. "Hi."

He lifted his head, and his somber expression immediately softened with his killer smile and a renewed gleam in his bright blue eyes. "Hi."

Her stomach knotted. He really was one of the most handsome men she'd ever met. "Drinking alone?"

He tilted his head along the bar. "I've had Dave to keep me company now and then. I'm glad you're here. Drink?"

"A glass of merlot would be great. Thanks." She slid placed her purse on the bar. As he raised a hand to get Dave's attention, Kate studied Mac's profile and tried to figure out his mood. He must have had a pretty trying afternoon if he'd spoken to Marian, and his sister and her family had turned up, too. Traitorous satisfaction unfurled inside her... at least he'd looked happy to see *her*.

Dave walked toward them, and Kate smiled. "Hey, Dave."

"Hey yourself. What can I get you?"

"Merlot, please."

"Coming right up." He put a glass in front of her and filled it with red wine. "How are things going with the fund-raising for the mother and baby unit? All the donations from the other night counted?"

"Yep, and we surpassed our target."

"So, what's next?"

"I'm not sure, but I'll definitely let you know if I need yours or Vanessa's help with anything. You guys have been fantastic."

"Always happy to help." He glanced at Mac. "Another?"

Mac drained his beer and set it on the bar. "Sure, why not? Do you mind if Kate and I take our drinks upstairs?"

Kate stilled. Upstairs? To his room? Heat immediately flooded her face, and her skin tingled with awareness. She stared straight at Dave, battling to maintain an expression of nonchalance. What was Mac thinking? Even if Dave kept quiet, the only way to the stairs leading to the upper floor was through the bar. Half the town would know she'd taken a drink with him in private…behind a closed bedroom door.

Dave raised his eyebrows and looked from Mac to Kate. "Well, sure, if that's what Kate wants. Kate?"

"Uh-huh." Further words clogged her throat.

His eyes shone with amusement. "Then that's fine by me. You kids have fun."

Fun? Nothing about going with Mac to his room would be fun…would it? Her mind raced with all sorts of fun that *could* be had, but she very much doubted Mac's mind meddled in the same places as hers.

Mac stood and smiled. "Ready?"

She nodded. "Sure."

Picking up her wine, she turned toward the staircase and kept her back ramrod straight, even when the heat of Mac's palm at the base of her spine penetrated through her coat and shirt. Eyes front, she ignored the numerous glances sent their way. Whatever happened next, she was a big girl and could handle anything Mac said or did. She liked him. He liked her. Yet, until she knew for sure he'd approach Marian gently and with care, Kate's defenses would remain firmly in place.

They walked along the short landing, then stopped outside one of the bedroom doors. "This is me," he said, pulling some keys from his pocket and opening the door. He gestured for her to enter. "After you."

She walked into the small and tidy room and noted his guitar leaning against one wall and his neatly made bed. The window was partially open to the darkness, his bag stowed beside a desk bearing a stack of papers and a red notebook.

"They're my father's."

She started and turned. "Pardon?"

He nodded toward the desk. "The papers. That's his research on Marian. It's those papers that started all this."

"Right."

"Do you want to take a look at them?"

She faced him, surprised he would ask. "They're private."

He shrugged and closed the door before standing in front of her. "I appreciate you being in this with me. I don't want to keep anything from you. I want everything out in the open between us."

Kate's heart quickened as his gaze roamed over her face. He gently eased the glass of wine from her hand and put it beside his beer bottle on top of a chest of drawers.

Her pulse beat faster as he returned to her and put his hands on her waist. Kate's heart thundered as his focus dropped to her mouth. "Mac—"

"I've wanted to do this all day. May I?"

She stared into his beautiful blue eyes, her body trembling as she saw the desire in his gaze. Her physical surrender to him was inevitable...even if she was forced to keep her emotional surrender firmly under lock and key. She nodded.

His lips tentatively touched hers as he hitched her gently forward. She gripped one of his biceps, her other hand clenching her purse. He slowly slipped his warm tongue into her mouth and their kiss deepened, causing her senses to flood with awareness. His scent teased her nostrils as he towered above her. Soft, deliciously arousing sensations swarmed through her body, and she leaned into him. Lips and tongues explored and appreciated until, reluctantly, she stepped back, afraid of just how far this evening could go.

"We need to talk, Mac."

He nodded, the desire in his gaze easing. "I know."

She shrugged out of her coat and laid it across the bottom of the bed before picking up her wine. "So…"

His gaze lingered on hers before he turned and picked up his beer. She sat on the bed, and instead of sitting beside her, as she'd expected, he pulled out the desk chair. "So, I had an interesting afternoon…a revealing afternoon."

"How so?"

"For a start, I managed to speak a little more with Marian."

"And?"

He smiled wryly. "And she's a hard woman to dislike. She was intent on convincing me of the importance of family. A few days ago, I would've probably gotten riled up again considering she'd given Dad up, but, thankfully I've changed and Dana's unexpected appearance would've cut me off anyway. It would be wrong of me to keep lashing out at Marian. She's not who she was decades ago. I, of all people, should cut someone slack for their past. God knows, I haven't been a nice bloke since Jilly died."

Relief lowered Kate's shoulders, and she lifted her glass in a toast. "Long may your understanding continue."

They drank, and she said, "Marian's a good woman, Mac. She deserves to know who you are, and the longer we keep that fact a secret from her, the harder it will be for you to tell it. You need to speak to her sooner rather than later. Unless your sister's visit has changed your mind?" Apprehension pressed down on her. What if it fell to her to tell Marian about Mac and his family? "If she has, I'm not prepared to keep your existence from Marian. I couldn't live with that, Mac. I'd never comfortably look her in the face again."

"I haven't changed my mind. If anything, Dana said a few things that made me more determined than ever to speak with Marian. I even told my Mum of my intentions."

Pleased he'd shared his mission with his family, Kate exhaled. "That's good. I'm finally realizing the advice I give to kids at work apply to my own life, too."

"And what's the advice?"

"That secrets sometimes need to be shared in order for a person to heal."

He stared, his gaze intense.

Her heart beat fast as their eyes locked. She felt a connection with this man. A true recognition of souls.

She looked around the room, purposefully burying her loneliness. "Has Dana gone home now?"

"She and the kids are staying at a B and B tonight and going home in the morning. I'm meeting them for breakfast at the Oceanside. A special treat before they leave. She's not exactly happy with what I've been doing, but I'm hoping she'll have calmed down a little by tomorrow."

"It's only fair she gets to put her point of view across. Once Marian knows who you are, you should also tell her about Dana and her children, too."

"I will."

She took a sip of her wine. "So, I assume you didn't ask me up here to tell me about Dana?"

He arched an eyebrow. "What other reason could there be?"

Heat assaulted her face, and she laughed. "I'm not insinuating—"

"I really wish you would."

Desire spread through her. Could she? To make love with him would change things between them. They would no longer be new friends or acquaintances. They'd be lovers and, for Kate, that would mean she'd want to take their intimacy further, have his trust in everything. She'd need him to speak with her about things, important things. Determination burned deep in her chest. She'd had her fill of secrets, of hurt and betrayal.

She took a deep breath. "What if Marian rejects you, Mac? What then?"

His smile faltered and his jaw tightened. "Then I'll leave. Go home."

She nodded. "Right."

He came toward the bed and sat beside her. He took her hand and circled his thumb over her palm, studying her fingers before meeting her eyes. "But if she wants to know about Dad, me and my family, then I'll stay around for as long as it takes to answer her questions and have her answer some of mine."

Kate stared into his beautiful eyes, and her desire for him intensified. Every part of her wanted to make love to him now, and possibly for a long time into the future. He was good and honest. He wasn't a liar or a cheat. He wasn't Dean.

She released a shaky breath. "Make love to me, Mac."

CHAPTER FIFTEEN

MAC STARED INTO Kate's deep, dark eyes. "Are you sure?"

Her smile was soft, almost shy. "Yes."

His body burned with longing even as doubt about making love to this woman coursed through him. Making love with Kate would be different than it had been with any of the women he'd shared a bed with since Jilly. He sensed after having sex with Kate, everything would shift inside him. That maybe he wouldn't want to leave the Cove, even if his grandmother rejected him.

Was staying where his father's mother lived something he was prepared to do?

Kate leaned away from him and put her glass on the bedside table, her shoulders tense. Then she touched his jaw, her stunning gaze boring into his. "What is it? I thought you wanted—"

"I do." He pressed a lingering kiss to her palm. "I also suspect I could be in real danger of falling in love with you. If that happens, what then?"

Her cheeks flushed, and tears glinted in her eyes. "Then I'll be glad, and we'll see how things play out. Right now, I'm not asking for anything from you other than to make love to me. I don't want promises. I just want a little care and tenderness. Now, put down your drink and kiss me."

God, he wanted her. Intimacy was a risk. Love was a risk. God damn it, life was a risk.

He pulled her close and kissed her. His body tensed as she slid her fingers over his shoulders and into his hair. Their tongues tangled, and as her nails teased his scalp, Mac's uncertainty dissolved. He hitched her closer until her breasts pressed against his chest. He kissed her harder, wanting her to know exactly what she did to him. What she and her support meant to him.

Slowly, he eased her on to her back and lay alongside her as his admiration and desire for her intensified. "You're amazing. Promise me you'll never let anyone tell you differently, or believe any differently."

Self-doubt shone in her eyes as he slowly unbuttoned her shirt. "You're strong, kind, loving and funny. You deserved more than your ex. You most likely deserve more than me, but I promise I'll never cheat on you. Not ever. I'm not him. I'm me."

She exhaled. "I know. At least now I do."

He opened her shirt and tugged it free from her jeans. Dragging his gaze from hers, he looked at her partially naked body and his breath caught. Her breasts were generous, bulging past the cups of her lacy white bra. Her skin was creamy and flawless. Leaning down, he kissed her collarbones, slowly making his way toward one of her breasts. She shuddered as he nipped and sucked gently at her silky-smooth skin.

His erection strained against his jeans as he slid his hand over her breast, along her rib cage and over the curve of her waist. "Beautiful."

He lifted his head and she reached up to tug his shirt free of his jeans. Moving away, he pulled it over his head and tossed it on to the floor. Returning to her, he let her explore his shoulders, pecs and stomach.

"You—" she huffed a laugh "—work out."

He smiled. "A little."

She raised her eyebrows. "Your body is not the result of a little. *My* body is the result of a little."

He smoothed his hand over her flat stomach and pressed a kiss to her belly button "—You think this is the result of a little?"

With her fingers at his chin, she lifted his face and pulled him closer. They kissed long, hard and deep, their hands busy exploring and discovering. Unable to endure the confines of his jeans any longer, Mac shifted on the bed and unbuttoned them. They took off their jeans and they came back together, their underwear the only remaining barrier.

He needed to touch her, to know she wanted him as he wanted her.

She lay back, and he slid his hand over her stomach to run his fingers along the top of her panties. She sucked in a breath and he smiled. The woman was so sexy, but she also possessed a mysterious control that turned him on so damn much. She trembled as he crept his fingers beneath the triangle of material and lower.

Satisfaction sped his heart as he stimulated her until her breaths quickened and she dug her nails into his biceps. Lower, and he pushed his finger inside. Soft, hot, erotic perfection. His erection throbbed as he continued to stimulate her, their lips joined once more.

"I need to touch you, Mac." She whispered into his mouth. "Let me touch you."

He fell back, and surrender washed through him. He wanted her like he'd wanted no one since Jilly. Kate had come into his life at a time when he battled emotions so fierce, so ugly, yet she'd broken through to him. The real him.

Now, lying with her like this, knowing she knew everything about him and still wanted to make love with him, he wondered if he'd really come to the Cove to find Kate. And no one else.

She smiled, the happiness and desire in her eyes increasing his urgency to feel her wrapped around him. Her hand moved over his chest, his stomach and then slipped into his boxers.

He closed his eyes as she curled her fingers around him, her movements purposely slow and intensely sexual. He gritted his teeth and pressed his hand to her back. She massaged him until his whole body ached with need. He moved his fingers to her bra clasp and released it with practiced ease.

Her hand halted and he opened his eyes.

She raised her eyebrows. "Kind of an expert at that, aren't you?"

He smiled. "One of my many talents."

She slipped her hand from his boxers and shimmied out of her bra, flinging it over her shoulder, her gaze dancing. "Then I'm looking forward to discovering the others."

She dipped her head and kissed him, moving her body over his until she lay on top of him, her perfect figure naked but for a tiny pair of panties. As they kissed and touched, their breathing became harried and their urgency more intense.

Just when he thought he wouldn't be able to resist taking her, she pulled away from him. Her gaze was dark with arousal, her pretty lips reddened. "Don't move."

She slid off the bed and walked to her purse. Fumbling inside, she took out a condom packet and ripped it open. As she came to the side of the bed, she removed her panties. Mac's gaze roamed over the entire, beautiful sight of her. God, she was something else.

She crawled on to the bed and sheathed him with the condom.

Eye to eye, body to body, she lifted above him before clasping his hands and lowering to his erection. He slipped inside her, and the breath rushed from his lungs.

She softly moaned and closed her eyes. With their fingers entwined, they moved, discovering one another's rhythm until they were in sync. She opened her eyes and Mac sat up, wanting to feel her in his arms, have her breaths merge with his.

The sensations built as their bodies heated. With each gentle thrust, his previous doubt of love ever appearing in his life again abated; with each of Kate's murmurs, more his old self re-emerged. He urged her on, wanting her to take the pleasure he so desperately needed to give her.

"Oh, God, Mac." She gritted her teeth. "I'm going to—"

She dropped her head back, her mouth open, and convulsed around him, her body shuddering and writhing. He thrust his hips forward and joined her, their hands dropping as they held each other tightly, as though both were afraid the other might not be real.

Second by sexy second, their bodies relaxed, and Mac opened his eyes. She stared at him, her glazed focus soft and loving.

He smiled. "You're..."

"So are you."

He kissed her and gently rolled her over

until they lay side by side, his arms wrapped around her. "Whatever happens next—"

"We'll deal with it. For now, let's just be. Okay?"

He nodded and brushed some hair from her face. He couldn't remember the last time he felt this happy, this complete. So entirely certain he was supposed to be nowhere else on earth but here, with Kate.

KATE STARED AT Mac as he dozed beside her, her heart filled with want of him but also a little foreboding. Until he told her what he planned to say to Marian, her whole heart would not be open to him. She had to be sure she could fully trust him with the hearts of the people she loved.

She'd been witness to too much pain, too much neglect and disregard for others' happiness. And so had he. Was it even possible that the two of them could be together when so much fear burned deep inside their hearts? Nothing less than a man who was good, true and considerate would be enough for her now. She needed someone who could comfort her when she was scared, support her when she wavered…and until Mac proved himself those things, she wouldn't be convinced Mac was that man.

No matter how much she increasingly longed for him to be.

She would spend her life alone before she lessened her resolve or risked her integrity.

She turned and ran her gaze over the stubble at his jaw, her fingers yearning to touch him. They'd made love, and that would naturally change things between them. By touching each other, holding one another and making love, their intimacy and expectations would almost certainly heighten.

She wanted him to know her on every level. The feeling was so alien, considering the fragmented relationship she had with her parents and sister. She wanted to trust Mac. Wanted him to know the good, the bad and the ugly about her, and wanted to know the same about him.

Life didn't come with guarantees. There could be no certainty they wouldn't hurt each other in the future, but this was now. So much was still left to be done as far as Marian was concerned, and Marian was her friend and confidant, and a woman she would have to see day after day, regardless of whether Mac stayed.

She swiped at her tears. It was no good. She needed to wake him so they could talk. She gently touched his face, lower to his neck and then his shoulder. He murmured something unintelligible before opening his eyes.

"Hey."

Her heart stumbled to see such tenderness in his gaze. "Hey."

His brow furrowed. "You okay?"

"Uh-huh." She nodded. "But we need to talk."

Concern immediately clouded his eyes. "About what?"

Her heart picked up speed. "Firstly, about me."

He shifted on to his elbow. "Tell me."

Her years-old confession stuck in her throat, yet if she wanted his honesty, his trust, she needed to share her secret with him as a way of showing him what he could mean to her. She took a deep breath. "I lost a baby, Mac."

Shock flashed across his face. "What?"

She briefly closed her eyes, drawing on every ounce of her inner strength before meeting his steady gaze once more. "I'd been seeing a guy casually and fell pregnant. My—" she sighed, tears burning her eyes

"—relationship with my mother was worse then than it even is now. She thought me scatterbrained, too interested in people rather than money. My diploma in social care and philosophy a total waste of time." She stared into his eyes. "If I'd told her I was pregnant, any modicum of respect she might have had for me would have vanished. I needed her back then, Mac. Even if I don't now, but I lost the baby…and I still didn't have the courage to confide in her."

"You dealt with a miscarriage alone? God, Kate." Slowly, he sat up against the headboard and eased her against him, wrapping his arms around her. "Has telling me this been worrying you?"

She nodded, tears sliding over her cheeks. "Yes, but I wasn't alone. I had Marian."

"Marian was with you when you lost your baby?"

"I was with her and George at their house when it happened. She stayed with me while George called the ambulance. They came to the hospital, and Marian didn't leave my side for the two nights I was there. Afterward…" She drew in a shaky breath and released it. "I didn't want to be alone. Didn't want to come home. So Marian opened her home to me. I stayed there for a lot longer than I intended. She cared for me like no one else ever has before or since."

"Which is why you're so afraid I'll hurt her."

"Yes."

He squeezed her tighter. "You lost a baby and I…"

"Lost one, too. But not in the same way. What happened to you was so much worse than—"

"Hey." He eased her around to face him. "You lost a child. Whether that be through a miscarriage, adoption or death, you lost a child. Just as Marian and I have. No more blame, okay? No more."

Relief and, dare she think it, love swelled her heart, and her tears flowed faster. "I was so afraid you'd think my grief silly when compared to what happened to your girlfriend and baby."

"Why? You lost a child, Kate. It seems to me you would've kept your baby, right?"

"Yes, despite everything, I was in a position to do that. No matter what my mother might have said, I would've kept my baby."

"Then that's all I need to know to understand the sort of woman you are. All I need to know to understand the unbreakable bond between you and Marian." He smiled gently. "You'll have kids, Kate, and you'll be an amazing mother."

"Maybe, but it's today that matters. Not next week, month or year. It matters what happens next with you and me…and with you and Marian."

An overwhelming liberty coursed through her, and Kate pulled his face to hers and kissed him. She poured all the anguish, pain and fear that she'd carried around with her for all these years into the kiss.

Eventually, she leaned back and rested her head against his chest, intertwining her fingers with his. "I can't go on any longer keeping who you are from her."

"I'll speak with Marian tomorrow." He touched his finger to her chin, lifting her head so their gazes met. His burned with determination and passion. "When people die, their lives don't end with them. I see that now. Jilly and my child still live on in my thoughts. Your baby does in yours. If there was anything I thought Jilly needed to do for closure before she passed, I would do it for her. The entries in my dad's diary reveal more than just words. They reveal his soul, too. Meeting

Marian mattered to him, Kate. He just didn't have the courage to see it through. I think knowing that will matter to Marian, too."

"Of course, it will."

Yet, her worry lingered. She had seen too much heartbreak and desperation not to learn that, despite people's best intentions, their actions were almost always about what *they* needed, not the person they believed they were acting for. How did she share that with Mac without sounding accusatory?

She dropped her gaze to her hands and nervously picked at a nail. "You know, I'm still coming to terms with my ex cheating with my sister, but I can feel something shifting." She looked at him, praying he understood her and wouldn't take offense. "But when I called my sister to tell her I wanted to help with her wedding, that wasn't for Ali or my mum, it was for me. I need to see her to get past this horrible loathing of what she did. I have to say what I need to say, have her look at me and accept completely that her actions changed me forever. That's all for me, not her."

"From what I've seen you do since I met you, your main concern is always for others."

"No, Mac. It's not."

"But—"

"Listen to me." She gripped his hand, tears pricking her eyes. "People often don't accept that everything they do, everything they say, has some kind of personal intention behind it. For example, with the fund-raiser the other week, my intention was to raise money for the mother and baby unit, but it was also about proving my worth as an employee, showing the town just how effective my ideas were, to help me believe I'm not worthless even though my sister and boyfriend disregarded my feelings."

His blue eyes darkened with uncertainty. "Why are you telling me this?"

She quelled her nervousness. "Because I think you need to be honest with yourself. You must accept that your need to find Marian is also most likely about the need to fill a void in you. Why keep your search from your family unless subconsciously you knew it was serving a purpose for *you*? Maybe only you."

The longer he stared at her, the colder his gaze grew. He abruptly moved away from her and stood from the bed. "You're wrong." He grabbed his boxers from the floor and put them on. "There's a part of me that wanted to find Marian for me, but the biggest part was for Dad."

"Is that true?"

He hesitated, two spots of color appearing on his cheeks.

Kate moved forward on the bed to close a little of the sudden distance between them. If he didn't understand her need for honesty in everything now that she'd told him about the miscarriage, she feared they had no chance of their relationship working out.

She spoke past the sickness churning in her stomach. "I'm saying this so that when you speak to Marian, you can tell her about you as well as your Dad. He's gone, Mac. You're here. Marian might be sad she'll never meet her son, but that also means he can no longer affect her. You can. She deserves to see you. The real you. That's all I'm saying."

He huffed a laugh as he buttoned his jeans. "All you're saying? I think you've said an awful lot."

Heat burned her cheeks as she slipped from the bed. There was no way he was going to dress through his irritation and leave her naked in hers. She whipped her panties and bra from the floor. "I should go."

"Fine." He pulled on his jeans. "I'll see

Dana in the morning and call you as soon as I can after."

Tears burned as she slipped on her jeans and grabbed her shirt from the floor. "You'll speak with Marian tomorrow?"

"I'll call you."

Kate's heart thundered. "I only told you what you know is true, Mac. I didn't mean to be spiteful or change your mind. I just want you to speak with Marian and be fully aware of why so you can be honest with her. Don't take the opportunity to know her family away from her."

A muscle flexed in his jaw. "I won't."

She shrugged into her shirt, silently pleading for him to understand her intentions. She didn't want him to regret any lack of honesty with a woman who could become such a big part of his life. She buttoned her shirt, her gaze on his. "You know I only want to support you, right?"

He raised his eyebrows. "This is support?"

She turned and snatched her purse up from the floor. "Yes. I like you, Mac. A lot. Do you think I'd reveal my failings, my occasional selfishness to someone I don't like, someone I don't believe I can trust?"

He stared, his jaw tight.

She lifted her hands in surrender. "Have it your way. Do what you have to do." She strode to the door and pulled it open. "But if you leave without speaking to Marian, or speak to her with anything less than love and care, don't expect me to keep my mouth shut after you've gone. Honesty, Mac. It matters."

CHAPTER SIXTEEN

MAC TOPPED OFF Dana's orange juice and re-
plenished his own before glancing toward the
Oceanside's windows where his niece and
nephew looked out across the water, their
hands most likely marking the once-spotless
glass. "I'm glad you brought the kids with you
on this trip. They certainly make you realize
what's important in life."

"Yeah, but with Jamie away as often as he
is, they also run me ragged. So…" She raised
her eyebrows. "Now you've told me what the
new woman in your life said about being honest with Marian, how are you feeling? I think
Kate has a point, you know."

He watched the light snow falling outside.
"She certainly made me take a long look at
myself, and I can't say I liked what I saw."

"How so?"

He met Dana's concerned gaze. "I need to
figure out what made me run headlong into
finding Marian, all the while knowing Mum

wouldn't like it and keeping my trip here secret from you."

"Have you come to any conclusions?"

"Yeah, some."

"Want to share them with me?"

He massaged the bridge of his nose. "Kate thinks we all do things with a personal intention, whether we realize it or not. If she's right, the reason I came here was so I wouldn't have to deal with everyone else's grief over Dad, only mine." He clenched his jaw against the shame of his selfishness. "Dad dying brought it all back."

"Jilly?"

He nodded. "It was as though I was flung back to the day she died. All the pain and grief came rushing back and evolved into this uncontrollable fury. I needed to lash out, and Marian Ball became my target."

"Oh, Mac." She squeezed his hand, her gaze sad. "That's totally understandable. You loved Jilly so much. To lose a baby, too…"

He tightened his grip on his glass. "Kate also made me think I need to take some time away from here before deciding if, or when, I speak with Marian."

"You're coming home?" She smiled, her blue eyes lighting with relief. "I think that's

a sensible idea. You need some perspective.
Now you've found Marian, there's no need
for you to rush into telling her who you are.
Years have passed, a few more weeks isn't
going to make any difference."

"Maybe."

Dana raised her eyebrows. "We *are* talking
about Marian being the only reason behind
your decision to leave Templeton, right?"

Mac tried not to squirm under the weight of
his sister's wily gaze, hating that his leaving
the Cove had so much more to do with Kate
than Marian. "What do you mean?"

"I mean, your leaving hasn't got something
to do with Kate, too, has it?"

He slid his gaze to Lily and little Mac as
they chatted with two people dining at a table
alongside them. The delighted older couple
smiled and clapped as his niece and nephew
executed hops and jumps in some kind of ab-
surd off-the-cuff ballet performance.

"It could have a little to do with her." He
looked at Dana, unease for what he was about
to say clawing uncomfortably at his chest.
"I like her, Dana. A lot. She could be..." He
swallowed. "Someone pretty special."

"Well, that's great..." She frowned. "Isn't it?"

Mac twisted his water glass around in circles on the table. "She's been honest with me from the very beginning, but I can't say I've returned the compliment."

"You've lied to her?"

"No, but I haven't told her there's every possibility I'll never want to come back here if Marian wants nothing to do with us. Kate's already had her heart broken. I don't want things to get any deeper between us before I'm sure I'm going to be around for the long-term."

"Aren't you thinking about you and her a little too seriously?" She leaned forward. "You've only just met the woman. You're under no obligation to her. You've not prom-ised her anything." She raised her eyebrows again. "Have you?"

"No, but I've slept with her."

"Ah."

Mac blew out a breath. "Exactly. With Kate, everything feels different. I want what-ever I start with her to stick."

Lily and little Mac returned to their seats at the table, and Mac welcomed the diversion. Dana's gaze continued to bore into his temple as he pushed the kids' juices toward them.

"Did you guys see anything interesting on the beach?"

Lily nodded. "Three mermaids and a whale."

Mac laughed. "Really?"

Little Mac shook his head. "No, you did not. We saw blue sea and lights from the fair." He glared. "You're lying."

"Am not!"

"Are too!"

Mac grinned and raised his hands, glancing at Dana, whose smile seemed frozen in place as she looked at her kids, her gaze full of warning.

Mac cleared his throat. "Why don't you go and ask that nice waitress over there if we can see the menu? I'm pretty sure they'll have something else you guys will like."

They scrambled down from their seats and hurtled toward one of the waitresses.

He faced Dana, and the force of her glare dissolved his smile. "Sorry."

"This is what I'm talking about." She drained the remainder of her orange juice. "You love those kids, right?"

"Of course."

"You're a great uncle to them, right?"

Mac frowned, wondering where she was going with this. "I try to be."

"*No*, you're a great uncle to them. That's who you are, Mac. You love kids. You love people. You love family. Either of us might have picked up the mantle to find Dad's mum, but it was you who went for it, regardless of your less-than-loving reasons."

Mac shifted in his seat and glanced toward the door. "And?"

"And that's why Kate's honesty has scared you. You don't like not being there for people… and I think a big part of you wants to be there for Kate."

He took a deep breath. "Which is why I need to leave. Kate deserves more than I'm prepared to give her. I'm not entirely thrilled she's stirred up the possibility of me being in a relationship again. Of opening myself up to something that could lead to God knows what."

Dana's eyes shadowed with sympathy. "The chances of you losing another woman how you lost Jilly are very, very slim, Mac. You're too good of a man to spend the rest of your life alone. You know that, right?"

He leaned forward. He feared he wasn't really ready for another relationship…that maybe he shouldn't have slept with Kate. "It's complicated. She's complicated. Plus, she makes me think about things I thought about with Jilly."

"Such as?"

"Such as…" He shook his head, willing his niece and nephew to come back to the table. "Kids, holidays together, a house…" He raised his eyebrows. "Even a dog. Chocolate Lab who'd I call Tyler. Such as having more than a life of bouncing from one gig to the next. Such as wondering if I might find a woman who makes me want to settle down and stay in one place for longer than a few days."

"Mac…" Dana reached across the table and squeezed his fingers, looking happy. "This is all good. Take a few days. Come home with me, but then, when you're ready, come back and talk honestly to Kate about everything you've been through. What losing Jilly and the baby did to you. Meeting our grandmother isn't as important as you moving forward with someone who could be your partner, your love."

He clenched his jaw, his dad's notes and diary entries replaying in his mind. "Says who?"

She frowned. "Says me."

He eased his hand from Dana's. "I have to see this through, Dana. I won't be happy until I do. Anyway, it doesn't matter what I might or might not feel about Kate. It scares the hell out of me to get involved again. You know how I fell for Jilly. If I fall for Kate, too…" He shook his head. "I can't go through that again. Kate and Marian deserve more than a man who's afraid of the future. If they come to rely on me and I end up feeling suffocated, afraid of letting them down…" He drew in a calming breath and slowly released it. "I need to go home. I need to really think about what I'm doing here and how it could affect other people."

"I agree."

He held her gaze before nodding, a silent understanding passing between him and the sister who had held him up for the two years after Jilly and their baby died. Lily and little Mac came to the table and Dana deftly lifted Lily on to her lap as they pointed to the menu and the treats they wanted. Nothing showed in their mother's expression that she might be more caught up in her brother than her children right then. Dana's ability to shield her children from her own troubles never failed to increase Mac's admiration of her. If only he were that strong.

Instead, when the going got tough, he fled. He'd fled from his family's grief to Templeton…and now he was going to flee from Templeton because he feared falling in love with Kate.

The one thing he was certain of was she deserved someone way stronger than him. He wasn't sure he'd ever be as flexible as Dana, wasn't sure he could be ten different people and, at the same time, exactly who the person with him needed him to be. How could he ever manage to be so much to so many people when all he ever thought about was how much he had to lose?

Hating the horrible pull deep inside his chest, Mac forced a smile and shoved his vulnerabilities aside. He reached across the table. "Hey, do I get a look at these pastries?"

Lily giggled and held a menu toward him. "Here you go, Uncle Mac. You get to choose first because you're our most favorite uncle."

He met Dana's eyes, and she winked, then he dropped his gaze to the menu. He'd go home with his family. The people who were his and hopefully always would be. Where he went next as far as Kate and Marian were concerned needed to be thought about long and hard. There was no way he'd allow either of them to love him without being sure he would be around for them for a very long time.

KATE STARED AT her computer screen, and the words of the memo to the center's head office blurred, her thoughts filled with Mac and his silence since their fight two days ago. Her concentration waning, she abandoned the memo and checked her phone. No texts. No missed calls.

Trying hard to hold on to her resolve that she had been right to say the things she had, Kate picked up her phone and headed for the small kitchen. Happy it was empty, she pushed the door closed and dialed Mac's number. Straight to voice mail.

She cleared her throat, fighting the nerves that tumbled in her stomach. "Mac, it's Kate. Again. Clearly I upset you the other night, but I was only trying to make you understand that this whole thing with Marian is as much about you as it is her. I'd really like it if you returned my messages. Hope to speak to you soon."

Hands shaking, Kate ended the call and slumped back against the counter, staunchly fighting back the tears that pricked her eyes. She would not cry. Crying was for people who let their hearts run away with them. She wouldn't surrender to the horrible, hollow feeling in her chest that had refused to abate for the past forty-eight hours.

The door opened and Nancy wandered into the kitchen. Kate quickly picked up the kettle and walked to the sink, turning on the tap. "Everything okay, Nance?"

"Everything's fine with me."

The "what about you?" hung in the air between them like an axe about to fall.

Kate turned, forcing a smile. "That's good. Kind of busy out there." She abandoned the kettle on the counter. "I'd better get back to work."

"What's going on, Kate?"

Damn it. Kate's smile wobbled as she purposefully faced Nancy. "Nothing. Everything's fine."

Nancy raised her eyebrows, her eyes full of concern. "You can talk to me, you know. The reason you've been so distracted the last couple of days wouldn't have anything to do with the new man in town, would it?"

"New man?"

"Kate, it's me you're talking to. We've worked together a long time and we're good friends. What's going on?"

Sighing, Kate leaned back against the counter. "Fine. It's Mac. He's not returning my calls. I might have said a few things to him the other night that he didn't exactly welcome." She drew forth every ounce of pride she had left from her rapidly dwindling reserves. "I just don't understand how men can cut women off the way they do. I thought he was different. How stupid could I be?"

Frowning, Nancy crossed her arms. "You like him that much, huh?"

"Liked." Kate scowled. "Past tense."

"Hmm. Well, if that were true, you wouldn't be glaring at that kettle as though it was to blame for world poverty and you wouldn't be snapping at everyone in the office. If he's not answering your calls, go and see him in person. Face-to-face is the best way to deal with men. Believe me."

"I just need to know if whatever was starting between us…isn't. Do you know what I mean?" Kate pushed the curls back from her face, hating the way her chest ached for something that had barely been there in the first place. "To spend so much time with me and then bolt without a goodbye or explanation… that's just low. As in my ex-boyfriend low."

"Where's Mac staying?"

"The Coast."

"You know you're the manager here, right?"

Kate frowned. "And?"

"So, take some of that extra time you've clocked up and leave early. Get yourself to the Coast. Just act nice and casual. Hopefully, he'll be there, but, if not, Vanessa should be able to tell you where he is. You know what she's like."

"I can't do that."

"Why not?"

Kate picked up a spoon, tapping out her nerves against the countertop. "It's too sad to go chasing after a guy that way. Really, really sad."

"No, it's not. There could be a perfectly innocent explanation why he isn't answering your calls. Give the guy a chance, Kate. You like him. He likes you. Don't give up on what might be a good thing." Nancy stepped closer and stopped Kate's tapping with a firm grasp. "Go. Now. Before the rest of us start betting whether it's safe to talk to you or not. You're cranky. Go and get uncranked."

Before Kate could respond, Nancy turned away and started busying herself making a cup of coffee. She stared at her colleague's back before lifting her chin and leaving the kitchen. She'd go to the Coast. Lord only knew what she'd, say to Mac, but the truth was, even with him ignoring her, she didn't regret her words or pushing for his honesty. If the man couldn't see what she said made sense, she wasn't even sure she wanted to be with him. But she most definitely needed another conversation with him.

"Stupid, stubborn, guitar-playing pain in the butt." She stalked to her desk and snatched her purse from the back of the chair. "This is your last chance with me, Mac Orman. Your very last."

She scribbled "Back in the morning" on a scrap of paper and placed it on her keyboard, then hurried from the office before she could change her mind. She walked to the Coast in half the usual time, and when she pushed open the bar door, the sparseness of the clientele was a clear sign she had no business being there at just past four in the afternoon. Shaking her head, she turned to walk back outside.

"Stop right there, Kate Harrington."

"Busted." Kate groaned before forcing a smile and turning around. "Hi, Vanessa."

The landlady raised her eyebrows. "Does it smell in here or something?"

"Of course not." Kate laughed, her shoulders rigid with tension. "I changed my mind about having something to eat, that's all. I can wait until later."

"Hmm." Vanessa wandered closer and slipped one arm through Kate's. "He's gone. Come with me and have a bite at the bar."

Sickness gripped Kate's stomach as she numbly allowed Vanessa to draw her deeper into the bar. "Mac's gone?"

"Uh-huh. Yesterday morning."

"Oh." Disappointment and hurt yanked hard at Kate's chest.

"Oh? That's all you have to say?" She nudged Kate toward a bar stool. "Sit."

Kate obeyed and placed her purse atop the bar, her mind racing and her heart hurting. "He's gone."

"And the only explanation he gave was he needed to do some thinking."

About me? Marian? Himself? Kate took a deep breath. "Do you know what about?"

"Nope. He's hardly the type to elaborate, is he?" She held up a can of Diet Coke. "You want one of these?"

Kate nodded. "Sure."

Vanessa poured it into a glass and handed it to Kate. "He didn't run out on you without calling first, though, right?"

Heat stung Kate's cheeks.

"Because if he did…" Vanessa shook her head. "He wouldn't be welcome back here, and that would be a shame. Dave and I were getting pretty close to a full-on smile from the guy."

"Yeah, me, too."

They exchanged a smile themselves before Vanessa raised her eyebrows. "You did tell Mac how much you like him, didn't you?"

"Yep, and then some. Which is most probably why he got out of town so quickly."

The door opened and Vanessa's eyes widened, her mouth dropping open. Frowning, Kate turned, her mind confused and her stupid heart in turmoil. Her breath caught.

Mac slowly walked toward her, his focus fully on hers. Kate tried and failed to drag her eyes from his, desperately wanting to act nonchalant. Instead, she froze, her thrill that he was back sizzling heat through her blood.

He stopped beside her, all six feet of him looming over her, his blue eyes dark and intense. "You're here."

Her throat dried, and she coughed to clear it. "Yes." Gathering as much bravado as she could, she finally dragged her gaze from his and faced Vanessa. The woman stared at Mac as though God himself had just walked through the damn door. "Vanessa? Could you make that two Cokes?"

Vanessa blinked, her smile slamming into place. "Sure. Coming right up. Are you back, Mac? Your room's still free."

Kate stared straight ahead, Mac's gaze burning into her temple as Vanessa poured his drink.

He stepped closer. "I'm back, and I'll need the room indefinitely. If that's okay?"

"Indefinitely...right...great." She put his drink on the bar. "I'll be in the kitchen if you two need anything else."

Left alone with him, Kate drew in a strengthening breath and turned. "Why don't you sit down?"

He slowly put his guitar and bag on the floor before sitting beside her. "I couldn't leave without speaking to you."

She picked up her drink, relieved it didn't tremble as she brought it to her lips. "I thought you'd already left."

"But I'm back now."

A ghost of a smile played on his lips. "It's like I'm connected to the place by an invisible rubber band or something."

She smiled softly. "I guess you are." She

sipped her Coke. "So, what is it you want to talk about?"

"You. Me. Marian." He brushed some of her hair behind her ear.

She resisted the urge to shiver as she focused on the bar. "Right."

"Look at me, Kate."

Her heart pounding, she faced him. His deep, dark, beautiful eyes held hers.

"I can't leave without speaking to Marian, but, more than that, I can't leave now I've met you."

She nodded, feeling a traitorous smile stretch across what felt like the breadth of her face. "I see."

He smiled, too. "So, will you speak to Marian with me?"

"Yes."

"Can we go back to your place?"

"Yes."

He slid from his stool and pulled his wallet from his back pocket. Extracting a five-pound note, he left it on the bar before picking up his guitar. He slipped the strap over his shoulder, picked up his bag and held out his free hand toward her.

Sexual tension hummed through her body

and overrode the common sense reverberating in her mind. She slipped her hand into his and led him from the bar.

CHAPTER SEVENTEEN

KATE ENTERED HER apartment ahead of Mac and tossed her purse on to a seat by the front door, deep yearning for Mac tumbling inside her. "Make yourself comfortable. Coffee? Are you hungry?" She tipped her head back to look into his dark blue eyes, her need to kiss him pulsing through her. "I can put a sandwich together. Or I could toss some pasta on to boil. Or—"

"Kate." He took her hand. "I don't want anything to eat."

"Right." She swallowed, far too aware of the warmth and breadth of his hand in hers. "Coffee?"

His eyes glinted with amusement. "Sure, but first I need to know if it's okay to kiss you. If not, I should maybe leave because I can't think about doing anything else right now."

Pleasure quivered through her, and her cheeks burned. She nodded. "You can kiss me."

Slowly, he lowered his lips to hers, and

Kate reached up to grip his hard biceps. She dug her fingers into the sleeves of his leather jacket and gently met his tongue with hers. He'd returned. To the Cove. To her. Her heart pounded as the familiar, spicy scent of his aftershave drifted into her nostrils, his hands on her waist making her feel all was right in the world.

After too brief a moment, he eased away and searched her eyes. "I'm sorry I left."

She reluctantly slipped her hands from him and crossed her arms as though protecting her heart. "Why did you?"

He turned and walked farther into the living room, then dropped on to the couch, his defeated gaze on hers. "I left because of what you said to me. The *true* things you said to me. Losing Jilly made me realize we need to grab every hope of family and friends we can. Not take those we already have for granted. Yet I chose to use my heartbreak to hurt someone else. Hurt Marian. But with you…" He slumped his shoulders. "Will you sit with me? This is twenty times harder than when I rehearsed it."

Anxiety and confusion coiled tightly inside her as she slowly walked to the couch and sat. "You say you want to grab family and friends, yet you slept with me and left, Mac. You hurt me, and you intend to hurt one of my closest friends."

"Intended...and I know. I'm sorry." He took her hand and raised it to his mouth, kissing her knuckles before resting their hands against his chest. "I came back because I had to. I couldn't get you out of my head. I couldn't..." He stared at her mouth. "I couldn't walk away without giving us a chance." He lifted his gaze. "Tell me I'm not too late. That I haven't blown my chance to be with you."

As much as his words sped her heart rate and gave her hope, Kate held on to her self-preservation and slipped her hand from his. She pulled back her shoulders. "I don't know until you tell me your plans. Are you going to speak to Marian?"

He released a heavy breath, his eyes somber. "Yes. I'm going to tell her who I am as soon as possible. Once she knows, her reaction will, hopefully, provide me with the answers I need."

"And how are you going to speak to her?"

"As gently and as tactfully as I can."

"And what exactly are the answers you're hoping for?"

"Why she felt giving Dad up for adoption was the best option at the time. Why she looked for him so many times and then stopped." He swiped his hand over his face and met her gaze. "Why she never married before George and why she never had more children. I don't think I've ever met a woman who should be a mother more in my life."

Kate softly smiled. "I couldn't agree more, and it would be good if she can answer all those questions, but I'm still afraid for her, Mac. I'm afraid for you, too."

"I'll be fine." He took her hand and squeezed her fingers. "And I'll do everything I can to ensure Marian is, too."

"Good. That's all I ask." Kate looked at their joined hands. "And what about you and me?" She lifted her eyes to his. "I need to trust you. I need to know you'll do all you can not to hurt me or let your grief get the better of you again. Do you think you can do that? Regardless of what Marian says to you, or what sort of relationship she wants with you from now on."

"I can." He looked deep into her eyes. "I feel so differently now I've found you. I can see that I could be happy again." He brushed his lips over hers. "That I can love again."

Kate nodded, yearning for everything he described. "I want those things so much, too. I want them for both of us."

"Then, that can only be a good place for us to start." He exhaled. "I have to see Marian now, and then it's our time."

She stared into his eyes and recognized the worry, the vulnerability. She'd suffered that same anguish of feeling rejected by her mother and sister. She raised her hand to his jaw and looked deep into his eyes. "It's going to be all right."

"I hope so."

She stood. "Let me make some coffee and then you can tell me how you plan to approach your formidable grandmother."

He huffed a laugh. "My plan consists of walking into the bakery and telling her I'm her grandson."

"You can't just blurt it out like that." Her concern for Marian heightened once more. "Doing that will most likely lead to her smacking you up the side of the head and ejecting you from the premises. She needs careful handling. She needs to know, from the very beginning, that you're telling the truth." She walked into the kitchen and set the kettle to boil. "Let's figure out the right time and place, and go from there."

"Fine." He stood and came to the breakfast bar that separated the kitchen from the living room, sliding on to one of her stools. "Any ideas?"

Kate pulled a couple of mugs from the hooks beneath one of her cupboards and spooned in some instant coffee granules as her mind churned. "I think we need to get Marian alone, so we can tell her about your family in privacy. She deserves the choice of if, when or how she tells anyone else. Her past is her own, not anyone else's to judge. Including us."

"Of course." He touched her hand where it lay on the countertop. "You know, it's just as well I ran into a contrary, too-much-to-say-for-herself girl the first night I arrived here. Maybe it was you who had to clear the way to being welcomed with open arms by the grandmother I never knew I had."

She leaned across the counter, her gaze on his lips. "Maybe it was."

He met her halfway and they kissed.

MAC SMILED AT KATE. He could see the cogs of her brain turning over, her thoughts showing clearly in her dark brown eyes. "You've thought of something, haven't you?"

"Yes."

"And?" Mac took the cup of coffee she handed him.

She picked up her own coffee, and they walked into the living room and sat side by side on the couch. "Well, I think it only right that we talk to Marian on her own territory, so she feels safe and in control. Considering all Marian does for everyone in the Cove, I don't want her to feel threatened or under any sort of pressure to do the right thing."

"Whatever the right thing is." Mac took a sip of his coffee, self-doubt churning. "I've no idea what that might be, and I wouldn't be surprised if Marian feels the exact same shock, anger and panic I did when I found Dad's notes." He inhaled. "She needs to understand I'm not here to accuse her or demand anything from her. Once she knows about me and my family, I'm happy for her to do what she will. This is about closure for me and, hopefully, her." He met Kate's steady gaze, the rapid beat of his heart telling him all too clearly that the goalposts had shifted since he arrived in the Cove. He was falling in love again, and there wasn't a damn thing he could do to stop it. "You've become a big part of what happens next for me. You get that, right? This isn't all about Marian anymore."

"And I'm glad, but right now, this *has* to be about her."

Mac silently regretted the selfishness of moving from Marian's feelings to his own. "So, I assume Marian's domain is the bakery?"

"Yes."

"But that place is *never* empty."

"She closes up on her own every night. We'll have a half-hour window between her locking up and George coming to take her home. The limited amount of time means we can tell her who you are and then leave, giving her the space she needs to process the information."

Mac sipped his coffee, doubting Kate's logic. "Shouldn't she have time to ask me questions? Lay down any ground rules? This feels too much like dropping a bomb and then fleeing before the aftermath sets in."

She looked at him, a faint color staining her cheeks. "You're right. It's exactly that. Doing it my way isn't fair to her."

The disappointment in her eyes seemed to reflect something more than simply his questioning her idea. Mac placed his coffee on to the small table in front of them. "What else is going on, Kate? Why did you want to talk to Marian and then immediately leave? If I was wrong to ask for your help, then—"

"You weren't wrong, and I'm glad you did."

"Then what is it?"

"It's what I said to you before about personal intentions behind the things we do and the choices we make. Suggesting you tell Marian who you are and leave serves my fear of not dealing with her shock, her possible heartbreak that the son she never knew is now dead and I knew about everything before her. I'm not sure how I'll cope seeing her upset." She shuddered. "When I found my sister and Dean in bed together, I ranted and raved, threw things and swore, but doing that healed nothing inside. When I lost my baby, I forced my pain and heartache to the back of my mind, refused to acknowledge how upset I was. I provoked arguments with my family and friends instead, but acting out didn't go anywhere near soothing the pain."

He smoothed his hand on to her thigh. "I can speak to Marian alone if you prefer."

Her eyes glistened with unshed tears. "I want her to love you, Mac. You deserve to know how wonderful a person Marian is. I hate the thought of her not trusting you...not trusting me."

He nodded, wanting nothing else than the words to take the anxiety he saw in her eyes. "I'll speak to Marian alone. She doesn't have to know you knew anything about my relationship to her. This is my job to do. Not yours."

"I just wish there was a definitive way to ease her into this. For news about your dad's passing and your family to not come as such a shock."

Mac drew his gaze over her face, falling a little deeper in love with her. With her generosity, her need to protect others from pain when she'd experienced such deep hurt herself. He couldn't help wondering if she had any idea how much her kindness had taught him. He touched Kate's chin and eased her face to his.

He gently kissed her and drew back. "I know only too well how families can be affected by shock. How loved ones can turn away from each other in the face of trauma, rather than draw closer. I turned away from my parents and Dana when Jilly died. I couldn't handle seeing the pity, grief and

worry in their eyes." He lightly kissed her
again. "We'll find a way to prepare Marian,
so I'm more of a distant rumble than a strike
from nowhere. That would be better for all
of us."

She swiped her fingers under her eyes.
"Agreed."

"So, maybe we need to find a way to test
the waters?"

"But how?"

"I don't know. I can't see how I'll manage
to go into the bakery again without blurting
out who I am. She already suspects I want
to talk to her about something." He smiled
wryly. "Just like my father always knew when
I was hiding something from him."

She briefly smiled before her eyes widened. "I've got it. I could go into the bakery
before George picks her up and tell her I'm
dealing with a case where a son is looking for
his birth mum. Marian's reaction will speak
volumes, and we'll know whether the time is
right for you to speak to her."

"Don't you think that's a bit underhanded?
The last thing I want is for Marian to be angry
with you."

"I'll be subtle. I can do this. I know I can."

"I don't know, Kate. It should be me in the line of fire, not you."

"But don't you see? She can't get upset with me without telling me her story. She'll either advise me or tell me about your dad. Either way, we'll know where we stand."

"The plan makes sense, but I can't let you—"

"You're not *letting* me do anything, Mac. I'm asking you to wait a while longer in the hope of causing Marian the minimum distress. You want that for her too, right?"

"Yes."

"Then we'll go with my idea of a hypothetical case. I'll go to the bakery tonight, and by tomorrow, you'll know if the time is right to meet your grandmother properly."

He drew in a long breath and slowly exhaled. "You really are kind of bossy, you know that?"

She grinned. "I do, and now I'd really like to boss you around in my bedroom."

He leaned toward her, easing her back on the settee, his need for her and everything she'd awakened in him rising. "Who needs a bedroom?"

CHAPTER EIGHTEEN

KATE SLOWED HER pace as Marian's bakery came into view. Her plan didn't feel quite so watertight now she neared her destination. The woman she so admired and loved was undoubtedly inside, oblivious to what was about to happen.

Pulling back her shoulders, Kate pushed on toward the bakery. As she'd expected, the building was in semidarkness, with only the low lights inside the glass counter and a light coming from the open kitchen door illuminating the interior.

Marian swept a broom across the floor. And as though she sensed Kate standing outside, she paused and straightened, then squinted through the window. Recognition registered, and she smiled and waved.

Kate offered a faltering wave in return, silently praying for the strength to see through her mission. She stepped toward the door as Marian unlocked and opened it.

"Well, Kate. What on earth are you doing here? You know what time I close up shop."

Kate grimaced. "I need some advice."

Marian beamed. "Then you've come to the right place. Step inside before you catch your death. These temperatures keep dropping the way they are, we'll be icicles before next week. Being by the ocean might be a godsend in the summer, but in February, a person can wonder if they're insane to live here."

The fading smells of sugar and cinnamon reminded Kate of how welcoming Marian and her bakery were to everyone in the Cove. Briefly closing her eyes, she prayed Marian wouldn't make her the first resident she banished from her domain.

"So, what's going on?" Marian lifted an upturned chair from one of the small pine tables in the center of the room and set it on the stone floor. "You look more than a little worried, my lovely."

"Not worried, more keen to help someone." Kate lifted a second chair and sat next to Marian. "I had an unusual call from a friend today."

"You did? About what? And what can I do to help?"

Kate's mouth dried, and she glanced toward the bottles of water and cans in the cooler. "Could I get some water? I'll pay, of course."

Marian waved her hand, her gaze serious, like a bloodhound sniffing out trouble. "No money needed. Help yourself."

Grateful for a few seconds of space, Kate willed her heart rate to slow. She needed to relax or it would take all of five seconds for Marian to realize this situation involved herself. Taking her time, Kate opened the cooler and stared at the various soda cans, water and fresh fruit before selecting a bottle of water. Schooling her expression into one of practiced objectivity, Kate rejoined Marian at the table and sat. "So, my problem."

Marian frowned. "Are you sure you're all right? You're looking mighty troubled."

"Uh-huh."

"And you're jumpy." Marian's eyes widened. "This advice isn't about anything illegal, is it?"

"No, not at all." Kate twisted the cap off her water and drank deep. She tightly gripped the bottle and forced her gaze to Marian's. "It's about an adoption."

Marian didn't as much as flinch. "I see. Whose?"

"It's confidential. I was just hoping you'd give me your opinion about something."

"Go ahead. I'll help if I can."

"Okay, well…" Kate cleared her throat and purposefully held Marian's gaze. "I know of a man looking for his birth mother. He thinks he might have found her, but he's unsure whether the mother will want to have anything to do with him. She signed a register for mothers who are willing to reconnect with the children they gave up for adoption, but that was years ago and, as far as we know, she hasn't taken any new steps to finding him since."

Marian's expression had turned into a frozen mask, her skin pale and her shoulders stiff. "Well, maybe she decided to leave the rest up to him."

Hope sparked inside her, and Kate nodded. "I suppose. So you think if he made contact with her, she'd be happy about it?"

"That depends." Marian's voice was low, the joy usually so prevalent in her exclamations, questions and praise absent. "What does he expect from her?"

The unanticipated question tossed Kate's hopes to the wayside. "I don't think he has an agenda."

"Are you sure?" Marian stood and snatched up her broom. She glanced at Kate before sweeping the floor with more gusto than when Kate had been watching through the window. "The boy must be expecting something. Has he considered why his mother might have given him up? If she was forced? The decision taken out of her hands?" She stopped, her gaze on the floor and her knuckles showing sharply as she gripped the broom handle. "Maybe the circumstances at the time meant giving him up would provide the best possible chance for the boy. If he blames her…"

Kate struggled to speak against her guilt. "He doesn't blame her. He just wants her to know he's okay."

Marian huffed a laugh and straightened, her cold gaze sending shock waves through Kate. "And then what? He'll disappear again as though nothing's happened?"

"No, it will depend on—"

"His mum, right? Everything that happens

next will be on the shoulders and conscience of the woman who made a life-changing decision years ago. That's not fair, Kate. Not by a long shot."

Regret for coming here twisted inside Kate. Neither she, nor Mac, had thought this through carefully enough. Kate swallowed, her heart beating fast as she stared into Marian's glassy eyes. Is this what families did to one another? Assumed and blamed without consideration for their loved ones' choices?

Kate stood, her legs trembling. "I should go."

"Why? You don't like my questions?" Marian raised her eyebrows, her gaze steely. "I haven't even given you any advice yet. I'm just putting some scenarios and considerations to you. This boy will be a stranger to his mother. A grown man with demands and problems. Expectations and heartaches. What is his mother supposed to do about that? How can she comfort and hold him when she walked away?"

"Marian, I didn't mean to—"

"What, Kate? What didn't you mean to do?" She came toward her, the broom still in her hand. "You've done nothing more than ask my advice, and I'm trying to help you.

If this man wants to find his mother, there's nothing you or I can do to stop him, but you need to arm him. He has to understand his face might remind her of a past she'd rather forget. God knows, life is not full of roses and sunshine. You only have to look at half the folks in this town to know that."

Kate bowed her head, her heart hurting to see such pain in Marian's eyes. "I understand."

"Do you?" Marian's voice softened, and she touched Kate's chin and lifted her face. A single tear slid down Marian's cheek. "That woman might have wanted that child more than she wanted anything in the world, but something about him, something about his conception might have made that impossible. The man needs to be prepared to hear things he might not like. That's all I'm saying." Marian released Kate's chin and smiled softly. "Now go. Get out of here before my George comes to pick me up and sees me all bent out of shape." She smiled. "You know the man likes me straight-backed and happy, right?"

Kate forced a small smile. "Right."

"Then off you go. I've told you all I can. What you tell this young man about his search is up to you. Good night, sweetheart."

"Good night..." Kate blinked back her tears. "I love you, you know."

Marian laughed and swiped her fingers under her eyes a second time. "Yeah, you and all the rest of this town. I love you, too. Now get out of here."

Kate hesitated and then hugged her, Marian's back pressed firmly to Kate's chest. "I'd be lost without you, you know."

Marian patted Kate's hand. "I know."

Kate released Marian and walked outside, grateful for the falling snow camouflaging her tears. Marian had mentioned difficult circumstances. Had something horrible happened to her friend?

Crossing the street, she walked to the promenade railing and stared out toward the dark ocean. How did she even begin to suggest to Mac what she suspected might have happened to Marian? Something heinous that no one in the Cove knew about. Something that maybe they should never know.

SITTING IN HIS room above the Coast, Mac leaned over his guitar toward the notebook on his bed. He whipped the pen from between his teeth, marked a few notes, stuck the pen back in his mouth and strummed through them again. Rubbish. Complete and utter rubbish. Laying the guitar on the bed, he picked up the notebook and flipped a page to the lyrics he'd written in a frenzied rush the night before.

They spoke of falling in love, heartache, risk, pain and the joyous rewards of finding that special someone. They also spoke of a man stripping himself bare in front of a woman. Laying his demons at her feet and praying she still loved him.

Uncertainty and fear rolled through his chest. No matter how much he wanted to explore a relationship with Kate, he couldn't shake the irrational notion of something happening to her as it had to Jilly. He knew everyone worried about losing a loved one suddenly and senselessly, but for him, the terrifying nightmare had become his reality.

The tentative steps he'd made toward loving Kate scared the hell out of him.

He'd made love to her, held her, kissed her and adored her, but thinking past the physical into the emotional sent chills through him. It was neither right nor fair to Kate to keep anything back if they wanted to make a go of their relationship, but he had no idea how to destroy the imagined horrors that stopped him from risking his heart.

Glancing at the wall clock above the small corner desk, Mac took a deep breath.

Eight thirty.

If Kate had gone through with her plan to catch Marian as she closed the bakery, he would've expected to have heard from her by now. He'd contemplated calling her but decided it would be best for Kate to return to him in her own time.

Impatient to talk to her, he put his guitar on the bed and walked to the window. A light covering of snow had turned his view of Templeton into a wintery paradise, but that was an illusion. The Cove was full of the same hurts and disappointments as any other town. Except Templeton had caught him in a mystifying snare, and Mac was no longer sure he wanted to escape.

He swung away at a tentative knock.

Praying Kate stood on the other side, he opened the door. He relaxed his shoulders. "Hey."

"Hey." Kate held his gaze for a moment before brushing past him into the room.

Her complexion was paler than usual, her beautiful dark brown eyes shaded with misery. The light gray shadows under her eyes and the tightness of her lips showed all too clearly that whatever had happened at the bakery, it hadn't been good.

She stopped dead center in the room, her arms crossed.

He cleared his throat. "You okay?"

She shook her head.

Unsure whether she wanted him to hold her, he made the choice to do so. Stepping toward her, Mac opened his arms. She exhaled and rushed toward him, her arms coming tightly around his waist, her head on his chest. "Oh, Mac."

Oh, Mac? He swallowed. What did that mean? Had things gone that badly with Marian?

He pressed his lips to her hair and tightened his arms around her. "What happened?"

An oppressive silence filled the room as he stared toward the window. A coldness swept through him, and he mentally rebuilt the armor around his heart that Kate had helped eased away, plate by plate. Now, he sensed bad news was coming. Something he wouldn't want to hear.

He lifted his chin and gently leaned back. "Tell me."

Her eyes searched his before she moved from his embrace. She walked to the window and stared into the distance before abruptly turning. "Something happened to Marian to make her give your father up for adoption. Something I'm not sure we should make her relive. Not when she's so happy with George. So happy in the Cove. It wouldn't be right. I know she listed her name to be contacted by her son if he came looking for her, but that was years ago. Maybe she changed her mind and forgot to take her name off the register."

Mac felt himself go rigid. "Something bad as in what?"

"I don't know. She didn't tell me, but that doesn't mean I couldn't read between the lines to know something's there. Our conversation sent Marian into a tailspin. She paled right in front of me. Her words spilled from her mouth at ninety miles an hour."

"What words?" He took her elbow, gently leading her to the bed. "Sit down and tell me what she said."

She slowly lowered to the bed and curled her fingers over the edges, her knuckles white. "I've been grappling for an hour with how to tell you, and, now I'm here, I still don't know." Her eyes glinted with tears.

"Kate, I'm a big boy. Whatever it is, I'll handle it."

"Okay." She exhaled a shaky breath. "I'm scared your dad might have been the product of a sexual assault."

"What?" Mac sucked in a breath, his hands curling into fists as he stared at her. "Are you sure?"

A tear slipped over her lashes and she swiped at it. "I don't know. If not that, then maybe Marian was in an abusive relationship that I'm guessing she wanted her baby to be no part of. She asked me what the son wanted from his mother. What he expected. Then it was as though a switch flipped inside her, and she started saying things about circumstances around a child's conception. What if the son's face reminds his mother of a time she doesn't want to revisit? If Marian wasn't abused, maybe her partner cheated on her. Or she was in love with a married man who refused to leave his wife. I don't know, but I do know, I've never seen her so wretched before. Not ever."

The breath left Mac's lungs, and he sank down on the bed beside her as sickness gripped his stomach. She rubbed her hand over his back as he leaned forward to rest his forearms on his thighs. He stared at the tattoos on his arms. The artwork served as a constant reminder of the dark and horrible places people were forced to go, to live in and, hopefully, survive. He'd commissioned these tattoos when he'd been angry, confused and uncertain of how to crawl out of his black hole after Jilly's death.

Lately, the markings had become almost invisible to him. He knew they were there, but their symbolism meant survival and hope for a brighter future.

But now, the darkness was back.

He raised his head and met Kate's concerned gaze. "If there's a chance my dad was the product of abuse, I won't bring that memory back to Marian, and I won't bring that kind of burden into my family."

"Of course not. It wouldn't be fair to anyone. If it's true, it won't be fair to you, either."

He shook his head, tears burning behind his eyes. "My mother asked me not to dig any deeper, said the same thing to my father as though she predicted something like this resurfacing. Why the hell didn't I listen to her?" He stood and paced the room, his shock turning to anger. "I never should've come here. I never should've started all this.

Mum was right. Dad's search should've ended when Dad died, but I pursued it through my own selfish anger. To vent everything bad that had happened in my life. Not Dad's. Not Marian's."

"Maybe, but it's good that you tried to reconnect with your grandmother rather than sever all contact the way I did with Ali. Don't you see your choices were so much braver than mine? You forged ahead, despite knowing things might turn out badly. I, on the other hand, turned my back and tried to forget Ali and Dean's betrayal ever happened." Her voice cracked. "I tried to forget my miscarriage. How is your way of dealing with things worse than mine? You said before that I taught you about intention. Well, you've taught me about courage. We're even."

"Even?" He huffed a laugh, not wanting her to comfort or protect him from himself. "We are not even, Kate. You've given me hope of a better future. I've given you nothing but worry and pain for a woman you've known for years. We're not even." He stalked to the door. "You should go. If Marian was hurt by whoever fathered her son…" He shook his head. "I will not call that son of a bitch my grandfather. I need to leave. I need to be far,

far away from here where Marian never has to know me or Dana."

"But that's not fair to Marian."

The hurt in her eyes slashed at his heart, but he hardened his resolve. "None of this is fair, but it's how it is."

"By leaving, by not speaking to Marian, you're taking her choice away. You can't look anything like your father's father or she would've reacted to you way differently than she has. Maybe your father didn't resemble him either. You've said yourself, you see your dad in Marian."

He trembled as he opened the door. "Please, Kate. Let me go."

He stared into the corridor, listening to the rustle and scrape of her gathering her purse and rising from the bed. Her footsteps came closer until she stopped beside him.

She touched his arm. "I'll go, but I don't agree with you not speaking with Marian. She deserves to know you and your family exist. I'll have to tell her. How can I not?"

"I know, but it will be a lot kinder to her having it come from you and not forcing her to look at me, my father's son." His chest aching, he dropped his study to her mouth. "You're an amazing woman. Don't ever be with anyone who treats you as anything less than a queen." He lifted his gaze. "Do you hear me?"

She nodded, her eyes shining. "Then you go on and be somebody's king. For me."

He turned away from her, unable to bear looking into her eyes for another moment and not surrender to the deep need to kiss her, hold her, make love to her one more time. She walked out the door, and Mac firmly closed it behind her, his chest burning with loss.

CHAPTER NINETEEN

Kate took a bite of her seafood linguini and, instead of groaning in satisfaction as she usually did at the Seascape, she had to force the food down. Lowering her knife and fork, she picked up her water and looked at Izzy, who sat across the table. "It's no good. I can't go on like this."

"Can't go on like what?"

"Keeping what I know from Marian. Wondering if Mac is going to show up again. My nerves are shot to pieces."

"So, what are you going to do? Mac's been gone for a week now, and you've heard nothing from him." Izzy's gaze was sympathetic. "I hate to say it, but I think you're going to have to accept you're unlikely to see him again."

Kate's chest ached with sadness. "You're probably right, but I won't keep his existence from Marian. I can't even go into the bakery. I feel as though one look at me and she'll know the last time I was in there talking about a supposedly hypothetical adoption case I was actually talking about hers."

"Don't you think she might've guessed that already, seeing as you're usually in the bakery on a daily basis?"

"Probably." Kate jabbed her fork into her food and pushed it around her plate. "I need to say something to her, Iz. This secrecy is eating me up."

"Then tell her. I know I'd have to."

Kate sighed. "I'll have to tell her everything. That Mac was in town looking for his biological grandmother. That he already knew she lived in Templeton, but had no idea how to broach the subject with her, or even if he should." She took a deep breath and exhaled. "Then he decided it was better to leave things be, but as I knew what was going on, I wasn't comfortable keeping it from her. There, simple."

Izzy shook her head, took a bite of her pizza and swallowed. "Nothing about this is simple. Nothing about *Marian* is simple. If your theory that something horrendous happened to her is correct, you have to be prepared for the fallout."

"This is so damn hard." Kate swapped her

water for her wine and took a strengthening gulp. "The pain in Mac's and Marian's eyes is haunting me. I have to do something to bring closure for both of them. I could tell when I spoke to her that Marian is far from over what happened to her. I'm not even sure she's come to terms with giving up her baby. She loves everyone. Will do anything for everyone. How hard must it have been for her to give up her child?" Tears clogged her throat and Kate swallowed. "It isn't right that there's a family out there she knows nothing about. She's already lost the chance to ever know her son." Kate looked at her watch. "She'll be closing up now. It's past six thirty." She met Izzy's gaze. "There's no time like the present, right?"

"And what about Mac?"

"What about him?" Kate grabbed her wallet out of her purse. "He's gone. It's over. I have to do right by Marian now."

"And if Mac comes back? What then?"

Kate's heart beat faster as she put her wallet on the table. "Then nothing. I made it clear I wouldn't keep this from Marian. If he hates me for telling her?" She shrugged. "So be it. I told him how much Marian means to me. God, I told him how much *he* means to me." She pulled back her shoulders. "And he walked away anyway."

Izzy stared at her, her expression inscrutable.

Kate frowned. "What?"

"I'm just worried, that's all."

"I know you are. So am I."

"Don't you think Mac's reasons for keeping this new information from his family are valid? I'm not sure I wouldn't do the same, considering all the time that's passed."

"So you think telling Marian that Mac is her grandson is the wrong thing to do?"

"I didn't say that. You *have* to tell her. It's just going to be incredibly hard, and I think afterward, things are going to be even harder. At least, for a while."

Kate shook her head, tears in her eyes. "I really thought I was starting to get things in order." She picked up her glass of wine and drained it. "I'm talking to Ali again. I'm even going to help with her wedding arrangements."

The concern left Izzy's eyes, and she smiled. "Well, that's fantastic. Why didn't you tell me?"

"Because I've had all this going on with Mac. I'll be going to see Ali in the next couple of weeks. Hopefully, when we're together, we can finally both move on."

Izzy picked up her water. "That's great."

Kate slipped a twenty on to the table. "Do you mind settling the bill? Now I've built up the courage to speak to Marian, I need to see her before I change my mind."

"Sure."

Kate stood. "She deserves to know she has a family out there. What she does about that is up to her, but my conscience will be clear." Kate held Izzy's doubtful gaze. "What now?"

"Nothing. I just care about you. I don't want Marian or Mac to hold you culpable for whatever happens next."

"Everything will be okay." Kate pulled on her coat and smiled softly. "Thanks for being here for me, Iz." Kate squeezed her friend's shoulder. "I'll call you later."

"Make sure you do. I won't be able to sleep until I know how it went."

Kate nodded before heading for the restaurant door.

Outside, snow fell softly, a light wind making Kate step up her pace. Nerves jumped in her stomach and her mouth felt as though it were full of sand from Cowden beach, but she had to go through with talking to Marian.

In the week since Mac had left the Cove, her work had suffered, her appetite and her sleep drastically reduced. She missed him with a depth that was ridiculous considering the time they'd known one another. But her emptiness only served to emphasize her belief in what they could've had. She had been so independent, so unconcerned about men and relationships since Dean's betrayal, but Mac had made her want to take a risk again… to feel again.

Now he was gone.

But Marian was here, living and working in the same town. How could she possibly avoid this conversation and ever look Marian in the eye again?

With that prospect at the forefront of her mind, Kate stopped outside the bakery. Marian was arranging trays behind the counter, her brow furrowed. Taking a deep breath, Kate knocked on the door.

Marian looked up, startled. Then her expression changed, first to alarm and then annoyance. Kate's heart hammered as Marian slowly walked around the counter and across the length of the bakery to the front door. Their eyes locked through the glass, and Kate held herself still. She would not crumble. She would not run.

Marian opened the door wide. "I was wondering when you'd come back to finish our conversation. I've asked George to pick me up half an hour later than usual every night for the last week in case you came back. You'd better come in."

As THE TRAIN pulled into Templeton station, Mac thought over the conversations he'd had with his mother and Dana. His abrupt arrival back home had caused suspicion in his sister and relief in his mother. How stupid he'd been to think he could keep this secret to himself. His heart and mind had ached every day since he'd left the Cove.

And as for his feelings for Kate? He wanted her in his life. Desperately. God knew, she was already permanently in his heart.

Shouldering his bag, he grabbed his guitar from the vacant seat beside him and headed toward the exit. Tonight he would do everything he could to speak with Marian. After that, he would track down Kate and pray to God she still wanted him. That his panic, guilt and indecision hadn't ruined something with the potential to be amazing.

Hurrying from the train, he made his way through the station and out into the street. Approaching the first cab in line, he climbed in the back. "The Coast Inn, please."

"Right-o."

Mac settled back against the seat and stared at the passing streets, his heart picking up speed when they drove along Templeton's main road and out the other side. The taxi pulled into the Coast's parking lot, and Mac gathered his belongings and stepped out onto the pavement. He pushed a ten-pound note through the window. "Keep the change."

Mac headed inside, where a trio on stage was playing soft jazz, which went some way to calming his nerves. He looked around and caught a few nods from people he'd gotten to know a little.

He inhaled the scent of wood and beer, fried food and candle smoke, the smells somehow helping his need for familiarity and comfort. Why did it feel as though he'd come home when he'd just left his real home? Was Templeton where he was destined to be?

"Mac?"

Mac started and turned toward the bar. "Hey, Dave." He walked closer. "How are you doing?"

Suspicion clouded Dave's gaze, his palms flat on the bar. "I didn't think we'd see you again."

Mac leaned his guitar against the bar and dropped his bag to the floor. "Neither did I. Change of plans."

"And those plans brought you back to the Cove again? Maybe you're changing your mind about this small town you didn't have much of a liking for when you first arrived."

"You could say that." Mac held the landlord's gaze.

He got the distinct impression he had a long way to go to convince Dave and Vanessa he was a good guy, but Mac wasn't one to give up on people easily. Testament to why he was back in Templeton. "Any chance my room is still free?"

"It could be."

Mac raised his eyebrows. "Could be?"

"It's empty, but it isn't ready for guests."

"Right. Well, any room is fine."

Dave crossed his arms. "You've got a different look about you. You being here wouldn't have anything to do with Kate, would it?"

The landlord's wily observation brought unwelcome hurt, and Mac drew his focus to the band. "Partly. There's other stuff I need to deal with, too."

He turned and Dave dropped his arms. "I'll let Vanessa know you're back. I'm sure she'll be happy. Why don't you sit and have a beer while we sort out your room?"

Fearing a beer might impede his desire to talk to Marian right away, Mac shook his head. "I've got something I need to do. Could I leave my bag and guitar somewhere?"

"Sure. You can store them behind the bar." Dave walked to a board behind the bar where the room keys were hung. He lifted one of them and handed it to Mac. "Here, take this. Your room should be ready by the time you get back. You know the procedure if we're locked up for the night."

Mac took the key. "Thanks. See you later."

The sooner he spoke to Marian, the sooner some of the load weighing on his shoulders would lift. Although that mind-set was doing a pathetic job of alleviating his nausea.

He headed out and soon came to the bakery. Mac fought his hesitation and peered through the glass.

His heart stopped.

Kate.

Her hand in Marian's.

Their expressions uncertain.

Was he too late? Had Kate told Marian about him? Damn it. Yet, how the hell could he blame her? Kate had told him she would share his story with Marian, and Kate's integrity was just another reason to add to his list of why he loved her.

He had to get inside and explain himself.

He knocked on the door.

Kate and Marian leapt apart and stared wide-eyed toward him. Mac struggled to keep his face impassive. He drew on the strength it had taken him to get through Jilly's funeral. His fixed composure then had gotten him through those horrible hours.

Marian shot to her feet, her smile wide as she came toward him and pulled open the door. "Mac! You're back."

Shock crumpled his demeanor, and he stiffened. She was glad to see him?

He returned her smile, his heart thumping. "Hey, Marian."

She gripped his arm and propelled him inside. "Come in, come in. It's so great to see you."

Mac stumbled to a stop and stared at Kate. Slowly she stood and gently shook her head, her gaze full of warning.

Marian didn't know. Kate hadn't told her.

Relieved, he turned to Marian. "Am I disturbing you?"

"Not at all." She gripped his arm. "Both of you take a seat. I'll fire up the espresso machine. What a night this is turning out to be. Two young people brought together in my little bakery after hours…" She hummed a couple of notes. "Well, fancy that."

There was no mistaking the glint in Marian's eyes as she whipped her gaze between him and Kate. Matchmaking was on the older woman's mind. Mac inhaled and slowly released it. He needed to tell Marian why he was really here before he even thought about mending his relationship with Kate.

He cleared his throat. "Marian…"

"Sit." She pulled out a chair next to Kate, even as she remained standing. "And you, Kate. Sit down. Both of you."

Kate stood stock still, her eyes wide and her mouth slightly open. Mac wasn't sure she was actually breathing.

He slid his focus to Marian. "I came here to speak to you alone."

The older woman's smile. "You did?"

Guilt burned at his cheeks and he nodded. "Yes."

"But…" She looked between Mac and Kate once…twice…three times… Slowly, she sat, her face paling. "No." She gripped the table. "No."

"Oh, Marian." Kate rushed forward and slid her arm around Marian's shoulders. "It's okay."

Marian shrugged her off, and Kate stepped back, fear of Marian's distress showing in her eyes. Marian glared. "It's not okay. You should go. I think it best you leave me and Mac to talk alone, don't you?"

The icy tone of Marian's voice raised every hair on Mac's body as he watched Kate gather up her purse, as she looked from Marian to Mac. Hopelessness swirled in her pretty dark eyes, and her hand trembled when she lightly placed it on his arm before brushing past him toward the door.

Once the door shut, Mac sat next to Marian and looked her square in the eyes. She stared straight back…and her determined expression had never reminded him of his father more.

CHAPTER TWENTY

KATE SLOWLY WALKED away from the bakery, glancing over her shoulder in futile hope that either Mac or Marian would call her back. Even though she wasn't part of their story, she had been drawn into Mac's need for closure, and the possibility of Marian's pain... or her elation.

A sob gathered in Kate's throat. If the prospect of Marian's upset wasn't bad enough, there was also the chance she could lose two people she cared about deeply because of their shared tragedy. One of whom she most definitely loved...and the other with whom she could be *in* love.

Tears burned as anguish pressed down on her, making her want to burst back into the bakery and tell Mac and Marian how important they were to her. Offer to heal their pain in any way she could. Yet, deep down, she knew to do such a thing would be destructive without Mac and Marian talking first. They were the main players on the stage, not her.

But that didn't lessen her sense of responsibility. She wanted to be there for them. She continued walking and swiped at her tears. They were both good, loving people. So very alike in their passion and protectiveness of the people they loved. It brought joy to Kate's heart that Marian and Mac were family.

And so, for now, it was up to them. Just as it was up to her to do something about her sister. Mac's bravery in talking with Marian made Kate want to show the same courage and set up a date to visit Ali. She pulled her phone from her bag and dialed her sister's number, sneaking another hopeful look behind her. The street remained empty.

Ali picked up. "Kate? Hi."

Kate fought to concentrate on her own life for now. "Hi, Ali. Listen, if you don't have any plans, why don't I come and stay with you next weekend? Things have calmed down at work, and I think I deserve a whole weekend off. What do you say?"

"That would be great!" Ali's excitement reverberated down the line. "You could bring this guy you've been seeing. We'll go out. Have something to eat. A few drinks."

Kate ducked into a shop doorway and leaned heavily against the wall. "I told you that was over before it even began."

"I don't believe you. There was something different in the way you spoke about him."

Kate closed her eyes. Wasn't it ironic that the last time she'd spoken to Ali, she wanted to keep Ali from meeting Mac, and now that he wasn't hers, she'd love nothing more than to introduce him to her sister. Mac had changed her, made her grow, and now she was 100 percent certain that she'd never allow anyone to hurt her again like Ali and Dean had.

"I'll be coming alone," she said.

"Oh. Well, if you're sure?"

"I am." Kate stepped from the doorway and hurried toward her apartment. "There are things I want to discuss with you. Things I'm not sure it would be good for Denny to hear when I get there."

There was a beat of silence before her sister sighed. "I understand."

Kate pulled back her shoulders and drew strength from Mac's courage in returning to Templeton. He hadn't run this time. Instead, he'd done the sensible thing and gone away, thought things through, maybe even spoken with his mother and sister. Now he'd returned to make things right.

She would do the same.

Kate inhaled. "We need to talk about what happened, Ali. Why it happened…and how much you hurt me. There are things I need to say to you so I can finally move on. I also want to apologize for enforcing our estrangement, calling you names. Neither of us handled the situation as we should have."

"But it was so long ago, Kate. Can't we just bury it?"

"No. I've been going through some stuff. I've learned what can happen if you bury things that have hurt you. I won't do it, Ali. I don't want to."

"Okay." Her sister sighed. "How about I ask Denny to disappear on Friday night and we'll have a night in like we used to? I'll get wine, some nibbles, and we'll listen to Whitney Houston." She laughed, the sound nervous. "Remember those nights?"

Kate smiled softly, love for her sister swelling inside her. "Of course I do. Those were the best nights."

"I love you, Kate. I'm so sorry…" Ali sniffed. "Really, really sorry."

"I know you are." Sorrow clutched at Kate's heart. "I'll see you Friday, okay?"

"Okay. See you then."

Kate ended the call and let herself into the apartment block. Curiosity about how things were going between Marian and Mac whirled in her mind as she rode the elevator to the fourth floor. She stepped into the corridor, worrying that she might have lost both Marian and Mac for good.

She admonished herself. Whatever happened, she had played a part in bringing two wonderful people together. That was something she could have pride in, at least.

Entering her apartment, she tossed her purse on to the couch. Everything would work out as it was supposed to. Hadn't she taught herself, through the pain and disappointments she witnessed in her work, to believe everything that happened was for a reason. A test of strength. That, for the most part, people were stronger than they gave themselves credit for. Mac had proven that to be true and so had Marian.

Now, it was Kate's turn to do the same.

MAC FOUGHT THE urge to put his arms around Marian as she covered her face in her hands.

He felt helpless and guilty, and the need to let this wonderful woman know him and his family made him wish he could fast-forward through the next moments so he could learn if Marian wanted to be part of the family.

Slowly, she lifted her hands from her face. Her eyes glinted with tears in the semidarkness. "He's dead? My son is dead?"

Mac swallowed the lump that lodged in his throat. "Yes, but his life wasn't in vain. He was a good father, Marian. A hardworking laborer who taught my sister and me the importance of manners, hard work and honesty." He stared into her eyes. "I need to be honest with you. When I came to the Cove I was mad. Really mad."

She frowned. "With me?"

He smiled wryly. "No. Not that I realized it at the time. I was mad at life, and Dad's death was the last thing I could take. I'd been pretending I was okay, that I'd handle losing him, but his death broke the seal on my anger. I chose to blame you for everything that had happened to me. That was wrong, and I'm sorry."

She nodded, drew a napkin from her apron pocket and dabbed at her cheeks. "I don't know what to say. I can't think…" She shook her head. "I'm not sure what I can do for you and your family now." She pressed her hand to her stomach. "My George…he doesn't know about this. He doesn't know about your father."

Breaking through his apprehension about touching her, Mac covered her hand where it was curled into a fist on the table. "From what Kate's told me about your relationship with your husband, your love for one another, I'm sure George will want nothing more than to support you. Whatever you decide to do next." He squeezed her hand, praying she recognized his sincerity. "I'm not expecting anything from you. Nothing at all. My father was a good man, but he also had trouble finding the courage to see things through. Especially personal things. It was him who found you, Marian, not me. I just finished what my father started. What happens next, what you do or don't tell me, is up to you. I promise."

She drew away and folded her hands into her lap. "Does Kate know about your father? That's a stupid question. Of course she does. The way she looked at me when she came here with a story about an adoption case…" She raised her damp eyes to the ceiling. "There's no fool like an old fool."

"You're not a fool. Coming to you with a hypothetical case was Kate's attempt to spare us both pain."

Her brow furrowed. "What do you mean?"

"She loves you, Marian. Fiercely. She told me what you did for her, what you were to her through losing her baby—"

"She told you about that?" Her eyes widened and then softened, a small smile playing at her lips. "I'm sorry. Carry on."

"Kate wanted to give you the opportunity to talk to her in confidence and, at the same time, stop me from talking to you when there was every chance you'd send me away. Kate was doing what she does best."

Marian swiped at her tears. "Looking after people. Caring for them."

Mac nodded. "Yes."

Marian glanced toward the window. "George will be here shortly, so we haven't much time."

"Then let me tell you a little bit about your family, and I'll go. Just letting you know my father had a good life, a loving family, has given me the peace I was looking for." He stared into her eyes. "I hope, eventually, knowing we exist and Dad had his faults but did his best to ensure we were cared for will bring you peace, too. He loved us deeply, Marian, and I'm sure when he found out he was adopted, his capability of more love was what led him to look for you."

She nodded, her shoulders relaxing. "He sounds wonderful."

Mac smiled, his heart hurting. "He was. I understand that now. My bitterness was clouding my understanding of him…of the situation. But now I see everything clearly." He took a deep breath. "Those two little monkeys Dana brought into the bakery are Lily and little Mac…your great-grandchildren."

Marian sucked in a breath. "My…" She closed her eyes, and tears slipped over her cheeks. "I have great-grandchildren."

Unable to resist hugging her a moment longer, Mac stood and carefully slipped his arms around her trembling shoulders and squeezed. "We're a good family, Marian. We want you to be a part of that. Please, take all the time you need. There's no pressure. If you want to write to me or call me, then do, but if that's too much, I'll respect your wishes. Whatever they might be." He stood back and lowered to his haunches. "I'll go, but take this." He reached into his leather jacket and pulled out one of his promo cards. "My number, email and address are on there. When you're ready—"

"Wait." She blinked, and her tears dried, her gaze determined, as though the spirit he had become used to seeing in her when she worked the bakery had reemerged. "Don't go. Not until I've at least explained what happened all those years ago. Why I had no choice but to give up your father."

Foreboding dried Mac's throat, and he straightened before returning to his seat. "There's plenty of time. You don't have to—"

"I do. I can't let you walk out of here when you were brave enough to tell me who you are. You've seen me with my customers, with the residents…" Her pleading gaze bored into his. "Am I wrong to guess you've thought me a charlatan? Someone who gave up their baby yet embraced the Templeton community as though the people here are my family?" She shook her head, her jaw tight. "Of course you have. As would I, had I been in your shoes."

"Marian—"

"The people here are my family, Mac. Each and every one of them." She rolled her eyes. "Even the ones who are a pain in the butt, or who come in here asking for my advice and then go off and do the complete opposite." She smiled. "They're all my children. They're every single child that could have been mine. When George brought me here, he changed my life by making me a part of this fabulous community. I'm home, Mac… and it's wonderful."

He leaned back as some of the tension in his shoulders dispelled. "I get that."

"Do you?" She raised her eyebrows, her expression questioning. "Really?"

"Yes. Templeton is pretty unique."

"In what way is it to you?"

He sighed. "Maybe it's not so much the town, but the people. I've never considered a small place as somewhere I'd like to live. I thought I was a city guy through and through, but during the time I've spent here…" He shook his head, unable to find the right words to explain how quickly Templeton—and Kate—had gotten inside him. "It's made me want to hang around a while longer. See if it's somewhere I might want to live permanently."

She smiled softly, her eyes glinting with mischief. "Kate's pretty fabulous, isn't she?"

Warmth hit his cheeks, and he met her smile. "Yeah, she is."

"Well, let me tell you what Templeton has

done for me. Just like your father looked for me, I looked for him on and off for years."

"I know. You signed a register to say you'd be willing to be contacted by him if he ever wanted that."

She nodded. "As my search came up empty over and over again, I assumed I wasn't meant to be anyone's mother and learned to live with that." She smiled. "But when I met my George and he brought me here, I finally understood I was meant to find George and mother the youngsters in the Cove instead. I've been blessed, Mac. Truly."

"I can see that just by looking at you. You've got a special kind of light." He leaned forward. "A light I'd like you to share with my family, your family, if you ever want to."

Her eyes filled with tears and she nodded. "Thank you, but first you need to know why I gave up your father."

Mac leaned back. "Okay."

She briefly closed her eyes before opening them again. "I was barely sixteen when I fell in love with a man three years my senior. He promised me the moon, and I believed him. Eventually, over months, he segregated me from my family and friends. Made me believe school was a waste of time and I didn't need an education. He made me believe I needed nothing but him." She smiled sadly. "Just another thing my George proved wrong about love. When George brought me here, he didn't keep me to himself. He encouraged me to join in with everyone, let them get to know me. Told me I was too good, too smart, too wonderful for him to keep to himself." Pride shone in her soft brown eyes. "That's a real man, Mac. A man willing to share a woman with the rest of the world. Show her off and trust she won't go too far or forget him. That's a good man. A brave man."

Mac's mind turned to Kate. God, he'd want to share her with the whole world if she was his. No one like Kate should ever solely belong to one person. "I understand."

"Good." She grinned. "Then you're a real man, too. Anyway…" She inhaled. "Eventually, I ran away with this man. His abuse started slowly. Name-calling turned to shoving, shoving to slapping, slapping to…" She swallowed. "You get the picture. For years after I found the courage to leave him, I couldn't understand how the hurting happened. Believed *I* let it happen. These men are clever, Mac. Very, very clever. They groom and then charm and then, once you're entirely theirs, they pounce."

Mac screwed one hand into a fist, the other gripping the side of his seat. "What happened to you wasn't your fault. You know that, right?"

She huffed a laugh. "Good Lord, I do now, and woe betide any man who raises a hand or a curse word to me, or any one of my children in this town. I'd come down on him like a ton of bricks. Mark my words."

The fire in her eyes relaxed Mac's fingers. "And then I guess you got pregnant."

"Yes, and that baby gave me all the fight I needed to leave. There was no way on God's earth that man would hurt my baby. I went home with my tail between my legs, but I hid the pregnancy from my parents."

"You hid it? How is that possible?"

She smiled softly. "It's possible, believe me. I never got too big, and bigger clothes were easy enough to find in the charity shops. You need to understand, my parents were devoutly religious. I was desperate. I had nowhere else to go. No one else to turn to."

She shook her head, her chest rising as she inhaled. "Maybe my parents knew and decided to ignore it. I don't know, but if they did, I'm convinced they would have cast me out. All I knew was, I needed nourishment, a place to sleep while I carried that precious babe. When the pains started, I took the bus to the hospital and gave birth. Having finally gotten away from my boyfriend, the decision was mine what happened next. I knew there was a chance my ex might look for me, and I wanted my child far, far away from him, where he could never hurt him." A tear rolled over her cheek. "The rest, you know."

"And your parents? Did they forgive you?"

"No."

Sickness gripped him. "Never?"

"Never."

The heartbreak in her eyes escalated Mac's growing care for her and, once again, he stood and wrapped her in his embrace. His heart hitched when she moved her hand to his arm and smoothed her fingers back and forth. "It was a long time ago, and it seems to me, looking at you, my baby boy soared and did good. Real good."

Mac rested his chin on her head and smiled. "He sure did."

"I spent many years alone, drawing comfort and friendship from anyone and everyone I met. At the grand old age of fifty-six, I met George, the true love of my life. We were at a mystery readers' conference, and I don't think we stopped talking from the moment he sat down beside me until two weeks later when I threw caution to the wind, packed up and came to live with him in Templeton."

"You left your whole life? Just like that?" Mac raised his eyebrows, "I'm not sure I could be that brave. You were that certain about George?"

"Yes." She smiled. "As I think you are about Kate."

The bakery door opened, and Mac stepped away from Marian. He turned and met the protective gaze of a man around Marian's age. Mac forced a smile, suddenly nervous and put out his hand. "You must be George. Mac Orman."

Slowly, the man came forward and gripped Mac's hand, his gaze wary. "I am, and what exactly are you doing with your arms all around my Marian?" His focus switched to his wife. "Are you all right, my love?"

Marian stood and swiped her fingers under her eyes. "Never better. Now why don't you grab my purse from out back while I see Mac to the door?"

George released Mac's hand and looked

again between him and Marian. "Mac. Aren't you the young man I heard got up on stage at the fund-raiser the other week?"

Mac nodded. "The one and only."

"People have been saying you've got some good playing in you." George smiled. "Fine playing, in fact. You planning on staying in town a while?"

"I—" he looked at Marian "—don't know."

Marian came forward and clasped his elbow. "Of course he is. For one thing, the boy is halfway to falling in love. Why would he leave now?"

George chuckled and took Mac's hand in his. "If my Marian says you're halfway to falling in love, son, you're already all the way there." He dropped Mac's hand. "I'm sure I'll see you around."

Mac watched George wander toward the back of the bakery and huffed a laugh. "You're made for each other."

"Yes, we are." Marian steered him toward the door. "Now go and find Kate."

Mac stopped, his smile dissolving as he looked into his grandmother's eyes. "You really want me to stay around a while longer?"

She cupped his jaw in her hand. "Yes. Just

give me some time to get my head around the
fact I have family and tell George, okay?"

He nodded, hesitated and then gently kissed
her cheek before heading through the door.
Once outside, he turned back. Marian smiled,
her hand touching the place he'd kissed.

CHAPTER TWENTY-ONE

KATE STARED FROM the travel bag on her bed to the open doors of her wardrobe. Even though she'd arranged to see Ali a week from now, the need to do something to prove to herself that she was consciously moving forward meant Kate would take her time packing—over a whole week—to keep her vow at the forefront of her mind.

If it took seven days to convince herself that losing Mac and, possibly Marian, in one fell swoop was for the greater good, so be it. If they came together it would do so much to bolster Kate's belief that hurt and pain led to bigger and better things. That losing her baby, experiencing heartbreak and betrayal, had made her stronger, wiser and better able to help herself and others. That was something she could most definitely live with.

Strolling to her chest of drawers, she pulled a drawer open and extracted a couple of T-shirts and some underwear. Her hands shook as she laid the garments in the bag. The thought of not seeing Mac again had such a frightening effect on her. She didn't know him, not really, so why did she feel as though she'd known him her entire life?

Abandoning her packing, she walked from her bedroom into the kitchen, where she'd purposely left her phone so she'd stop looking at it every five minutes. She picked it up.

No missed calls. No texts.

How was she going to get through this next week? Maybe it would be best for her to go to the bakery tomorrow morning and grab her usual bacon roll and coffee. Brazen it out with Marian, let her say whatever it was she needed to say. Whatever the outcome, Kate would know where she stood with at least one of the two people she cared so much about.

As for Mac…

The peal of her apartment intercom bounced from the walls. Kate stilled, hope painfully rising in her chest. "Please, God…" she murmured, her eyes tightly closed. "Please let me talk to him one more time."

She opened her eyes, walked to the door and pressed the buzzer. "Hello?"

"Kate, it's Mac. Can I come up?"

His rich, smooth voice slipped down the line and straight into her heart.

Her breath hitched. "Of course. I'll leave the door open."

She buzzed him in, replaced the receiver and opened the apartment door. Then she rushed around her living room, stuffing the DVD cases of *Love, Actually* and *Notting Hill* under the couch. She didn't want him to know she'd been considering blubbering over two of the best romantic comedies of all time later that night.

Grabbing her coffee mug, she hurried into the kitchen area and tossed it into the sink, the clang of china against porcelain making her flinch. *Calm down. Calm down.* She took a few breaths and then reached for a bottle of red wine from her rack. Just as she pulled two glasses from an overhead cabinet, Mac's footsteps sounded outside her apartment door.

Still holding the glasses, she turned and prayed her smile didn't look as manic as it felt. "Mac. Hi."

He closed the door behind him, his eyes on hers. "Hi."

Kate crossed her arms, her sadness things hadn't worked out between them squeezing her heart. His expression didn't speak of sunshine and flowers, happy reunions and undying declarations of love. She swallowed. "Wine?"

"Sure." He walked slowly through her apartment, taking off his jacket before tossing it on the arm of her couch.

Her hands trembled as she unscrewed the wine and filled the glasses. She wanted him so badly it hurt. Why did she feel the moment he stood too close, she'd burst into tears? It was the idea of losing him once she'd found him. It was the notion of being alone again when she no longer wanted to live that way. She wanted to live with Mac.

When she smelled him, she turned. "Oh."

He stood so close, flecks of silver showed in his brilliant blue eyes. He took the glasses from her and put them on the counter. Her heart raced as he drew his study slowly over her face and lingered on her mouth before lowering his lips to hers.

Her body turned to traitorous mush as she leaned into him, a whimper escaping into his mouth. She kissed him, her fingers moving over his shoulders into his hair as she urged him closer. Heat washed through her as her body lit with arousal and her mind whirled.

Please, God, let this mean he wants me. Let it mean he's not leaving.

His hands moved to her waist and, with one fluid motion, his lips left hers, and he sat her atop the counter. Instinctively, she opened her legs, and he stood in between them, his gaze burning into hers. "I told Marian about my dad. About me. Dana and the kids."

"And?" Kate hardly dared to breathe, afraid he might step away from her when she wanted him this close forever. "What did she say?"

He smiled gently, the seriousness in his eyes melting to something infinitely softer. "She wants me to hang around a while longer."

Kate's heart jolted. "Really?"

"Yes." He pushed a stray curl from her cheek and tucked it behind her ear. "If that's okay with you, too."

She swallowed. "Of course it is."

"Only..."

"Only what?" Panic sped her heart. Didn't he know, couldn't he sense, how right it was for him to be here? For them to be together to learn more about one another...to *love* more about each other. "Only what, Mac?"

He inhaled a long breath and released it. "Marian needs time to process this."

Confusion whirled through her as the light

in his eyes dimmed and his brow furrowed. "And that's not okay?"

"I'm worried once she's thought about everything, once she's spoken to her husband…" His hands still gripping her waist, he tipped his head back for a long moment before dropping his chin. "I'm worried she'll ask me to leave. To go far away where she won't have to see me. The trouble is, I don't know if I'll be able to do that. Not now. Not now I've met you. I'm falling in love with you, Kate."

Relief pulsed through her, and she grinned. "I think I might be falling in love with you, too."

He huffed a laugh, dropping his forehead to hers before pulling back. He kissed her again. Long and deep, his fingers digging deliciously into her flesh to bring her closer. Then he drew back. "You make me strong. You make me imagine a happy future. Something I never thought would ever exist for me ever again. You're healing me, Kate."

She leaned closer and kissed him, tears burning her eyes. "And you're healing me. I'm going to see Ali next week so we can finally put the past where it belongs. Now I've found the closure I was looking for…in you. In you and everything you've done with Marian since you came here. You've made me see how things can be if you don't run away or pretend they never happened. Things happen, and we have to face them."

"And from now on, I want to face them with you. I've taken my room at the Coast. I can stay there until Marian knows what she wants to happen next. After that—"

"You can move in with me." The words burst from her mouth so quickly, heat burned her cheeks. She blinked. "If you want to, that is."

He laughed and kissed her again. "Oh, I want to. I want to very, very much."

She smiled against his mouth. "Shall we go to bed?"

"Absolutely."

Wine abandoned, Mac lifted her from the counter, and Kate's breath caught as she wrapped her legs firmly around his waist, her hands gripping his broad shoulders. She dropped kisses to the tendons in his neck, the stubble of his jaw, drew his bottom lip between her teeth and enjoyed every ounce of happiness that swirled through her.

Kate pulled back and looked deep into Mac's eyes. All she knew in that moment was the man holding her was the man she wanted to be with. Always.

EPILOGUE

Three weeks later

KATE STARED TOWARD the Oceanside's door, her foot bouncing on the floor. Where were Marian and George? Where were Dana and the children?

Mac slid his fingers over her thigh and gripped tight. "Stop. They'll be here."

She faced him. He stared back at her, a smile playing at his lips. She sighed. "How can you be so relaxed about this?"

"How can I not? In the last three weeks, I've spent time with you and I've spent time with Marian. George knows who I am and has welcomed me. Marian can't get enough of hearing stories about me and my family. About Dad. Nothing can go wrong."

Inexplicable foreboding continued to bother her as apprehension lingered on the unresolved aspects of her splintered family. "I just don't want any of this to fall apart for you. You've done so much to get to this point."

"It won't."

She glanced toward the door again. "Things are better between Ali and me, but we still have a long way to go, Mac. Who's to say Dana won't be as happy with all this as you are?"

"Hey." He touched his finger to her chin, turning her face to his. "It's going to be fine. I've spoken to Dana and—"

"Uncle Mac!" The scream of Mac's five-year-old niece, Lily, sliced through the civil drone of the diners' voices. "We came to see you again."

"Hey, you." Mac stood and bent down to scoop his niece into a hug. "I swear you've grown three inches in the past month."

She giggled, and Kate looked at Lily's mother and brother as Dana and little Mac walked toward their table. Dana's smile seemed frozen in place, and Kate inhaled against her nerves as she slowly rose and forced a wide smile. "Dana, it's nice to finally meet you."

Mac's sister nodded, her shoulders high and her smile strained. "You, too. I hope we're not late."

"Not at all. Come and sit down. Wine?"

"Wine. Yes. I'd love some."

Kate smiled as Dana slid into a seat around the circular table. Kate picked up the wine and filled Dana's glass, before topping off her own. She held out the glass to Mac's sister. "Here. Cheers."

They clinked glasses as Mac returned to his seat and his niece and nephew ran toward the windows at the far end of the restaurant. Kate drank deep before returning her glass to the table, trembling ever so slightly. She glanced at Mac who carefully watched her, before he turned to Dana. "So, you're here."

Dana blew a breath. "I am. I tried to persuade Mum to come, but she refused. Said it's best for us to get to know Marian first."

"If that's Mum's choice, there's nothing either of us can do about it." Mac picked up his wine and sipped. "She'll come around, eventually."

"I hope so." Dana turned to Kate. "How are things going living with my free-spirited brother?"

Kate laughed and relaxed her shoulders. The gentle teasing in Dana's eyes bolstered Kate's confidence that the evening might go well, after all. "Fine. I've learned he finds it

hard to sit still for five minutes and I'm finding scraps of song lyrics all over the apartment. But, apart from that…"

"Hey." Mac frowned. "I am here, you know."

They laughed as a shadow fell over the
table. Kate looked up, and her stomach flip-
flopped. Marian. Her eyes shone with happiness and as she stared at Mac, her growing
love for him obvious, Kate's heart jolted with
pleasure to see her dear friend so happy when
things could have gone so very wrong.

Mac immediately stood and wrapped his
arms around his grandmother, pulling her
tight to his chest. "Hi, Marian."

"Hi." She gently placed her hands on his
back. "We've been hanging around outside
for the last five minutes."

Mac drew back. "Why?"

"Nerves. Something I'm not used to, but
they seem to have become my closest friends
since this morning." Marian turned to Dana
and held out her hand. "Marian Cohen. And
this is my wonderful husband, George. You
must be Dana."

Dana stood and took Marian's hand. Kate
noticed that Dana's fingers slightly shook,
and she wasn't the least surprised when Marian held Dana's hand tightly in both of hers.

"It's so lovely to meet you. And you and Mac look so alike." She glanced around the restaurant. "Aren't the children...ah, there they are."

Kate looked toward Lily and little Mac as they stood with their noses pressed to the glass, no doubt watching the dark ocean. She cleared her throat. "Why don't we sit?"

George held out Marian's seat, and they all sat.

Prepared for a few moments of awkward silence, Kate took a deep breath to start a conversation...about anything.

Marian got there first. "So, Dana, do you work? I'd love to learn more about you."

"I did until Lily came along, but now I'm lucky enough that my husband's job means I can stay home and be a full-time mum. I wouldn't want to do anything else."

"Well, that's wonderful." Marian glanced toward the children once more. "They are two of the bonniest babies I've ever seen. So full of life."

Mac leaned forward. "Yeah, and mischief."

"Is there any other way children should be?" Marian raised an eyebrow at her grandson. "Don't you think for one minute, Mac Orman, that I don't know you're the cool uncle who winds them up as much as possible when you're with them. I've got your card marked just by looking into those eyes of yours."

Everyone laughed, and the atmosphere calmed. Kate leaned back in her chair as the conversation flowed and they placed their orders. She stared at the faces around the table and wondered if this was a family that would teach her how things could be. If this was the family that, along with Mac, would make her believe that her goals were relevant and that it was okay that she wasn't money-driven like her mother and sister.

That it was okay if she dreamed of marrying, having children and being content to stay at home with them like Dana. She couldn't think of anything more fulfilling, anything more that would heal the pain of her past and lead to acceptance that she was a good person, a caring person, a person who could be the mother her children deserved.

The waiter walked away, and everyone but her and Mac rose from the table. She looked up. Had she missed something?

Disappointment sped her heart, and she faced Mac. "Where are they going?"

He smiled and nodded toward the windows. "Marian could hardly sit still, she wanted to see the kids so badly. Dana's taking her over to introduce Marian and George properly."

"Oh." Relieved, she said, "And what does 'properly' mean?"

"Dana just made Marian's day, week, month and year by saying it was time Lily and little Mac were introduced to their great-grandmother."

"Oh, my…" Kate grinned and looked across the restaurant as Marian picked up Lily and George picked up little Mac. "Look at them."

"I can't stop looking at them."

Marian and George pointed toward the ocean and beyond as the kids stared at them or followed to where their nana and grand-dad pointed in the distance. Suddenly, Dana turned, her happiness clear in her bright eyes and flushed cheeks as she put her thumb up to Mac.

He slid his hand on to Kate's thigh. "I have something to ask you."

"Hmm." She couldn't drag her gaze from Marian. The woman had taught her so much. Had shown her so much love and support. She couldn't think of a better reward for her kindness than having found a new family. "What is it?"

"Kate?"

She faced him. "You've made Marian the happiest woman alive, do you know that?"

"I do. The trouble is…" He drew his gaze over her face, let it linger at her lips. "There's another woman I want to make happy, too."

She smiled and pressed a kiss to his lips. "You do."

His gaze glazed with concern. "Do I?"

"Yes." She cupped his jaw, her heart swelling with love for this once-upon-a-time stranger who'd strolled into town and captured her heart. "Of course."

"You can have everything I have, Kate. You can be a part of it, share it, be with me as things change and evolve."

"What are you saying?"

He took her hand, and her heart picked up speed. His expression was so sincere, so hopeful. He looked happier and happier as each second beat with her heart.

"Mac?"

"Marry me, Kate."

"What?" Her heart stopped, the music and chatter of the diners dissolving.

"Marry me." He grinned. "As soon as possible."

"But—"

"I love you. You love me. Time, Kate. Time

is what we waste. Not experiences. Not love. Not loss. Time. I won't waste any more. Will you?"

"No," she whispered.

"What?" The happiness in his eyes snuffed out like a blown candle. "No?"

"No."

"Oh. Right." His fingers started to slip from hers. "Okay."

She tightened her grip and laughed. "No, Mac. I won't waste any more time. As for marrying you? Yes, yes, yes!"

He laughed and stood, pulling her from her chair and into his arms, her feet leaving the ground as he hauled her higher. "The lady said yes!"

The entire restaurant burst into applause, and when Kate shook her head, her gaze met Marian's. She grinned. Her friend stared at Kate and Mac, her hand pressed to her chest and her tears glinting at her cheeks.

Kate looked at Mac and pressed a firm kiss to his lips. "You, Mr. Orman, are someone so darn special."

* * * * *

Get 2 Free Books,
Plus 2 Free Gifts—
just for trying the Reader Service!

HARLEQUIN®
SPECIAL EDITION

Get 2 Free Books,
Plus 2 Free Gifts—
just for trying the Reader Service!

HRLP17R3

Get 2 Free Books,
Plus 2 Free Gifts—
just for trying the Reader Service!